Ascension Island and the Ice Maiden

By Daniel Stapleton

Vincent had heard of the letterbox walks but hadn't given them any further thought until now, and they perhaps presented an opportunity.

CW01497214

Dedication

This book is dedicated to Phil Inman who befriended me, and introduced me to Ascension Island and the letterbox walks many years ago. We kept in touch once back in the UK, and in my darkest hour, he wrote to tell me himself and a workplace prayer group were praying for me, which helped. When I became a Christian I found, not surprisingly, he was as well. We hadn't always managed to keep in touch very well over the years but I got back in contact when writing this book. He rang me several times while I was writing it and his calls always came exactly at the time, I needed encouragement in my life generally. Not least Phil volunteered his time and editing skills to help take the rough edges of my grammar, style and punctuation for which I'm very grateful.

Daniel Stapleton
Nuneaton, England
June 2020

Contents

Chapter One – An important consignment

Deborah was anxiously awaiting the arrival of the cargo ship. It was more than important; it might prove crucial. She had staked a lot on its arrival and ironically if everything she'd ordered turned up, she might well lose her job and with it, her lovely home and life on this idyllic island, Ascension Island, in the middle of the South Atlantic Ocean, that's if her instinct had let her down. Today was the fourteenth day since the ship had left port. Consequently, since no-one had come into contact with it on its slow voyage, the voyage itself would have conveniently been a quarantine period for the crew for when it arrived.

She browsed a series of internet news sites and all the news remained bleak. Britain and Europe seemed to be losing the battle against the pandemic which was now gaining a foothold on other continents. Also, while the British, Europeans and Russia were fully engaged in dealing with the pandemic the global superpowers were moving to a war footing. America had accused China of germ warfare while the Chinese had made counter claims. A number of Chinese satellites had been destroyed and no-one had claimed responsibility for what they'd described as hostile acts of aggression that someone would pay for.

The UN, an organisation Deborah had never rated as being of much use, had been leading negotiations. But there hadn't been a breakthrough and there had been more than one walkout. War seemed inevitable and it seemed the madness of it would sweep the globe and destroy life as mankind knew it. Except perhaps here, a long way from everywhere and small to boot.

The following day she learned that the pandemic had now taken a firm hold across the world except for the North American Continent, so far. There were however, rumours that the Canadians and Americans had only partially contained it and law and order was on the brink of collapse. Here on Ascension the majority of the island's population had left or were planning to leave on the last flight. The St Helenians, 'the Saints' had left first, though many said they hoped to return. Deborah supposed it was probable only a tenth of the population would remain, she needed to check with Sabrina for accurate figures. While she was sad to see so many people leave, because she knew some of them as friends although others not at all, she had no intention of leaving herself. She found the island was healing to her and she knew that was what she needed.

The South Atlantic Ocean

On the Merchant Ship 'Hansel' Vincent paced up and down the deck. The weather was warm and they weren't making good progress but neither were they making bad progress and they would arrive in time, fifteen days after having left port. For him 'in time' meant before the war started. He had been listening to all the radio news he could and none of it was good. The rest of the ship's company were as anxious as he was but they wanted to press on and then get back to Cape Town as soon as possible. They had heard of the pandemic but decided even a slim chance of survival was better than none at all. None of them expected to suffer the effects of Nuclear War if there was one and they might be right but they had families to return to and he didn't. He'd never been to Ascension Island before and once they arrived, he'd have to make up his mind if he wanted to stay for what might be forever, or try his luck back home. The thing was he was haunted by recurring nightmares of being part of a gang of rag-tag nuclear apocalypse survivors living on the streets wearing gas masks and shooting anything that moved. He'd sometimes wake up in a sweat after the nightmare. He put it down to combat experience rather than a premonition. However, since it was likely he'd be re-called into military service as soon as the ship returned and the war seemed almost inevitable, he wasn't interested in finding out whether it was a premonition or not. This might just be the first time he wasn't fighting someone else's war, or fighting at all.

It was just after dawn the following day when Ascension Island was sighted in the distance. It looked to be a small mountain with a halo of cloud around it's top. Oddly, those clouds were the only ones for miles around. Slowly and surely, they drew nearer to the island and it looked verdant and green with some tall pine trees. Then the ship turned to port and as it followed the coastline the island appeared to gradually change into a reddish brown arid volcanic landscape with several reasonable sized cones, but none anything like as big as the mountain itself. Then there were some pleasant sandy looking beaches. Then there was a longer and continuous stretch of beach and various buildings just in from it and there was a jetty and what appeared to be a small harbour.

The 'Hansel' dropped anchor just offshore. The harbour and dockside crane were smaller than Vincent had expected and he realised unloading wasn't going to be quick because everything would have to be double-handled using pontoon barges.

The captain of the 'Hansel' saw a RHIB [*rigid-hulled inflatable boat*] approaching from the island and watched it moor alongside his ship. A couple of islanders were boarding his ship to greet him. He was surprised to see that the woman who was up the rope ladder first was also wearing a large automatic pistol in a holster, and then he remembered that he'd been told Ascension was under martial law.

"Morning Captain, Deborah Black, deputy administrator. Can we have a quick private talk?" she asked him.

"Of course, I'll clear the bridge" and once he'd done so, he invited her to sit down and then said "We can talk now."

"Firstly, I'd like to offer you and all of the ship's company a safe haven here for as long as you want it, in the hope you'll escape the war and the pandemic. Secondly, I'd like to know a little bit about your crew, especially if they are going to stay with us."

"That's very good of you, though we are all keen to get back to Cape Town. We all know our chances of survival might be slim but we'd rather die with our families than live without them." The captain paused and then said "Vincent Irving has no family and I'm guessing he might want to stay here. I don't know much about him and in fact nobody seems to and he keeps himself to himself. I hired him as an Able Seaman but really his experience level is more like an Ordinary Seaman for the most part. He's got some sort of extensive ex-military background but he's also very capable with a small boat. I once asked him if he was an ex-marine but he simply replied that he wasn't without venturing any further information. He doesn't mix with the other men but when one of them got into trouble in a bar in Angola a few months back he probably saved the man's life and left his crew member's attackers seriously injured. I had to pay a bribe to the police to let us leave without charges being pressed even though they knew my crew member and Vincent were the innocent parties. Vincent just shrugged his shoulders when the whole crew thanked him for helping their crew member and friend. The man himself told me that he thought Vincent could easily have killed the attackers but looked as if he chose not to and broke some of their bones instead. Sailors have a tendency to get into trouble in bars from time to time and often get into drunken fights or get robbed and when they don't, they watch someone else who is. Yet my crew member said Vincent's fighting looked more like something you see in a Hollywood movie than a real bar fight. Anyway, he's worked hard for me, rescued his crew member and I doubt will give you any trouble, in fact he'll be an asset to anyone, especially your island." The captain told Deborah.

"Thanks Captain. I have some things to attend to on the island but I'll be back promptly once the unloading has finished so you won't be delayed departing, and if you need me to bring anything back for you then radio my office and I'll see what I can do," she told him before leaving.

9

Vincent ensured that everything was safely unloaded including crate after crate of what appeared to be cast iron, rather than plastic pipes. His work was completed, but he hadn't yet managed to disembark. He was interrupted in these thoughts by a message telling him that the captain had called all the ship's company onto the bridge. Vincent made his way to the bridge and aware he'd not had chance to ask anyone what was going on, when he saw her.

'Her' was an attractive well-tanned woman who had an extreme air of authority about her. Vincent was also surprised to see that she had a large pistol in a holster, on a waist mounted belt. It wasn't a Glock 17 which the British Forces had been using for decades, but its service issued predecessor, the nine-millimetre Browning. Seeing it reminded him that Ascension Island was sort of semi-military, or at least had been at one time. He also thought that probably you didn't need to live here very long, being practically on the equator, to get a first-class sun tan.

"Good morning. My name is Miss Deborah Black, and I'm the deputy Administrator for Ascension Island. I want to personally thank you for delivering our cargo" She then paused and looked at the crew including Vincent before resuming speaking. "Also, and exceptionally due to the global crisis, I want to offer sanctuary here for any or all of you for as long as the crisis lasts. Martial law was declared a short while ago but there are only a few of us who are actually armed with live weapons." She told them in a very firm, but well-spoken, English accent.

The captain looked at his men and one by one they politely shook their heads, except for one. The captain smiled, because as he'd expected, Vincent would leave them, to stay here.

Vincent boldly stepped forward. "I'd like to stay maam." Then he turned to face the rest of the ship's company, stepped forward and shook each by the hand and gave each a small manly hug and pat on the shoulders. Vincent had rightly guessed he'd be the only one to stay and he'd planned on that possibility of staying without considering he'd need an invitation to do so. Still, he thought to himself, everything is above board and legal this way. Then without further ado he went to his bunk and grabbed a holdall bag that contained everything he'd brought with him and everything that he owned that was paid for. The captain passed him a thick envelope which he assumed was what pay he had due him and shook his hand. Vincent then followed the woman and he left the ship, and another of his old lives behind him, without looking back. Since he knew almost nothing about the island, he didn't really have any expectations. He quickly realised he wasn't about to check into a hotel or anything like that. He hadn't been smitten by Miss

Black but he was interested. There was something about her that was appealing, unusual, and besides that he found her physically attractive.

Vincent went down the rope ladder hanging over the side of the ship and watched the swell rise and fall a couple of times before timing his leap onto the RHIB. His timing was good and he didn't get his feet wet. It was less than a few minutes before the RHIB had sped forward, circled the 'Hansel' and slowed as it pulled up to the jetty. He watched the woman reach for a rope hanging from the quay steps and then when the swell reached its maximum height, she stepped from the RHIB to the quay steps, hanging onto the rope and then quickly up the steps. Someone else from the RHIB followed her and then it was his turn and as the others had before him, he managed to disembark without getting his feet wet. It always felt a little bit funny at first being back on the land after being at sea, but he knew he'd soon get used to it.

Now he was on the island it seemed like there was no time like the present for finding a bit more about that woman.

"Excuse me mate. That woman over there, Miss Black, does she have a boyfriend, a partner, or anything?" Vincent asked a quayside worker who had just got out of the cab of the small crane.

"She's nicknamed the 'Ice-Maiden' and no-one even gets close to her, so my advice to you is to forget her and any fantasy of seeing her white bits" the man replied laughing when he'd finished speaking. But Vincent couldn't forget her and since the Island was small it was inevitable, they'd meet again. Besides if she wasn't attached to anyone here it might mean she hadn't found anyone to interest her.

Deborah allowed herself a moment to watch the man from the ship she'd allowed to stay on the island. She suspected he'd a longer and more chequered history than any of her hasty official enquiries had told her and even those enquiries had contained a number of ominous gaps. That was the reason she'd undertaken this task in person. She wanted to see him face to face. Faces told her more than records could and while records could be falsified or supressed, she trusted her own judgement. He looked to her to be everything he was supposed to be and a lot more besides. She instinctively felt she could trust him, that he was dependable, a good friend or an enemy to regret. There was also something about him she couldn't pinpoint but more a gap than a concern. Least of all she found him appealing, a rare trait in any man she'd seen for a very long time indeed. Well, he was here to stay and be part of the island. If she'd hadn't have liked the look of him, she wouldn't have invited him and no-one would have been any the wiser apart from the captain. She moved forward from her vantage point, to talk to him.

"Mr Irving, here is a key to a bungalow which you can now call your home . You will need to report to myself, at my office over there, at eight o'clock sharp tomorrow morning." She told him and before walking away added "See you in the morning."

As she stepped inside the administrators building, she pulled her radio out of her dry bag and spoke into it "Henry, this is Miss Deborah, are you available for a small task that will start in Georgetown and finish in Two Boats?" she asked.

"Yes Miss Deborah" Henry replied.

Deborah paused for a moment because she knew she was asking for Henry, the Chief of Police, to do her a favour. Well not quite, she'd pose her request such that he wouldn't feel under obligation and could decline if he wanted to. "Henry, a Mr Vincent Irving has chosen to take an extended stay here with us on the island, rather than return to Cape Town on his ship. If you'd like to, you could collect him from the square and drop him off at Two Boats for me. He's been given a key to one of the recently vacated bungalows and that's where he will be living from now on. Perhaps you could also suggest to him that he might need to set out by seven in the morning so he will be on time to meet me at eight."

"No problem, Miss Deborah" Henry replied. He then drove slowly towards the quayside in Georgetown and raised his eyebrows. Occasionally Miss Deborah had invited him to do what was a favour but she'd never asked him to provide a taxi service before. It could be that she wanted this man kept an eye on, being new to the island and everything, or it could be for some other reason. Nope, that wasn't it, being kept on eye on. If she'd wanted an eye kept on him, she'd have said so. It must be that she liked him and wanted to help him, that was unusual, still it was no problem for him to drive to Two Boats and he was always happy to do anything for her because she was the best boss he'd ever had.

Vincent had been given a key and the address of a house he could live in at a place called 'Two Boats'. He didn't have any kind of map but did have his holdall which contained all the clothes he owned along with a few personal possessions. He had some cash and his wages but that wouldn't last him long and he'd need to get a job. He was standing in what passed as a main road in what he'd been advised was Georgetown. There was very little vehicular traffic and no taxi rank let alone taxis. Ascension Island was more basic, more primitive and more of a bad idea the longer he stood in the hot equatorial sun. To cap it all he was feeling thirsty. He supposed he could ask someone for directions and see if he could thumb a lift or simply walk. Just then a police vehicle pulled up alongside him and the copper opened the passenger door and called out to him.

"Vincent Irving, I've been invited to give you a lift to Two Boats, and I'm obliging, so get in and put on your seat belt" the policeman told him.

Vincent looked at the naturally dark-skinned policeman and guessed he must be a Saint Helenian and not just an ordinary copper but an Inspector or something like that by the look of his uniform insignia. He certainly had a strange accent; unlike anything he'd ever heard before in his travels. "Thank you' he replied and putting his bag on the back seat, sat in the front seat.

The policeman didn't introduce himself but began to speak to Vincent. "Miss Deborah, the Deputy Administrator, must like you because she's never invited me to give anyone a lift before. She's good like that Miss Deborah, giving me the choice when she wants me to do a favour for her. Mind you, don't mistake her kindness for stupidity, she's smart. Now, it won't take very long to get you to your house in Two Boats, about fifteen minutes, maybe less. There's a small shop there and you should be able to buy anything you need today. You aren't likely to run out of money before you get a job in the morning. That's right, there are quite a few jobs here and Miss Deborah has told me to suggest you set out at seven tomorrow morning for Georgetown, thumbing a lift, and to be in her office for eight, preferably clean-shaven. That's my advice, the clean-shaven part. You'll find everyone stops for hitch hikers here on Ascension and you shouldn't have to walk for too long in the morning sun." Then having arrived at Two Boats and stopping outside a bungalow, and without waiting for a reply he beckoned Vincent out of the car and once he'd seen Vincent remove his bag, he waved goodbye and drove slowly away.

Vincent checked the house number against the numbered tag on the key he'd been given and then unlocking the door, entered the house. He closed the door behind him and walking into the lounge abruptly sat down in an armchair. Well, he thought to himself, I've been stuck in worse places than this. It was warm and dry and it would be home, most likely for ever once the war started that's if there was anyone left alive to fight it. Though who could tell what was going to happen? Still, this was likely to be safer than most places because it was so remote and there wasn't much here. He didn't mind that there were few people here, he liked his own company and he liked peace and quiet. Looking around the kitchen he found the kitchen cupboards and even the fridge was well stocked. He made himself a mug of tea and sat down to drink it at a dining table when he noticed an envelope addressed to 'The new occupant'. He opened the envelope and read it.

13

Welcome dear new occupant of your new home. This was once our home and we were very happy here on Ascension Island. However, we have left to spend our last few days, perhaps even a week, with our family in England before life as we know it ends. We entered this world with nothing and will leave it with nothing so everything here is now yours. God bless you.

Vincent took a sip of his tea and took, for him, a rare moment of serious reflection. He didn't really know why he had chosen life here rather than death one way or another when the war began. He was certain it would begin and thus end most life on earth unless the pandemic killed everyone first. He also wasn't sure they were two separate things, the war and the pandemic. The pandemic might be germ warfare to soften up everyone. He further reflected that his life hadn't amounted to much and he had many regrets. The regrets were mostly about the things he had done, rather than the things he ought to have done but hadn't. That thought itself was a bit like the stuff he'd said as a child when forced to attend church with his parents. He never thought it had done him much good, being forced to go to church, but he might be wrong. The very name of this place was straight out of the Bible because it was discovered on the calendar day the early church celebrated the Ascension of the risen Christ to heaven. Or was it re-discovered on Ascension Day having previously been discovered previously? He wished he'd taken a bit more interest in the captain's mini history lesson. Still, he supposed they'd all know the history here and he could catch up with it someday. Of course, it wasn't really his choice to be here as such but rather the only place that might give him an escape. He didn't really know why he needed to escape, to carry on living, he could have just waited for death to take him. Still now he was here he'd need to make the most of it. In fact, he could probably make a fresh start, and make this a proper fresh start. No-one knew him and between the pandemic and the war, no-one would ever find out his past, unless he chose to tell them. Well, there might be a time for confessions later, but for now he'd behave himself and get stuck into a job and grow old, brown and wizened.

Turtles

After finishing work for the day Deborah decided there was something she could do tonight, that she'd not yet managed to do since she'd been on the island. She was going to see if she could see a turtle laying eggs. She didn't know much about turtles or how a nuclear war would affect the sea and thus the turtles. She hoped the turtles and the hatchlings would all live on much as before. But just in case they didn't she wanted to see one even if her first time proved to be the only time. She knew it was a bit early in the nesting season, if not before it was really due to start, to see a turtle but all she had to lose was her evening.

Deborah left her home just after nine at night and decided she'd wait a couple of hours before giving up if she'd not seen a turtle. She walked, at a leisurely pace for her, to Long Beach. At the beach she slipped off her sandals and slowly walked in the sand near the water's edge. The moon was high in the night sky and while not quite full, was providing a reasonable level of illumination. She had a torch with her but didn't want to use it and scare off a turtle that was making its long slow climb up the beach, though the beach wasn't particularly steep.

Long Beach hadn't been given its name by chance and it took longer than she'd expected to walk its full length. Once or twice, she thought she might have seen a turtle but it was just a shadow. It was only on her second walk to the far end of the beach that she once more thought she saw a turtle. Yes, this time it was a turtle. Like a large round rock, the turtle moved slowly up the sandy beach. She watched the turtle from a distance while also gradually shortening that distance, getting nearer to it, but not close enough to cause it to change its mind and course of action. It was likely the turtle was older than she was and might even be twice as old. It was also likely that this turtle might have hatched on this very beach before, during, or not long after the airfield runway was built by the Americans near the end of the second world war. Of course, this turtle might not be that old but of the others that would come to lay their eggs on this beach, unless interrupted by this war to end all wars, several would surely be of that age.

Eventually the turtle had gone as far up the beach as she had intended to and after turning around slowly but surely, she began to flick the sand with her flippers as she dug her nest. Deborah knew that this was exactly what the green turtles did, and she'd seen photos and video clips but nothing could come close to this first-hand experience. After quite a long while the Turtle's digging pattern changed and she guessed the turtle was now digging the final part of the hole in which she would lay her eggs. It seemed slightly rude mannered to watch the stream of eggs being deposited by the turtle but Deborah was moved by this stage in the creation of new life. She wondered what sort of world the hatchlings would emerge into in about two months' time and whether their long swim would be contaminated by nuclear fallout in the sea. It seemed likely there would be fewer human hazards, such as discarded fishing nets and plastic waste for not just these hatchlings but all turtles to have to contend with in future years. She then wondered whether in years to come the islanders might once again catch the turtles to eat them, having tired of a diet of mostly fish. If the future turned out to be a post nuclear apocalypse future, there might not be many conservationists, rather just survivors struggling to survive. She hoped the turtles would survive.

The Turtle had finished laying her eggs today but would return again on other days to dig another nest and lay another clutch, that's if what a nest of turtle eggs were called, Deborah thought. Then the turtle slowly made her way back down the beach and Deborah felt alone in the world. She remembered a time when she wasn't all alone, a happier time. As she walked back along the beach and to her home she tried to hang onto this memory as a positive one. A memory of new life and new beginnings when there seemed little hope.

Chapter Two – You're in charge now

Well, that was everything signed and sealed, now it just needed to be delivered. But before the delivery Will wanted to have a few quiet moments of reflection. Deborah was more than a safe pair of hands. She was a capable leader with just about as broad a background and experience anyone could have hoped for and was a Major in the Territorial Army. Of course, in some ways she was as big a mystery to him as the day he'd first interviewed her in London. She was known as the 'Ice Maiden' long before she'd arrived here yet no-one had been able to pinpoint when or where she'd first been called that. He'd never personally found her cold but nor had he found her warm either. He wasn't allowed to find out anything about her from her security clearance application and certainly she'd been security cleared at the highest level more than once. His intuition told him there was a death, a bereavement, in her not-so-distant past, before Gibraltar most likely but she was under no obligation to tell him anything about her past – that was for the security clearance people alone. In any event he was very pleased to have had her as his deputy on the island and time and time again she'd proved sound in her decision making and leadership. She'd quickly built and sustained first class working relations with the Americans though one or two had been disappointed everything was conducted professionally and not more personally on account of her being such an attractive woman.

What had impressed him most though were her recent efforts which she'd sought to conceal from him. She'd acted in the best interests of those islanders who were planning on remaining, of which she would be one. She'd gambled everything and it had paid off, at least as far as anyone would know. The cost, only large in island budget terms, would be immaterial once the missiles started flying and life as we all knew it came to an end; that's if everyone hadn't died from the pandemic first. He supposed though that every underground and above ground hardened facility was now being readied for occupation for the duration. He'd heard from a source, Corsham had already been occupied for several days. Of course, she'd not quite managed to get everything the island would need and he'd filled in those small gaps himself with additions that hadn't occurred to her. Yet without her initiative and gamble he simply might have been too busy to have done much in time. Of course, a while back he had put in place a few long-range plans of his own but that was good planning without risk taking and not putting his future on the line. Well, enough reflecting, it was time now.

"Morning Deborah, we need to have a serious chat so please come in and sit down" Will told her over the phone.

Deborah wrung her hands and braced herself for bad news. She supposed Will had found the paperwork relating to her massive delivery. Or maybe he'd seen some of it being unloaded. Though he was supposed to be playing a round of golf on the world's worst course, and the only one on the Island, when she'd had it unloaded and placed in various storage sites. Once in his office she told him "Ok Boss, go ahead" while remaining standing.

Will motioned her to sit down and waited until she did, before speaking. "You're in charge now, I've appointed you the Administrator. Since I declared martial law and as the only person with an armed forces commission that means you're also in charge on that score too, though I suppose you were already, but answerable to me. Hal spoke to me before he left and since he somehow managed to get you American citizenship, he's raised some sort of paperwork to give you absolute authority over all things US as well. Of course, you can always resign and come back on the plane with me this evening but I don't think that's what you want is it?"

Deborah shook her head, being momentarily speechless.

"I don't blame you, not least because I'm flying into trouble to see my extended family, when I should have flown out with Hal and persuaded my family to meet me in America. Hal could even have arranged it for me. Anyway, enough of my tale of woe. There's some Top-Secret files you need to read, mostly about the bunker and a few other things you never managed to find out about." Will smiled before speaking again. I bet you thought you were in for the high jump on account of your big spend on survival equipment including miles of cast iron pipes that arrived the other day." He told her. "If you think back to when you first arrived here, I told you there wasn't much I either didn't know about before it happened, when it happened, or shortly after it happened. Well, I approved your order when the UK bounced it back to me, though I think you missed a few items off your big shopping list that I added for you. When the time comes, you'll smile or be relieved as you discover what I ordered. In any event Hal placed a big order of his own of which he's left details for you to read when you get chance. Some of it he's stored in the bunker, some in his own warehouse. I think he already told you that the Base Exchange, the BX, was well stocked and if the shit hit the fan, you could help yourself first and redistribute the rest."

Deborah managed to nod a reply. Will stood up and beckoned Deborah to stand up as well. "Will the 'Ice Maiden' spare her old boss a big hug before he embarks on a round of good-byes, not forgetting I need to paint the lizard?" She nodded once more, and gave Will more of an embrace than a hug. It had been a while since she'd hugged anyone and since Will was on the chubby side, she was slightly surprised to find that unlike herself he was somewhat soft and squashy. When they parted, and held hands both could see the other had been crying. Deborah didn't like crying and she didn't want to be crying now and she quickly wiped her tears away.

Will then passed her a folder that amongst its contents included an envelope that she could see contained a security combination. He then simply gestured for her to sit at his desk before leaving with a simple "Good bye and good luck."

Deborah was shocked. She'd been so busy for some time that she hadn't really given much thought to what might happen beyond her own plans. She'd expected to be right about the war and everyone was planning for it, mostly to leave, or in some cases being ordered to leave but she'd not given Will much thought. She hadn't decided whether she thought he would leave or not and it was always going to be something to think about the next day or the day after that. Well tonight was the day of the last flight that would leave for some time, or perhaps for ever. Will, her boss, now her ex-boss was going to be on it and she was in charge of everything. She didn't mind being in charge of everything but neither was it something she'd sought. While she'd always had a manager, she was one herself. She'd also pretty much got on with her job with little or no interference or explanation to anyone because she was organised and efficient. Well, the future was going to be different and while she had planned for it, those plans would need to be adjusted, hopefully only slightly.

Deborah opened the envelope and opened the stuff that looked like, and might even be, tin foil, and looked at the number. She opened the desk drawers looking for a combination change key and once she'd found one, she immediately changed the combination number from Will's choice to her choice on the safe. She wrote the number on a piece of paper and re-used the tin foil stuff to wrap the paper up. Next, she got a new envelope put the newly wrapped combination in it and sealed and double enveloped the envelope. She looked at the contents of the folder and could see there were the original letters of her new appointments. She went to the photocopier and made several copies of them. Lastly, she opened the safe using her new number and placed the folder in it, less the envelope she'd prepared and without looking at the rest of the contents picked up her Land Rover's key and closed the office door behind her.

"Sabrina, Will has just appointed me the new Administrator and Military commander. Hal's given me some other powers as well. I'm going to file a combination change with the Police and give them a copy of my letter of appointment, here's a copy for you. When I get back, most likely tomorrow, there's some's things we need to work through quite quickly."

"Congratulations Miss Deborah, I'll still be here bright and early as usual." Sabrina told her and smiled. Once Deborah had left Sabrina smiled a bigger smile and wondered how Deborah hadn't seen that coming - She certainly had.

The rest of Deborah's day was busy, mostly visiting the Americans who she needed to ensure were fully on board with Hal's plans. They all seemed content, almost cheerful and took her through a range of procedures and handovers relevant to her newly found position of authority. When she finally got home it was dark but then it always got dark early on the island. Later in the evening the last flight to leave the island was taking place and she needed to be at the airhead to say her final goodbyes. She decided she'd wear a dress, and then realised that since she was armed with a pistol that might be slightly awkward. She supposed she could find something that worked well with a belt and perhaps a lightweight jacket because despite it being warm, it would feel cool compared to the heat of the day.

Later that evening she drove slowly from her home in Georgetown down to the airhead and found that she wasn't alone, yet the departure lounge wasn't packed and Deborah realised this was because there weren't that many people left to say goodbye to the people leaving. She'd look at the official figures in the morning but judging by the number of people leaving, the island population would now be much less than a hundred. She supposed that everyone on the plane knew that they were flying to an almost certain death but wanted to spend their last weeks, perhaps a fortnight, or only days, with family or extended family in the United Kingdom. The Americans had left on their last military flight at the end of last week apart from the few that had chosen to remain, who she realised she was now managing civilly and leading militarily.

Then it was time and a 'crocodile' of people slowly left the departure lounge, some waving goodbye, several crying and just the occasional person not even looking back. Usually, she was airside when a plane was departing but today, she wasn't, but simply stood with everyone else that was staying behind, in an act of solidarity because while she was in charge, she was also one of them, a 'Remainer'. At one point she was surprised to see a police Land Rover pull up with its blue lights on and some sort of drama taking place. Inspector Henry Pollack had now taken over full responsibility for arrivals and departures since the Royal Air Force air movements staff had left and would be supported by one of his two police sergeants so she'd leave them to handle it. A few people left the departure lounge at this point but most stayed and waited until they could see the plane's door close and then watched it taxi to the runway threshold. Unlike most airports where the planes queued for take-off there were no taxiways, and no queues here and there hadn't been a queue since the Falklands conflict and that was well before her time. Finally, the plane's engines increased to full power with a roar and the plane accelerated down the runway and took to the air long before it was near the runway's end. Deborah pondered how different it was from Gibraltar with its much, much, shorter runway that was extended into what was once sea, yet in both cases in a matter of less than a minute any plane having taken off was flying over the sea. Well, that was it, she thought and then she drove back home and feeling tired was soon undressed, lying on her bed and under her mosquito net quite naked and asleep.

In the morning Deborah was up while it was still dark outside but she knew it would get light very quickly, it always did. She quite liked the way the day and night stayed approximately the same length of about twelve hours each, all year round, because the island was very close to the equator. She liked it because she didn't have to change her daily routine throughout the calendar year. As she opened her fridge door and took out a carton of orange juice, she supposed that this was something that would change. There were all types of dried and concentrated juice in storage but not only would they not taste as good as this they would run out one day and she doubted they'd ever grow enough oranges on the farm to use them for juicing. She sighed slightly at that thought. She was just about to think about what herself and Will needed to plan for the day when she remembered that he'd left and she was wholly in charge now. She ate a bowl of muesli and pondered that was something that would run out as well, though she'd personally ensured there was a large supply of it in her war food stock. Would the war start today? She doubted it, but she needed to be at work and continue to plan for it.

Entering the Administrator's building while it was still dark outside, she almost sat down at her old desk but remembered in time and sat at her new desk in her new office. Deborah decided that her first act would also be one of defiance and one that while not necessarily popular with the Remainers was one she'd do anyway. She reached up for the framed photograph of His Majesty the King and removed it and put it on top of a cupboard. She looked at the hook on the wall and decided she'd transfer a framed print from her old office to replace it. But that could wait until later, there were more important things to do first and she did so now.

Deborah looked on her computer screen at the scant details she'd found out about Mr Vincent Irving. He had a reasonably impressive but short period of service in the South African Armed Forces but had ended up working as a leading or able seaman on various ships. There were no police records for him but his career history, life history even, had some very large unexplained gaps. She'd rung an old colleague in Gib' who owed her a massive favour, yet who was only willing to repay it with information on the basis that he'd didn't think it would be discovered before nothing would really matter anyway. His secure email said he couldn't be certain but there was a chance Vincent had served in the French Foreign Legion at one point and reached the rank of Sergeant. Some of his records looked fake but of a high quality. It was a mystery why he's taken to working on various tatty ships but the fact that he seemed to need a place to live might be as good a reason as any other, though it was possible, he'd sometimes been a gun for hire to provide seagoing protection against Somalian pirates. There was no family background apart from his early years, and no trace of what had happened to his parents. The impression gained was that he was a good person to have as your friend and one of the worse people to have as your enemy. He'd almost certainly not pass security vetting to British Standards yet could probably keep a military secret better than anyone who was security cleared, and maybe already did keep military or other secrets.

Well, she thought, she wasn't really any the wiser, for pulling in her favour, but then nor was she worried either because no concerns were raised or warnings given. Her gut instinct told her he'd be ok so long as he was kept busy and was reasonably well looked after. She looked at her watch and momentarily smiled at its craftsmanship, well he should be here soon. Then she heard Sabrina arrive and decided she'd speak to her straightaway.

"Morning Sabrina, I'm glad you've stayed on the island because I'm promoting you to the post of Deputy Administrator. I know you were very much part of 'the power behind the throne', as some put it and will relish a challenge. Your appointment letter will be the first document I sign today. You'll get a pay rise but I guess that's not going to make a difference for very long. Still, I want you to enjoy some sort of benefit while such things exist. I'm not planning on moving house and I'm going to persuade Henry to move himself and his family into The Residence. However, if you've seen a place you want to move into let me know and in any event, this evening I'll take you shopping for free at the American Base Exchange, the BX, before all the good stuff goes" Deborah told her.

What Deborah didn't tell her was that she was also somewhat sad for Sabrina in that she also knew she had no-one else or no-where else to go to. Deborah didn't really know what men found attractive in a woman's looks but she thought any man would have found Sabrina attractive. Besides, she had a large firm bust that appeared conical, that no man could fail to notice.

Perhaps that was the problem, they never got past looking at her bust to see the woman who possessed it.

"Thanks very much Miss Deborah, it's lovely we can carry on working together, you're the best boss I've ever had" Sabrina told her smiling. Sabrina never found Deborah cold and she hated it when people referred to her as the Ice Maiden. Maybe she'd never really got over the death of her fiancée, not that she was supposed to know about that. She then smiled at the thought of shopping in the BX, Hal had taken her shopping there last week and had sworn her to secrecy because neither of them had to pay for the things she'd taken. Perhaps she could get an identical watch to the one she already had and wear them alternate days or something.

Deborah's office phone rang and she answered it, but before she could speak the caller spoke.

"Morning Boss, Doc Caskey here. I've got eight islanders in quarantine and one unexpected visitor. The visitor will probably die of whatever virus the Pandemic is or something else I can't fathom. Nor can I be certain all the islanders will live. Do you want to have a walk down the road and have a chat about this over coffee?" he asked.

"Yes, I'll meet you at the hospital" she replied. Deborah was anxious as she walked down the road to the hospital. If someone had brought the pandemic virus to the island it could wipe out everyone or kill enough people to make long term life on the island unviable.

"Morning again boss, come on in to my office" Doc Caskey greeted her when she arrived at the hospital, and added "the coffee's hot and if I don't run out of cream in a month's time it will most likely have all gone bad by then unless it survives being frozen, so help yourself.

"Last night one of the cabin crew got off the plane as if to help the passengers get on but in fact, they had no intention of getting back onto it. It wasn't apparent that was the case until the plane was about to leave and at that point the aircraft captain decided he wasn't prepared to wait for his missing cabin crew member to be located. It's possible he already knew she had no intention of re-boarding the aircraft. One of the ground handling team found them in the airside baggage area and called the police. Two of the police arrested them and took them to the cells. In the middle of the night, actually about zero three hundred hours, it was obvious the woman was sick and the duty policeman called the duty medic. The duty medic didn't like the look of them and called me and along with my wife we suited up and moved our uninvited guest, the duty medic, the ground handling person, the police sergeants and a further four people they've been in contact with, into quarantine. I've injected them all with what in all honesty is a cocktail of vaccines that might not do a damn thing and they all might die. If we've missed anyone, we might lose most or all of us to this Pandemic, if that's what it is." The Doc told her.

"Ok Doc. There's nothing else to be done then is there?" Deborah asked.

"No, well I'll keep you informed" he told her.

"Thanks Doc. I must dash now, as I'd forgotten an early morning appointment I made yesterday before I realised what Will had planned for me. Thanks for the coffee" she told him before leaving hastily. However, Deborah decided rather than rush back to her office she'd find Henry and invite him to move house.

"Morning Chris, is the Inspector about?"

"He's not here Miss Deborah, but he won't be far away so I'll call him for you." Chris replied and then advised that "He'll be here in a few minutes. Would you like to wait in his office or shall I send him to yours?"

"Thanks Chris, I'll wait in his office" Deborah replied and then entered Henry's office and sat herself down. It wasn't long before Henry arrived and joined her.

"Morning Miss Deborah, how can the island police be at your service today?" he greeted her.

"Morning Henry, I'll come straight to the point I'd like you and your family to move house and live in the residency. I realise I'm supposed to live there but it's too big for one person and you're one of the few, if not only, island families and my Chief of Police, so it's all yours."

Henry was taken aback by Deborah's offer but he didn't feel it was something he could accept. "But Miss Deborah, no Saint has ever lived in The Residency, it wouldn't be right for me to live there."

"Well then, you and your family will be the first Saints to live there and my saying so makes it right. Besides in 1867 it was built to be the naval sanatorium and it's only in more recent years it became a posh house. It's a lovely place and your children will enjoy it. In any event I'm insisting and if after, oh, say a year, you are all unhappy there you can move back to Georgetown and it can stay empty, which would be a real waste." Deborah told him.

Henry shook his head at first and then smiled and said "If you make it an order I'll move in at the weekend."

"Ok Henry, it's an order and any problems let me know." She told him, before shaking his hand and waving him goodbye.

Chapter Three – Appointments, Planning and Spire Beach

Vincent was awake and realised it was still dark and his watch alarm told him it was six in the morning. He wondered where he was and then remembered he was on Ascension Island and starting a new life. As he gradually recalled the events of yesterday, he knew he needed to have a shave and make his best second impression and hoped his first wasn't that bad. Then he remembered the woman called the Ice-Maiden who he'd been told liked him, which was good because he liked the look of her. After what in his military experience was called a triple-S (a shit, a shower and a shave) he grabbed a quick breakfast and realised that at some point during the day he'd need to shop for some groceries. He looked at his watch and it wasn't yet seven o'clock. He grabbed his rucksack and locking the bungalow door, put the key in his pocket and walked down the road.

Vincent looked around and he soon found what was the main road and even a helpful signpost for Georgetown. He'd done some hitch-hiking in the past and hadn't struck on a formula for success so was surprised that the first vehicle that reached him stopped and the passenger door opened and he got in with a smile.

"Thanks for stopping. Are you going in the direction of Georgetown?" Vincent asked.

"Yes, I certainly am and you must be new here and just about the only person that is a new arrival, so I guess you came off our last supply ship yesterday?" said the man, who didn't offer his name.

"Yes, that's right. Thanks for giving me a lift" Vincent replied and sensing that the man didn't want to make any more conversation remained silent until they pulled into Georgetown, whereupon the man stopped, shook Vincent's hand and waved him goodbye. It was light now and since it wasn't yet eight o'clock, he decided to have a short wander around. Then having remembered what the administrator's office looked like and finding it, he entered it at exactly five minutes to eight. Having explained to an elderly receptionist his appointment was with Miss Black, a woman with a large bust then appeared and asked him to follow her and seconds later he was directed into a large and reasonably plush office and found he was standing in front of Miss Deborah Black.

"Morning Mr Irving. Take a seat. Having decided to stay and under no compulsion to leave I guess you've realised you will either be here for some months until the world crisis blows over, or indefinitely if it doesn't." Deborah paused for Vincent's response which was a nod of his head, and then continued. "I'm in charge here and I ran some background checks on you before your ship arrived because I didn't want my island lumbered with any undesirables or tourists. You've undertaken military service and you're a leading seaman and can handle small craft well. The checks didn't tell me why you're such a rolling stone but I guess that rolling stops now. As of yesterday, I am also now the commanding officer of the military here as well as the governor of all UK interests and base commander of all US interests. I have several office staff members but no military staff though I've armed the police. I can offer you a couple of different jobs and you can pick which one you want, they'll both pay about the same amount of money, a house goes with the job and each has some kind of vehicle to go with it for a six-month contract. You can either be the Island's new road sweeper and litter picker upper or you can be my military second in command and swear an oath of allegiance to the King, organise the defence of the Island, and so on." She told him matter-of-factly.

"I'll swear the oath and take the job that goes with it." Vincent replied.

Deborah smiled warmly at Vincent and Vincent gave her his best beaming smile back and flashed his eyes welcomingly. Deborah then passed him a bible and a small piece of card on which was written the oath of allegiance. Vincent swore the oath and while he was concentrating on this short act, Deborah stole a more detailed glance at him and unexpectedly she found him more appealing then when she'd first seen him. Then he'd finished and was looking her in the eyes.

"Ok" Deborah said and then began to speak again "I think you met Inspector Henry Pollack yesterday when he gave you a lift to your new home. Well for the next couple of days he'll show you around the island and he'll let me know how you are getting on with your new responsibility. Also, while you're the military second in command, he's the chief of police which means you have equal ranking with each other but I've known Henry for a long time and I've only just met you, so don't give him any trouble else you'll be sweeping roads after you get out of the police cells." Having finished speaking Deborah smiled at Vincent again but he observed this time it was a different sort of smile, more of a 'don't fuck with me or I'll make you sorry' smile.

Vincent stamped his feet together and replied "Yes maam Deborah". He pronounced the word maam like a sheep baaing, just as he'd learnt a long time ago. He was serious and Deborah realised that.

Once Vincent was outside, he let out a sigh. She was a hard-arse bitch he thought at first. Then he had a re-think and supposed that she was a woman in a tough job in tough times and needed to ensure she had absolute respect from everyone, especially someone she didn't know such as himself. So, on balance he decided she was ok and perhaps something of a challenge on account of her having amazing emotional self-control. She'd given nothing away to him that she didn't want him to know yet he'd managed to surprise her slightly by his own candour and respect. Well, if he could surprise once with impeccable behaviour, he might be able to do so again, until of course she expected nothing else and by then she might relax a bit with him.

Sabrina had been waiting for Deborah to finish with that Vincent bloke and she was troubled not so much by the news from the UK but rather the lack of it. "Miss Deborah, I'm not getting any news from London and our usual contacts aren't replying to our e-mails." She said.

"Ok, I'll be through in a minute, I just want to grab a tea." Deborah replied. Once she'd got her tea she sat down with Sabrina and after a while she shook her head. "I'm guessing the country is moving to a war footing and London's been, or being, evacuated. We're most likely on our own from now on. I could try a few numbers on the secure line but we haven't really got a need to ask them anything and there's nothing we can do for them."

Once Vincent was outside, he saw Inspector Henry beckon him over to a Police Land Rover and then he was encouraged when he remembered Henry had told him yesterday that Miss Deborah had liked him.

"Good morning, Henry. Is it ok to call you Henry or should I call you Inspector Pollack or something else?" Vincent asked politely.

"We are working together as equals and Henry is fine Vincent. Two days might seem plenty of time to see everything and go everywhere on this small island but we'll need to undertake some journeys on foot some distance from where we can park. I've picked up a pair of binoculars, a scope and a compact camera, all of which you can keep for as long as you are here on Ascension, which might be forever. What I thought we'd do is drive around the outside of the Island as much as we can and then work in and out of the edges and then finish with everything in the middle" Henry told him, also passing him a map advising him to 'thank Kate for that when you see her'.

Vincent replied with a simple "Sounds good, let's get started" and jumped into the passenger seat of the Police Land Rover. They then began with a short drive out to the end of Long Beach and then turned back through Georgetown to the airhead, around the runway threshold and then up to the top of South Gannet Hill. Then doubling back once more Henry stopped on the runway dispersal area before making a radio call and then driving all the way down the runway and then they doubled back, leaving the runway and along a road through what Henry described as the American base before turning off onto a road which at one point was both straight and flat. The next road provided a sharp contrast in being both extremely twisty and mostly uphill with the occasional downhill section for a while. Henry informed Vincent this was the NASA road and led all the way to the old NASA tracking station site. At the old NASA site, it was cooler than anywhere else they had been and occasional fog banks, which Vincent realised was actually low cloud, slowly brushed by them. You could see for miles and Vincent spent a long time looking around and was about to make some notes when he realised, he had neither pen or notebook with him.

Henry looked at Vincent and grinned before handing him a hardback exercise book and a pen.

Vincent made some sketches and notes and then they had a lunch break including some cans of Coca-Cola Henry produced from a cool box.

They returned back down the NASA road and Henry explained they'd go up Green Mountain tomorrow. Vincent looked at the map and could see they next drove on the New Mountain Road and through what was once the RAF accommodation site of Travellers' Hill, then through Two Boats and onto North East Bay Road. Henry pointed out a live firing range near to Broken Tooth Crater, before continuing along the road itself which was a dead end at the old Ariane down range tracking station site, requiring them to double back. On returning to Two Boats, they drove along the Old Mountain Road in the direction of Georgetown, the one road Vincent recognised but just past One Boat they turned right onto English Bay Road driving right down to the beach. Then turning around but turning right onto Pyramid Point Road but which anyone who'd been on the island for decades still called the Nike Zeus Road. The road led to what Henry explained was once a missile tracking station for the abandoned Nike Zeus Anti-Ballistic Missile system and which early in its life tracked test missiles fired from the American White Sands range. He wasn't absolutely sure what was there now or what it was currently capable of, but expected before the month was out, if it could do anything, they'd find out what that was. Then they turned around back onto English Bay Road and then right onto the Old Mountain Road into Georgetown and then back to Two Boats.

"Nike, like the trainers?" Vincent asked.

"No, after the mythological Greek goddess of Victory. The trainers came at least a decade after the first missiles" Henry replied and added "Well Vincent that's been a fairly full day and to help you learn about the island and remember things, here's a new copy of a very old guide book about the island. It was written by a Mr John Packer in the nineteen fifties. Have a good evening and I'll collect you from your house in the morning so no need for you to go to Georgetown" Henry told him before shaking his hand and driving slowly away.

Vincent unlocked and opened the door of his new home and sat down. He'd have a shower, a bite to eat, and then he'd have a read through the book he'd been given.

The next day Vincent was up bright and early. He was waiting outside for Henry to pick him up. He had packed a rucksack complete with a micro-fleece top in it because he'd been told it was a lot cooler up the mountain than anywhere else on Ascension.

"Henry, why do some people call Miss Deborah the 'Ice Maiden'?" Vincent asked.

"Well Vincent it's not a name any of her close colleagues or friends call her. She'd been called that when she worked in Gibraltar and somehow it followed her here. Then since she already had a nickname, no-one saw fit to give her a new one. So occasionally someone uses it when she's done something that person doesn't like. Personally, I've always found she has treated me well, even though she is slightly aloof, maybe shy." Henry told her.

"Thanks Henry, one other thing, do you have an agreeable nick-name?" Vincent asked him.

"Ford. Some of the Saints call me Ford, after the founder himself, I guess it's more than agreeable, and even complimentary in a sense." Henry told him smiling.

Vincent laughed and told him "I think I'll stick with Henry but if anyone else mentions 'Ford' at least I'll know who they mean."
Once they started on the drive up the mountain road Henry explained he'd wouldn't be talking much because it was a tricky drive with a whole series of hairpin bends, once known as the ramps, to negotiate and steep drops with little or no crash barriers. Although the drive was slow and awkward Vincent enjoyed the increasingly panoramic view of the island, albeit only of one side. What he could see was the airhead and an interesting selection of volcanoes. Henry decided to stop at one particularly good vantage point so he could point them out and name them for him.

"Ok Vincent, I believe the clock ray method will work for you. One o'clock the airhead, ten o'clock is South Red Crater and a letterbox walk, two o'clock is Dark Slope crater, just below but not really three o'clock is the Devils' Riding School and I think the only one of the letterbox walks created by RAF servicemen. Eleven o'clock is South Gannet Hill, which we drove up yesterday" Henry pointed out to him before executing a perfect hill start.

It wasn't long after that before Henry parked at the Red Lion, which despite its promising sounding name wasn't a public house. "I think what we will do is walk around the mountain on one of the lower paths which will give you a good view without being troubled too much by low cloud" Henry told Vincent. Then added "there are several different walks around the mountain but I think we will take the one called Elliot's Path. This path or walk, dates back to the year 1840 and circles the mountain at about two thousand four hundred feet, or if you prefer about seven hundred and thirty metres. Its original purpose was to enable a lookout to be maintained in every direction even when the mountain top is covered in cloud so it's ideal for our purposes today." Henry told him before leading the way.

It was a pleasant walk around Green Mountain which took them nearly three hours to complete the full circumference of, but this involved frequent stops for Vincent to make a note or a sketch or take a photo or for Henry to provide an interesting fact. The mountain itself contained lots of diverse plant life which Henry explained had mostly been imported and of which some was edible including raspberries and cape gooseberries. However, what would have encouraged Vincent would have been a fresh apple or a long drink of coconut milk. Vincent asked Henry about Coconuts and was told that about a decade after Elliot's path was made some coconuts were planted but only one survived and while it never bore fruit it did give the location and name to a bay which was also one of the Letterbox walks.

Henry advised that he'd finished giving Vincent the 'grand tour' and from now on he could do his own exploring and if he got lost or had a question, he could contact him or one of his officers at the police station by: radio, telephone, or in person. Then having stopped outside Vincent's home they shook hands and Vincent noticed a Land Rover parked outside. "Your new wheels Vincent, the keys are in it but if they aren't, I bet you know how to hot-wire it" Henry told him laughing before waving him goodbye.

Vincent looked at the Land Rover and could see it was what looked to be a nearly new military lightweight. He couldn't understand how it could be new since they hadn't made them for years and guessed it had either been in storage or had been refurbished at some point. It would do the job though and he liked it.

Vincent spent the rest of that day writing up his notes into a short verbal briefing he could deliver to Miss Deborah Black. Then if she wanted it typed up, he could get someone to type it up on a computer for him or if she wasn't in a rush, wait for him to type it up with his best two fingered typing. What the island really needed though was not a plan but someone to deliver it. He'd suggest something like a 'Dad's Army', he'd call it the Island Defence Volunteer Force and he'd create and deliver a training programme to make it work. It would be good for the island and it would give him something meaningful to do while he was here until he could find something more interesting. His programme would need to be toned down a fair bit from teams he'd put together in the past and it only remained for him to persuade Miss Black to accept his idea.

"Good morning Maam. I am ready to deliver my verbal briefing on the task you gave me" Vincent told Deborah in her office the next morning.

"Please proceed Vincent" she replied.

"Any attack would initially be by air or by sea, followed by a land assault. However, I don't think an air attack is realistic because it will require more than one tanker and a lot of air-to-air refuelling for any ground-attack aircraft to reach here and that isn't going to happen in my judgement. There's the possibility planes from an aircraft carrier would attack but I think all fleets will be engaging other fleets and they're not going to attack us here because we're not worth attacking. I think it's more likely any attack will by sea followed up with a landing party from a submarine or some sort of merchant vessel. I don't think we are going to see any warships because they'll have been busy engaging each other and there is nothing much we can offer them. However, if a hostile warship does turn up, I doubt they'll have any shells or missiles left to launch a bombardment so again I'd expect the threat would be from a landing party.

"Of the coastline most of it isn't suitable for a landing so we'll only ever need to keep a lookout on the beaches and the harbour. The reality though is that we'll see a ship before we see a landing party. Any landing party might try a night landing but they'd be wiser not to, besides they'd have to have their ship come close to the island during darkness for them to make an assault which I think is unlikely. So, I don't recommend maintaining a night watch unless we see something on radar or sonar, during the day, assuming both are in working order and we have enough electrical power to run them." Vincent paused before continuing "The real threat though is that aside from you and I and the police, there is no-one capable of mounting a defence. I am therefore recommending volunteers be trained in the use of firearms and basic fieldcraft to form an Island Defence Volunteer Force (IDVF) and that this is something I could do within a short space of time, and then maintain as time went on, Maam."

Deborah listened to Vincent's report and was surprised. She wasn't however, surprised at his assessment, rather that it was almost exactly what a report undertaken by British Armed Forces, that she'd recently reread, had stated. She also knew that only herself, Will and a small group in the Ministry of Defence had read that report. She was also impressed with his idea of creating and training a volunteer defence force and was at a loss to understand why she hadn't thought of this, after all she was an Army reserve forces officer herself.

"Very good Vincent, I'm impressed. I accept your report and recommendations in full and you can proceed right away. I'll ring the Island police station to let them know you can draw the key for the armoury and tell Sabrina to give you the number to deactivate the alarm system. I'll also ring someone at the Americans' site so you can have access to their armoury as well, though I'm not sure if they even have anything in it" she told him. Then opening her desk drawer removed a large package which she pushed across the desk to him. "A Browning nine millimetre for yourself and a box of ammunition. I think from now on you should be armed at all times."

Vincent nodded and carefully removed the pistol from the holster, ejected the magazine and very rapidly cycled the mechanism and fired the action. He then refitted the magazine, holstered the pistol and fastened the holster and belt around his waist, having resisted the temptation to shove it in the back of his shorts. He was familiar with the Browning which had been around longer than he had and wasn't British or American by design but Belgique.

Once he'd finished Deborah looked at him and spoke once more. "I believe you have the keys to your Land Rover now. I'm not sure yet who we have left on the island who might fix a problem with it but I expect it will be reliable and not need fixing for many years." Then, once he was gone, she checked a book on her bookshelf about the history of the Island, and it was as she'd remembered, during the Second World War there had been a voluntary defence force and now they'd be one again, this time for what she supposed no-one would call the Third World War but rather the nuclear apocalypse or something like that.

Guns and volunteers

Vincent was pleased his efforts had been appreciated and left straightaway to draw the armoury key from the police station and to get directions to it. Once he'd got the keys and found and entered it, he used the alarm code to switch off the alarm, locked himself in and had a look around. Well, there wasn't a shortage of small arms but they were all very old. Not antique old but twenty plus years old and most likely either left here sometime after the Falklands conflict or supplied when the British forces replaced the L1A1 SLR SA70 with the SA80. He pulled a rifle off a rack and while not surprised to find it well-oiled was surprised to find that it appeared to be practically brand new, in fact he decided it was brand new.

There were several of the old type of Sub-Machine Gun, and a similar number of Light Machine Guns. He wasn't sure how many volunteers he'd get but they'd probably be a lot less than the number of arms here. He just hoped there was plenty of ammunition and that it wasn't past its use by date. He also guessed that since there were a lot more weapons than people on the island, let alone his defence force, he could utilise the extra magazines so everyone could carry several. It occurred to him though, if they were in a situation where they were putting that many rounds down, they'd be in dire straits and heavily outnumbered.

News had spread fast across the Island that there was to be an Island defence force. When he arrived outside Georgetown police station at the advertised time volunteers could join it, there was a group of about a dozen people. They consisted of half Saints with the rest mostly Brits and a couple of Americans. The Saints were an interesting mixture because half of them were women, something Vincent hadn't expected but which didn't bother him in the slightest.

"Evening all" Vincent said with a smile as he greeted his volunteers, adding "For this evening we're going inside the police station who have kindly let us use their facilities. One of the policemen will take your name and address; except if he doesn't consider you'll be suitable in which case his judgement is final. If he thinks you're borderline, he'll add a question mark after your name and you'll be given a chance and I'll make the final decision on whether or not you'll be fully trained. We aren't expecting to have to get into a firefight with any attacking forces but if we do it's likely some, or most of us will get injured or killed but we'll do so with honour. Likewise, if anyone decides that they've made a mistake in volunteering this evening they can also leave now without embarrassment." Vincent told them and waited. No-one left and no-one was rejected and they all smiled at Vincent after providing their details to the policeman, though since he greeted most of them by their first names, Vincent assumed he knew them already.

"Ok team, because from this point onwards WE are a team" Vincent told them emphasising the word 'we'. "Every team has a leader and I'm your leader. You don't need to call me Sir, although Miss Deborah, as our commanding officer, has made me a Lieutenant. But you will do as I tell you because all our lives may depend on it. You will also do exactly and precisely as I tell you and when I give an order you will reply by shouting 'YES VINCENT' except when I gesture you with my hand over my mouth which indicates you must make no sound. And remember if I say 'shit' you start straining. is that clear?"

"YES VINCENT" The team replied in unison as if they'd been saying it for weeks.

"Very good. This is a good start and you might just turn out to be the best team I've trained. Now gather round and I'll show you some guns, which from this point onwards we will always refer to as 'small arms'. You will learn how they work, how to get them working again if they stop working and how to take them apart and put them together again even in pitch darkness. Now watch and learn." Vincent told them.

Vincent then spent several hours stripping and assembling the British weapons with his team, with a refreshment break after the first hour or so. At the end of the evening, he explained the pros and cons of each weapon, including how much they weighed and that when it came to firing them if you had short arms you might be better off with the sub-machine gun rather than a rifle but if you had average length or long arms yet turned out to be a rotten shot you'd also be better off with a sub-machine gun. On the other hand, if you were an amazing shot but struggled with the length of a rifle, even with the shortest butt piece fitted he'd try and cut the butt down to make it more user friendly. Then in a move that surprised them all he gave them each a rifle with some a sub machine gun or a light machine gun as well. He told them to get used to stripping them and putting them back together and cleaning them using pencil lead rather than oil to lubricate the moving parts. Then he told them that from this point onwards these would be at least one of their personal weapons and they would be responsible for it.

Then wholly unprompted they all came to attention, well after a fashion, and shouted "YES VINCENT" and then one by one they shook his hand and left.

"That was a big gesture of trust Vincent" Chris, the taller of the two policemen told him.

"Yeah, well they need to know from the outset I trust them and they can trust me because one day our lives might depend upon it and if a shit-storm descends upon us, forming a neat queue outside the armoury won't be much use." Vincent said. "Besides I liked the look of every one of them and I reckon I'm a reasonable judge of character. Thanks also for your help and hosting us tonight Chris, I appreciated it. Good night."

Vincent drove home slowly back to Two Boats and reflected on the job before him. He decided he'd need to have a proper look at the Broken Tooth live firing area before he used it. He also wanted to be able to put in place some means of calling everyone out, like a phone 'call tree' unless there were enough radios for everyone to have one. He also planned to teach them basic fire control orders before having some kind of simple practical exercise.

The day following Vincent's training evening with the newly formed defence volunteers, Deborah was on her short drive across town which she drove only so she'd have her vehicle outside the office in case she needed it, when she noticed that there were a few islanders armed with small arms of varying types. When she walked into the Administrators building since Vincent was already in the office that she had allocated him, she knocked on his door and poked her head around the door frame.

"Morning Vincent are your volunteers' weapons live armed?" She asked him.

"No maam, morning maam. No volunteer will be issued with any ammunition except for supervised live firing practice until you have: inspected them, satisfied yourself of their proficiency in the use of their weapon or weapons and authorised live arms as the commanding officer." He told her.

"Thank you, Vincent. Also, how good do you think they will be?"

"I can honestly say Maam that they may prove to be the fastest learning and most highly motivated team I've ever put together."

Deborah thanked him for his work but was sceptical that the volunteers would be as good as he was leading her to believe, or perhaps he'd had to train fairly hopeless people in the past. Well time would tell but she hoped they'd never be put to the test.

It was just over a week later from the founding of the Island Volunteer Defence Force and Vincent had just got home from working and was about to have a shower when the house phone rang. Since there was hardly anyone on the island to ring him and since he hardly knew anyone, nor had yet put in place a phone call tree for the volunteers, he hadn't really given the phone much thought. He was barely even aware of its existence and it had never rung before. He walked over to it and picked up the receiver and spoke into it saying, "Hello."

"Vincent, there's been an accident on the cliffs down to Spire Beach, just past half way down. One of a group of walkers, Eddy Mannock an aircraft handler, is badly hurt and I need your help" Deborah told him.

"What do you need me to?" Vincent replied, forgetting to add his usual 'maam'.

"I don't know" Deborah replied then adding "a rescue team have already left with a stretcher but it's a really awkward descent. They have to be careful that halfway down they need to go left or end up going over a cliff and end up as casualties themselves. Then even if they reach the casualty before it gets dark, they won't get back very far before it will be pitch black. They'll be manhandling a stretcher with only head and hand torches for illumination and it will be very slow going, and well it might just take too long for the casualty."

"What's the water like at the beach? Can you get a RHIB in?" Vincent asked.

"I'm not sure, its gravelly with a short slope so it gets deep quickly. There's a heavy swell at the moment and our only RHIB has the seats in the middle such that you can't get a stretcher on it." She replied.

"Hmm. Ok. Is there another boat we can use?" He asked.

"Well, all the fishing boats used by the big game fishermen went back with them to St Helena and all the boats left are small. Except we still have what was the RAF's launch, can you meet me at the quay in Georgetown in a quarter of an hour and have a look at it?" Deborah asked.

"Yes, I'll be there" he replied and then put the phone down. Vincent looked into his rucksack and checked his torch worked ok and then ran to his Land Rover, put his seatbelt on and hustled the Landie through the village and onto the Old Mountain Road. Vincent was vaguely aware of a speed limit on the island but he'd never had to worry about it because he was never in a hurry and always drove slowly. The road was by far one of the better ones and Vincent managed to get the Land Rover up to about eighty-five miles an hour, at least that was the speed displayed on the speedo, and he even overtook a car on his drive to Georgetown. He then slowed down a fair amount as he entered the town and made his way to the quayside.

Deborah heard a Land Rover being driven very quickly and hoped it was Vincent and looking at her watch saw he'd taken less than five minutes to arrive. "Thanks for getting here so quickly. I've radioed the rescue party and told them to go down to the beach after they've rescued the casualty and to wait for you. This is Arnold. He's going to row out with you to the old RAF launch and go with you. I've given him a radio in a dry bag so once you're on the launch he'll keep in radio contact. Good Luck and don't take any silly risks" Deborah told Vincent before making eye contact with him.

Vincent nodded and was just about to reply when he felt her eye contact. Her eyes had betrayed her heart; there was a warmth in them, she cared for him and was worried, she'd let her guard down and he could see there was a need in them. "Yes maam" he told her before following Arnold down the quay steps and into a small rowing boat, and in his haste narrowly avoided getting soaked as the swell rose up the steps. It only took a few minutes to reach the launch and once they'd moored the rowing boat on the buoy they clambered onto the launch.

"Hi Arnold, have you used this launch before?" Vincent asked.

"Yes, but not very recently sir" he replied.

"Ok, well I never have, and please call me Vincent, unless I do something stupid in which case call me what you like" Vincent told him, smiling, while looking for the starter button for the engine. It was getting dark already and they were both relieved when Vincent got the engine started and found some lights. Arnold cast off from the buoy and they were on their way. The swell was forecast to increase and the small launch rose up and down the waves of the swell once they were clear of the harbour. The launch seemed to have a near full tank of fuel and Vincent put the engine on a notch just below full power and they were making almost fifteen knots, a lot slower than the RHIB would have been. Vincent wasn't sure if going North and North East would be quicker than going South and then East because while it was a shorter distance, he didn't know which direction had the most favourable currents. He figured it would take about three quarters of an hour to get to Spire Beach maybe less but if less, longer on the way back. He didn't have any kind of nautical map but knew the water was mostly deep and the currents were mostly off the shore. Of course, he knew there'd been ship wrecks in the past and they had been mostly sailing ships. All the same he'd have to take care not to get too close to the shore until he reached Spire Beach because there might not be anyone to rescue the rescuers.

It was over half an hour before Vincent and Arnold thought they could see Boatswain Bird Island which meant they were close to Spire Beach now. Arnold made a radio call and then tapped Vincent on the shoulder. They then saw a flare shoot high into the now dark sky and Arnold spoke into the radio but Vincent couldn't catch what he was saying. He did throttle back slightly and turned into the coast a bit more. Then they saw another flare, nearer this time and Vincent turned directly towards it, still on a steady throttle.

They arrived just off Spire beach and Vincent edged the boat nearer to the shore until he thought the keel was just brushing a gravelly sea bed. It was tricky keeping the boat in position as he saw the rescue party wading out to the boat as the swell rose and fell. Arnold helped two of them on board and then they helped get Eddy, in the stretcher, on board assisted by a group of others in the sea. Too many thought Vincent, we're overloaded or near overloaded. He carefully increased the throttle setting to near maximum and the boat slowly edged forward. He hoped the swell wouldn't wash over the boat because it was already lower in the water than it should be and also a bit crowded for effective bailing, should the need arise.

"Thanks for coming Vincent, I knew we could count on you" a man told him which when he looked to see who it was, found it was none other than Henry.

"Evening Henry, I think getting back will be harder than it was coming here, the swell's picked up. How is the casualty?" Vincent asked.

Henry pulled a face and shrugged before speaking "He doesn't look good and he's lost a lot of blood, it will be touch and go but the Doc should be able to fix him up if we can get back inside an hour. He'll be waiting for us. I've bandaged the wound and it's not bleeding through the bandage."

Vincent nodded and put the throttle on the full setting though it seemed not to make a lot of difference other than change the tone of the engine. It was risky holding full throttle for a prolonged period of time on an old engine of what he termed 'unknown providence' but it sounded ok and Eddie's life might be at stake so it was a risk he felt he had to take. The swell increased and after a while the launch would slow down as it climbed a large wave and then speeded up with a lot of prop shaft rattling after cresting the wave and going down to the trough. At one point there was a sudden burst of excitement and then some laughter. Arnold shouted to Vincent that a flying fish had just hit someone on the head and bounced off them and fallen back into the sea.

Vincent looked to Port and saw a red light. It was the tracking radar at the Pyramid Point facility and he knew it was a safer journey now, past Long Beach to Georgetown quay. The waves remained high and when they arrived the swell was now over a metre, if not a metre and a half high, and it was impossible to safely unload the stretcher with Eddy on it. Arnold put the radio to his ear and then advised Vincent "They are going to try and use the dockside crane to lower a line for us to fix the stretcher to and then once we're certain he isn't going to fall out they will lift him up and land the stretcher on the quayside. Henry will help them with the pick-up of the line. Get in as close as is safe to do so and once he's clear the rest of us will use the quay steps if you can get close enough, after that you can moor up here and I'll help you."

Vincent had never seen anyone in a stretcher hoisted by dockside crane before but it seemed to work well though he found it was tricky keeping the launch steady and he kept wishing it was more powerful. At one point as the swell dropped Vincent saw a large Octopus on the quay steps. Finally, with everyone off the launch he and Arnold moored it up, with more expertise on the part of Arnold than himself. He was soaked and for the first time since being on the island he felt cold and shivered as he climbed up the quayside steps.

38

Deborah watched Eddy hoisted from the launch and transferred from the quayside to an American ambulance and driven the short distance to the hospital. She watched the rescue party disembark along with Henry and his sergeant and Henry came over to speak to her straightaway.

"Evening Miss Deborah. Vincent done us proud, it was tricky at the beach and a rough sea journey back here and I'm glad he's with us. Eddy doesn't look good and has lost a lot of blood but he was still conscious so I expect he'll live. We are all wet and cold so why don't you invite everyone back to my place for a hot cocoa?" he suggested.

"Ok Henry put the kettle on we'll soon be with you" she replied and then she went to each group of people and told them to go to Henry's new home, the residency, and she'd meet them there.

Vincent and Arnold were on the quayside and she watched them intently and saw them shake hands. She saw Vincent shiver and walked up to him. She was just about to embrace him and give him a big thank you when she changed her mind telling herself 'No Deborah, not now, not yet, maybe not ever'.

"You pair look cold. We're all very grateful to you and you must join us at Henry's home for a hot cocoa. I'll drive you, jump in." Deborah told them, and after a longer drive than Vincent had expected, albeit with the vehicle's heater blasting out hot air, they were at Henry's. The atmosphere was fairly light-hearted and there was a lot of chat about the rescue with the casualty seemingly forgotten.

Vincent hadn't been to this part of Green Mountain and was surprised to find that Henry and his family lived in what must surely be the poshest house on the island, half way up Green Mountain itself, and called the residency.

"Nice place Henry, have you lived here long?" Vincent asked him.

"No Vincent we have only just moved in, say hello to my wife Pam. Pam this is Vincent the island's newest arrival and it seems a man of many talents including handling a small boat in a strong swell." Henry replied.

"Pleased to meet you Vincent" Pam said.

"And to meet you" Vincent replied. He then looked around for Deborah and found she was holding a large tray of mugs and a jug of what he guessed was cocoa from the aroma he could just about detect. She saw him looking at her and she smiled, walked over to him and poured him a mug of cocoa. Vincent felt cold again, not having fully dried out, and he realised that the Henrys' home was a fair way up Green Mountain and on the cool side, especially when you were wet in places and cold already.

Then Deborah surprised Vincent with an impromptu sideways hug and rub of his arm with her warm body and hands. Then she draped her jacket over his shoulders telling him "This is dry and might warm you up a little."

Vincent was grateful for the jacket and was just about to reach out and put his arm around her waist when she moved away from him. He looked around and when he caught Henry's eye, he was introduced to everyone that had been with him in the boat. Another policeman and what he guessed must be the man's wife arrived and spoke to Henry and Henry smiled and thanked them.

"Here you are Vincent, the keys to your Land Rover which has been delivered here for you to save you having to hitch a lift back to Georgetown" Henry told him smiling.

Vincent thanked him and abandoning any hope of getting better acquainted with Deborah, said his goodbyes so he could get home and have a warm shower and wash the now dried salt off his skin.

After the incident at Spire Beach

"Morning Maam," said Vincent.

"Morning Vincent" Deborah replied and then paused before speaking again. "If you are comfortable doing so Vincent, you could address me as Miss Deborah, the same as everyone else does."

"Yes, Miss Deborah. Also, I have a question for you. Why were the walkers going down to Spire Beach?"

"I expect they were checking on the letterbox. Spire Beach is one of the letterbox walks and sometimes a walking group will check the box is still in good order, the ink pad moist and so on, or just walk to it for the walk itself." She replied.

Vincent had heard of the letterbox walks but hadn't given them any further thought until now, and they perhaps presented an opportunity. "Would you like to walk one of the letterbox walks with me one weekend Miss Deborah?" he asked while displaying the most neutral smile he could manage. Deborah didn't reply and he was just about to ask again when she did with a sad look that made him feel sorry for her.

"That's very kind of you to ask me but well, err, this isn't a good time for me so, well, err well thanks but no thanks" she told him adding. "I'm sorry Vincent and I have a lot of things I need to get done now so perhaps we can talk another time."

"Yes Maam" Vincent replied and he left her office to the one down the corridor which he'd been given. Fuck! He thought he was making progress and he was but now the door was shut again. This fucking war would kick off any day now and that would be that, for weeks, months, years even. She was holding back on him and herself and there wasn't much he could do about it until another opportunity presented itself.

Deborah felt sad. She'd made a small move and he'd responded and then she'd thrown the barriers back up. She might as well have slapped him in the face and he didn't deserve to be messed about. Just at that moment Doc Caskey appeared at her office door and once she'd beckoned him in, he closed the door behind him.

"Morning Boss, good news and bad news. Eddy had a reasonable night and I'm confident he'll be ok but with an interesting scar to bear witness to his mistake. The unwelcome visitor died last night and I can't be certain it was a virus that killed her. The problem is I'm guessing we'll need to move into the bunker soon and the islanders will still need to be in quarantine, this is their tenth day so you, or me if you prefer, need to decide whether to move them or not." Doc Caskey said.

"How do you know about the bunker Doc?" Deborah asked.

"Well obviously Will told me, will that do for now?" he replied and added "I think it's still a secret for practically everyone else on the island, besides you are going to have to tell them soon, aren't you?"

"Yes, I think I'll have a key personnel meeting first, you'll be invited of course" she replied and added "I'm really hard-pressed today but I'll make time for a proper catch up in the morning if that's ok?"

"Ok Boss, but don't overdo it, remember to delegate and begin to build a bigger management team than Will and Hal had because you'll need it. See you tomorrow" he replied.

Deborah left her office so she could talk to Sabrina. "I need your help to produce a list of key personnel on the island and first wondered if Will or Hal had such a list? Then if they did, can you get them and can you cross out everyone on them who's no longer on the island?"

"Yes Miss Deborah, Will did have a list which I found yesterday and I'm looking for the list Hal left me and then I'll produce an up-to-date hybrid list from them both" she replied.

"Oh Sabrina, there's one other key task and that relates to our IT. We need to make sure everything we are storing is on our own file server or even C drives or portable drives or USB sticks because the 'cloud' is likely to go up in smoke once the war starts. Also, can you see if there is anyone who can ensure the IT network on the island will work at least for us and that we don't have switches, routers, hubs, bridges or whatever that will only work by leaving the island and coming back again. I can't think of anyone that can do this but perhaps there's an American that can at least come up with some ideas and at the very least get all of our stuff migrated from the 'cloud' back to solid ground here. Thanks."

Chapter Four – The letterbox walks

Vincent decided that for the few days left, if that, before the war started, he'd try and do some of the letterbox walks even if he did have to do them on his own. He liked to exercise or just be outdoors, even a ship's deck, and hadn't enjoyed sitting in an office most of the day. He hadn't really found out much about the history of the walks, other than the oldest walk was called 'The Letterbox'. Also, for quite a long time there were just ten other walks. They were founded by a British Broadcasting Corporation (BBC) Engineer on the island, Sean Newbery in 1979 making a total of Eleven. A twelfth walk was added in 1986 and then more walks added after that with ten on Green Mountain itself, although the walks and paths on the mountain dated back to a much earlier time each having its own name but without being actual letterbox walks.

The Letterbox was the first and original letterbox and had had about three lives or positions as it were. It was a long walk and while the one he most wanted to do; it would have to wait. The second walk created was Sisters Peak and he'd manage that after finishing work. Lady Hill he decided he'd get up extra early to walk because it was quite local and not that difficult. Several walks were volcanic domes or craters and of those, Broken Tooth, appealed to him the most being accessed over mostly black lava rock. The last walk on his short list was the Devil's Riding School dating back to 1986 and being created by RAF guys of that era. All the other walks would most likely have to wait a while before he undertook them, including Spire Beach.

Beep, Beep, Beep, Beep. Vincent woke up and switched off his alarm clock. It seemed early to him. But of course, it was early because he wanted to walk up Lady Hill, the first letterbox walk he would undertake. He jumped out of bed, got dressed, washed and cleaned his teeth and made himself a mug of tea, with UHT milk, and had a bowl of muesli. While eating his muesli he pondered what breakfasts might be like this time next year, dried fish most likely. He grabbed his rucksack, checked his Browning pistol and found a pen and piece of paper. He wrote on the paper 'Vincent, climbing Lady Hill back before 0900 hours or send help!'.

It was a short drive to the base of Lady Hill and after leaving his message in his Land Rover he put on his rucksack and switching on his torch started the climb. There was a fairly easy track to follow, even by torch light and the climb wasn't that steep. While he'd generally thought of a hill as being green and grassy, Lady hill wasn't like that, being comprised of orangey red crushed rock. Vincent supposed that in daylight he might even have been able to run to the top. Sure enough, it took him well inside an hour to find his way to the top. He had a look inside the Letterbox by torchlight and read the names of the people that had all made this climb before him and the dates they had done so, written in an exercise type book. He then added his name and the date and time of his visit.

He looked at his tatty old cheap watch and noted it would be a while before sun rise and he decided he wanted to stay on the summit and wait for it. While he was waiting, he reached inside his rucksack and took a drink of the chilled juice made from a powder and water that he'd mixed and filled his flask with. Then he realised it was getting lighter and there it was, sunrise. He looked at his Walking Maps booklet and thought that just maybe he could manage another walk today and then get into work late. Deborah could hardly sack him and despite giving him a small demonstration worthy of her nick-name he must still be in her good books.

After a flick through the booklet, he decided to tackle Broken Tooth Crater. He could drive back to Two Boats and take the North East Bay Road and then park on the dry water course and walk the rest of the way as you were supposed to.

It was quite hot when Vincent parked up and set out walking. The trail was easy to follow and the volcano crater was easy to keep in sight. He was making good time up to the point where the dry water course ended and it was necessary to cross a short stretch of solid lava. It was a fascinating sight to behold because the lava flow just stopped in what seemed like a mid-flow and it was quite high. It had the appearance of having stopped flowing seconds ago. Despite, being fairly well travelled he'd never seen anything like this before. It was a bit of hop skip and jump across the lava flow and Vincent was pleased to have made good time in reaching the letterbox. After writing his name in the book in the letterbox, he decided to have a long drink and rest for a few moments before making his way back. Once he was on the move again, he soon got into a good rhythm of practically running across the lava flow when he misjudged his step and slid down into a gap in the lava flow and found himself in excruciating pain. For a second, he thought his leg might be trapped and he'd have to radio for help but he was able to slowly but painfully ease it out and haul himself up. There was a long-ragged cut that looked like it would need stitching to pull the wound together but he was sure nothing was broken. He'd some other grazes on one elbow and both arms, and his watch was smashed, but it was the leg that was the trouble. He didn't feel ok and he supposed he was suffering a bit of shock. It was slow progress after that to get off the lava flow and back onto the dry water course. There was some steady bleeding but not enough to really worry him, not yet anyway. He could use the first aid kit in his Land Rover to bandage his leg but his legs were quite hairy and when the bandage came off it would hurt all over again. No, he might just as well drive straight to the hospital. After walking at a much slower pace than he'd set out with, which eventually turned into a limp he reached his Land Rover and sat in it.

Ouch, that hurt, Vincent thought as he used his leg to let in the clutch and it hurt again as he let it out as well. He felt slightly dazed and decided he'd change gears without bothering to use the clutch for the rest of the drive. It wasn't good for the life of the gearbox synchro's but he'd be gentle. He was soon through Two Boats and on the familiar drive to Georgetown he was used to, only stopping outside the hospital instead of the administrator's building. He grabbed his rucksack and hobbled inside and hung onto the reception desk once he'd reached it. Just then he saw the doctor and Deborah appear together.

"Hi Doc. Oh, err morning Maam. Can you have a look at this gash on my leg please Doc?" Vincent asked the doctor while being surprised to see Deborah with him.

Deborah had been intent in preventing any alarm about the possible arrival of the pandemic virus on the island and it had seemed to her to be less conspicuous for her to drop by the hospital than for Doc Caskey to visit her office. Vincent looked a bit grey in his complexion and his leg looked a mess and very bloody. He also had some deep looking scuffs and scrapes on his arms. She didn't pause to think before speaking and blurted out "My darling what's happened?"

Vincent and the Doc, with perfect timing stopped dead and looked at her in disbelief of what they heard her say. Then they looked at each other.

Deborah blushed but quickly gathered her composure and said "I'll catch up with you both later, I must dash now" and left before either of them had time to comment.

The Doc looked at Vincent's leg before speaking "Well son, I suppose you know this isn't going to glue and we're going to have to sew these flaps of skin together. What did you do, fall in a lava flow?" the Doc asked.

"Yes, and yes, on the way back from Broken Tooth letterbox" Vincent replied.

"Mmm. Two letterbox accidents in a week. She'll ban them if there's another accident and nobody wants that because after the war, we'll need some challenging recreational activities. She has most of the weight of this island and its population on those pretty young shoulders and she's hanging onto other things she can't let go of so doesn't need any more drama. That slip of her tongue just now tells me that she's losing some control and in relation to you that might be a good thing but if she loses control in other areas, it will be a worry to us all. Very soon there are challenges ahead we all have to meet and pull through so don't mention her slip of the tongue to anyone or get your hopes up till we're the other side of the war. Oh and no more fucking letterbox walks on your own, doctor's orders, suppositories three times a day if you don't" the doc told him while patiently cleaning and then stitching Vincent's wound. Then he muttered something to a nurse and left them together.

The nurse smiled at Vincent as she applied a dressing then a bandage over the freshly stitched wound. "Ok, Mr Irving, don't mess with this. Try not to get it too wet and come back tomorrow morning for us to change the dressing. This will hurt for a few days so you won't feel like walking very far on it but just in case you are tempted my husband never jokes about suppositories and Deborah is one of our dearest friends. Have a nice day." "Yeah, thanks. See you tomorrow." Vincent told her.

Deborah sat in her office and bit her lip, 'Fuck'! Her heart had ruled her head for a split second and she'd accidentally revealed she had feelings for Vincent, to his face! What troubled her the most though was that she hadn't consciously realised that herself. Well, her options were: to try and explain it as a slip of the tongue when in reality it was obviously a 'Freudian slip', explain to Vincent she obviously was beginning to have some attraction to him, or do nothing and act as if it had never happened. Do nothing was always an option in any given situation or scenario but one which she almost never chose. Yet this time it seemed like the best thing to do. It wouldn't hurt her or Vincent for them both to know that while she had feelings for him, she wasn't going to do anything about them right now, but nor would she deny them. Mmmm, yes do nothing and not so much pretend it didn't happen but ignore the fact that it had happened.

Vincent walked gingerly to the Administrators Office from the Hospital with his leg hurting. He realised that he'd have to provide some sort of explanation for his accident while ignoring the fact that Deborah had accidentally called him 'darling'. He didn't think this would be too difficult as he was feeling very sorry for himself and he wasn't in the mood for making jokes or being smart or anything like that. So instead of going to what was his office he went to Deborah's. He decided he'd try and do all the talking.

"Morning Maam. As you can see, I've hurt my leg and the doc has sewed up the gash. I was kind of jogging across a lava flow and missed my footing," Vincent told her while pulling something of an embarrassed face that said 'I've been a silly bastard and know it so I don't need to be told so'.

46

"Ok Vincent I'm assuming you'll be ok to sit in your office and look at some notes I've made and make some phone calls. We have a secret bunker here that very few people know about and that I haven't told anyone about yet, or even looked at, but soon everyone will know about. I'm planning on running all the island's operations from the bunker including this office, the Administrator's office, for a short period of time. That should enable everything to settle in before we move everyone on the island into it for the duration of hostilities, assuming that happens. It will give us complete command and control as well as protection from everything. Sabrina will work with you today as I need to go and check out a few things down there myself. The main thing I want you to do is create a list of everyone or team, that needs to be on initial occupation, from a bigger list Sabrina will give you, run it past me by radio, and then after I've approved it call those people to a meeting. Does that all sound ok?" she told him while maintaining her best neutral and dead-pan expression.

"Yes Maam" Vincent replied.

Deborah realised that she'd managed to get off lightly with her slip of the tongue and Vincent looked pretty fed up and must be in a fair bit of pain. He looked like he'd smashed his watch as well. Perhaps that was something she could put right for him. She could say it was a thank you for going beyond the call of duty for the Spire Beach rescue. Yes, that would work, she could ring Frank this afternoon to arrange it.

Vincent walked slowly back to his own office and arranged a spare chair so he could rest his injured leg on it. Sabrina's list of names was lengthy and besides each name was a job title and whether the person was American or American staff or British and British staff. Having read through the list he decided he'd have no idea how to decide who needed to be on an initial occupation for the mystery bunker. He hadn't even been told how long an initial occupation might be. He hadn't bothered with the news since he'd been here and didn't have much idea how much time might be left before war broke out and everyone needed to move into the bunker and live in it. He decided to ring one of the names near the top of the list that he recognised.

"Morning Frank, it's Vincent here, we met the other day when Henry introduced us. I'm trying to help Deborah prioritise a list of key personnel and need some help with the list of Americans. Do you think you can help me?" Vincent asked.

"Sure thing Vincent, why don't you pop over and I will show you some other useful stuff?" Frank replied.

"Well err, the thing is I've hurt my leg and I'm trying to rest it enough so I can work the clutch pedal for the drive home at the end of the day." Vincent told him.

"How about if I collect you? Can you hobble outside, do you have a stick?" he was asked.

"Yes and no, I'll start hobbling now, see you in a minute." Vincent told him and then wondered why he hadn't got a stick, it might help. By the time he was outside and looking up the road Frank had arrived. After a quick greeting Frank had driven them to the American base area.

"Well Vincent, let's see how I can help you with this list. I'll type something up and print it before we have to revert to slate and chalk." Frank joked. Frank then spoke as he typed the list "You need me, Brad the lead radar operator, Alan, the only guy left for what I still call Nike-Zeus, but is now the Pyramid complex, the Doc, Andrew the only guy left for the English Bay Power Station and that Saint that all the other Saints look to as their unofficial leader. In fact, as well as printing it I'll e-mail a copy to Sabrina so she can add the Brits to the list and have one list. Didn't take long, did it?" he added.

Vincent was pleasantly surprised replying "No, it certainly didn't."

"Well since we've done the important stuff how would you like to wander over to the BX and pick up some nice things?" Frank asked and adding, "you look as if you need a new watch for starters."

"Yeah, well I'd like to but I don't have much money." Vincent replied.

"Well, here's the deal. Let's let Uncle Sam pay, because in a few days or weeks' time no-one will be around to have us account for this stuff and the only thing most of America will be buying is the farm. Besides, what we don't take and use now will simply gather dust. Before he left, Hal told me it would be ok to give everything away if things turned sour. Then he laughed and said but if it didn't and he came back, I'd have to arrange for some sort of 'accident' to cover the loss." Frank laughingly told him.

Vincent was surprised how jovial Frank seemed to be about everything. He supposed that having made the decision to stay on the island, what might be termed the 'outside world' had nothing to offer him. It didn't take long to hobble over to the BX which Frank unlocked and then locked behind them.

"I'll get a trolley for your stuff Vincent and wheel it for you." Frank told him. "Here's a nice blue watch, the Breitling Superocean automatic 48. It has a self-winding movement and doesn't need a battery so might just last you for ever unless you have another accident, so here's a spare with a different coloured face, green and you might as well have a yellow as well, just in case you're accident prone. They're titanium cases so light as a feather, nice, aren't they? Grab a couple of knives and multitools – you can never have too many, keep some in your vehicle, some in a grab bag, that sort of thing. There are some binoculars over here or spotting scopes if you prefer. Hey, how about a camera monopod you could use as a walking stick. Nice compact underwater camera and a big brother DSLR, a camera bag and some other bags. We're at the clothes section now, just pick a bunch of stuff in your size and remember after the war there's about forty other blokes that'll clean this place out, so shop early." Frank told him.

Vincent enjoyed the shopping trip. Over the years he'd had some nice stuff but sometimes he'd had to sell things when he was short of money or couldn't afford a repair or service bill, often the case with watches. He'd also had the odd thing stolen or had lost it. Now and again he'd simply given something away to someone he figured needed it more than he did. After they'd finished at the BX Frank locked up and they went to Frank's office.

"Thanks for that Frank, I really appreciate it. Tell me you seem more cheerful and less worried about the world crisis than most people on the island I've met, why is that?"

"Well Vincent, I'm on this beautiful island with my lovely wife, where there is no crime and I have several friends. There are no traffic jams and no pollution. There is good fishing and good walking and it doesn't rain very often but when it does it's soothing." Vincent nodded he understood by way of reply

Frank produced a couple of coffees and after they'd finished them, he gave Vincent a lift back and then transferred his shopping to the Land Rover for him, explaining there was no crime on the island and he didn't need to worry about anything getting stolen. He then said goodbye and left without being seen while Vincent limped back to his office.

It was just gone midday when Frank's phone rang, he picked it up and found it was Deborah ringing him.

"Afternoon Frank, its Deborah. I'm hoping you can help me out with a thank-you present for Vincent who served us proud with the Spire Beach rescue only to have a smaller but perhaps no less painful one himself earlier today. It's something Hal mentioned and agreed with me in that at an appropriate time I could re-distribute the contents of the BX. His intention was after the war when no-one would hold anyone to account, but I'm prepared to take a risk and would like to shop early for something for Vincent. I believe there are some nice Breitling watches that might make a welcome thank-you gift for him, what do you think?" she asked.

"Err. Well Miss Deborah I think Vincent may already have a nice watch." He replied.

"No, I don't think he has, I've only ever seen him wear an old one and he smashed that in his accident this morning, and if he does, I suppose having another nice one won't hurt, will it?" she told him and added "I'll meet you at the BX in five minutes."

Frank put the phone down and then roared with laughter before going to the BX to meet Deborah.

At the BX Frank showed Deborah where the watches were and he was glad he'd given Vincent watches from the under-counter stock rather than the display. "This is a lovely watch Deborah" Frank told her picking up the Breitling Superocean automatic 48 from the display. "It's an automatic and light as a feather with a Titanium case" he told her.

Deborah looked at the watch and it looked like just the sort of watch that might suit Vincent. "Yes, but perhaps in that Green colour" she told him.

"I tell you what why don't you take both for him and that yellow one as well. As you say he served the island proud at Spire Beach and we probably have more nice watches than we have people on the island. In fact, have a yellow one for yourself before they all go." Then seeing her hesitate he told her "I insist and if Hal returns and there's no war, I'll simply burn the BX down to the ground." And then he roared with laughter. Deborah was convinced though slightly bemused by Frank's jovial insistence and took all three watches but without taking one for herself and thanking him, left.

As soon as Deborah had left, Frank picked up the phone and rang Vincent telling him "You won't believe this but you're about to get three more watches, so keep the ones you just got in the Land Rover and make sure you have that old one back on and act real surprised when you get given the new ones" and he then said 'Bye' before Vincent could reply. He then rang Henry. "Afternoon Henry, Frank here, those nice titanium watches are flying off the shelves so you better get yourself and your men down here real-quick if you want one, or two. See you in five minutes then" and then he hung up before Henry could argue with him and then he roared with laughter till tears rolled down his cheeks.

With a carrier bag containing the watches, each in a massive display box Deborah stopped at the hospital. "Hi Luke I need a favour, it won't take long, and please don't say no," she told Doc Caskey, using his first name on account of her request being a personal favour from him. She then explained she wanted him to give Vincent an update on how Eddy was recovering from his accident at Spire Beach and then present him with the watches as a gift from the islanders. He nodded his agreement and was glad he'd picked up pretty much the same thing himself from Frank yesterday

50

and wondered what the fuck they'd do if Hal returned and peace was declared.

Vincent was sitting in his office when Deborah appeared in the doorway and began to speak to him. "Afternoon Vincent, Doc Caskey is here and myself and Sabrina would like to join you both for a few minutes" Deborah told him before ushering the Doc into the room.

"Afternoon Vincent. I'm a doctor not an administrator. Yet it seems to me that the island hasn't really given you a proper thank you for saving Eddy Mannock's life and risking your own life in that beach rescue in heavy seas. He is recovering well. Then while treating you this morning I couldn't help but notice you'd smashed your watch. So, it seemed to me and after speaking to Deborah and Sabrina that a new watch or maybe three that might last you a lifetime would be a nice thank you gift, so here you are." Then having finished his impromptu speech he turned to Deborah and rolled his eyes and then turning back to Vincent clapped his hands and Sabrina, and Deborah joined in clapping.

Vincent opened each watch case and was surprised to see the very same model of watches he'd been given earlier. He was wondering whether he should give back the three from earlier and realised he'd better say thank you.

"Well, I'm not really sure how to thank you for these lovely watches which I'm guessing will last me a lifetime. Thanks very much" he replied, while half expecting someone to announce he'd been set up for some sort of joke.

At the end of the day Vincent put the bag of watches in his Land Rover to go with the pile of stuff he already had and pondered what a strange day it had been. Over the years he had experienced good days go bad, bad days go good and strange days, but never a day that went from bad to good to very odd. Still, it had ended well, though he felt he might still need to give away some of the watches.

He soon found the pain in his leg increased dramatically when he used it to press the clutch in and let it out again. So, once he was on the move, he carefully changed gear without the clutch and drove slowly in fourth gear all the rest of the way back to his home. Once he'd opened the door, he dumped everything he'd been given just inside the door and sat on the sofa. He thought he might have an early night but then remembered he had a training session with his team. In a flash of inspiration, he decided he'd practice using the call-tree and get them to meet here instead of the Exiles building in Georgetown and once they were here, he'd get them to practice battlefield first aid in the darkness outside.

Chapter Five – The beginning of the end

Deborah was on her own when she made her first visit to the bunker. The initial access was straightforward, mundane even, from the Administrator's office at the airhead. Then with something almost as dramatic as Ed Straker's office in the TV series UFO, it was possible to open a hidden security access door that led to a very wide metal spiral staircase that eventually ended in front of a wide blast door. Once through the blast door there was a set of airlock doors to pass through before ending up in a long corridor. The corridor stretched a long way into the distance but Deborah knew it was ten thousand feet long because it was as long the runway that was above it. Apparently when the runway was first built the bunker tunnel was built underneath it as part of those works. Initially it was just planned as an air raid shelter but over the years it had been developed and widened. Whenever any work was undertaken to the runway, additional facilities had been added below it and leading off the corridor at the same time without causing much suspicion. Obviously, the engineers knew a bunker when they were building one but had no inkling of the level of sophisticated fit-out that would follow after they had left. The various fit-outs had all been undertaken by staff with the highest security clearance who routinely worked on similar projects around the world though mostly the UK or USA depending on what was being installed.

The bunker was exceptionally deep because it was designed to survive the runway being bombed above it. Every military or key civil operation that was conventionally run above ground on the island could be run below ground, here in the bunker, or at least that's what the briefing document stated. There were also some things that were only ever and could only ever, be operated from the bunker. Deborah realised that the bunker was designed at a time when the military strength of the island was much, much, larger numerically than the current total population of the island. From what she had read she knew there was enough food and water down here to last many months, along with just about everything else you could possibly want. It took her some time to check the whole facility and she'd have a better look when she returned to deliver her briefing and introduce the bunker to everyone else. She retraced her steps back to the administrator's office having very carefully checked everything was locked and sealed behind her.

Now that she'd seen the bunker and it was quite pleasant, as bunkers go, she decided that she'd move and run all key functions from the bunker starting from tomorrow on a working hours only basis and then move everyone else in afterwards, the exact day depending on how things developed.

Deborah also decided she'd need to call an all-island meeting and tell them they'd be evacuated to the bunker. There was no point in keeping it a secret any longer and she wasn't going to give anyone the choice of not evacuating. The meeting would be tomorrow morning.

"Sabrina, can you tell everyone on the island I'm calling an emergency meeting tomorrow morning, which they must attend. You choose the best time and place for it, maybe the Exiles Club, and see if you can get someone to arrange a microphone and speakers with a battery powered loud-hailer as a back-up. Thanks" Deborah told her. It wasn't laziness or indecision on her part not choosing the time and venue. Rather that her choices might not have been as good as Sabrina's in this matter. Part of Deborah's management ethos was to ask for the result she required rather than tell people what to do. As a young manager she'd found her approach worked better than she'd ever imagined and it was rare she needed to intervene, and almost never with experienced staff. She'd also had experience of working for senior managers who were much less flexible than herself. One in particular always had to do everything his way unless he didn't have an idea in which case it could be done her way.

A meeting of everyone

"Good morning everyone. My name is Deborah Black and I'm the island's Administrator and Military Commander-in-Chief for both the UK and the USA. Most likely most of you will have heard of me and many of you will have met me before and of course some of you are personal friends. You will also be aware of the global crisis and how that's changed things here, including Will's departure and my appointment. Not least you'll be aware Martial Law was declared. You already know our Chief of Police, but perhaps most of you haven't met our newest and only arrival, Vincent Irving, who I've temporarily appointed as deputy military commander and who was a key asset to the island in the casualty evacuation from Spire Beach the other week. Miss Sabrina Triumph who you probably know better than myself, has taken over my post as Deputy Administrator.

"We are now the entire population of the island, unless anyone is missing and after this meeting Miss Sabrina will take some details from you to confirm where you are living and any skills or knowledge you had in the past, perhaps a previous job that might be useful to us here. By that I mean just about anything such as a DIY plumber to DIY car mechanic or any medical training. This is important to us because we are 'it' and unless the global crisis has a happy ending, we'll remain 'it'.

"I can tell you that all the countries around the world that were slow or unable to halt all movement of people have been annihilated by the pandemic. The African, Middle East and Latin America countries were all hit very bad very early on, though it was much later that we found that out because some of them suppressed the news. The United Nations appear to be achieving nothing but perhaps their real failure was both in the recent and longer-term past than now. There's a slim possibility their negotiations will save the day but for now we have to plan for the worst-case scenario.

So, if the global crisis takes a turn for the worst and by this, I mean open armed conflicts, although we are a long way from everywhere there is a slim chance our facilities may be targets and thus subject to a missile attack. Any missile might have a conventional warhead or a nuclear warhead. However, we're actually more prepared for that than most of you might imagine because there is a substantial underground bunker-cum-nuclear fallout shelter on the island. You may have heard rumours of it, one or two may even have worked on it, or in it, and while it was a highly classified military secret, I've now decided to tell you a bit about it. Also, we are all going to occupy it, hopefully only for a short time. It will give us absolute protection and provides everything for us apart from, well, natural sunlight. It can operate wholly independently of everything else on the island while being linked to key infrastructure. It was designed for many times more of us than are here on the island now so we shouldn't feel cramped. The access we will use is from the Administrator's Office at the airhead. There are a couple of jobs that go with bunker occupation, known as shelter marshals – I'm inviting volunteers for those jobs, let Miss Sabrina know if you're interested, though some of you will already have key tasks that you'll need to carry on with.

I'm expecting to be advised when I'm to issue a 'move to shelter' order though I've not told my UK colleagues we're using the Bunker which I'm not supposed to have told anyone about. Their idea will be filling sandbags and making shelters within our own houses. I suppose I could ask them for permission to use the bunker but they'll be busy and even if I get a reply it might be one I'd have to ignore. So, there you have it. We really are all in this together and over the following days, weeks, months and years we'll get to know each other a lot better. I'll be using a mixed warning system to let you know when to leave your homes and head for the bunker. If anyone wants to move in early, and I'll be taking up working residency from tomorrow and living residentially from next Monday, unless the crisis quickens in pace, let Sabrina know and she'll let me know. Finally, rather than have an open question time, where I might have a job to hear your questions, I'm staying here for individual questions until the last one has been asked, however long that takes. I'll also publish a list of questions and answers, maybe tomorrow or the day after." Then having finished speaking Deborah was just about to sit down when there was a large round of applause. The applause took her by surprise because she was simply doing her job. She acknowledged it with several nods of her head and then recalled what a manager had told her years earlier that was along the lines of 'what you don't always realise Deborah is how well you lead such that others follow you unquestioningly. Also, if you pass a criticism on another team, your team accept it as absolute truth, which it may be, but they are then less skilled than you are in dealing with that underperforming team, just be aware of those things.'

Deborah saw the crowd disperse but was slightly discouraged to see a long queue forming of people wanting to ask her a question. As things turned out it wasn't so much a queue of questioners but mostly a queue of people wanting to thank her, or shake her hand, and one or two gave her a hug. She found the whole experience very touching and moving and wholly unexpected. All this time she was flanked by Sabrina and Henry on her right and Vincent on her left. Some of the islanders spoke to them as well and one of the older men took the opportunity to give Sabrina a hug. The man's wife looked slightly annoyed when he did this and the beneficiary was Vincent who received a hug from the woman. Vincent looked embarrassed afterwards and the woman smiled sweetly at him and less so her husband. Sabrina stifled a giggle.

Once the last person had left, Deborah thanked Sabrina and then Vincent and told them she'd see them tomorrow, then she spotted Henry's family. "Henry, I see your family over there, please call them over so I can talk to you all together". Henry did as he'd been asked and Deborah smiled at Henry's wife Pam and the young children. She knew that they were the only children on the island unless anyone had any more which seemed unlikely. "Hello Pam, hello children. You've grown so big since I last saw you. I wanted to talk to you because I want to make sure you don't have any secret worries you haven't told your Mummy and Daddy?"

"What's a bunker?" they asked in unison.

"There are all sorts of bunkers but our bunker is like an extra big house with work places and bedrooms but it doesn't have a garden or windows. It's made especially strong to keep us safe while we wait for the troubles of the world to pass us by." Deborah told them.

"Will everyone die that left the island?" Charlie asked.

"Nobody really knows for sure. They might die and they might not but whatever happens I don't think they will be coming back here. The world will be very different and lots of things will change but we will have to wait and see what that looks like."

"Could you and Miss Sabrina have babies so they could grow up and be children so we could have some more friends?" Elizabeth asked.

Deborah realised she'd forgotten how candid and searching the questions of young children could be and she needed a moment to think of an answer.

"Well, Elizabeth, that might be difficult at the moment but who knows what might happen in the future" she replied.

"That's enough questions you pair, it's past your bedtime. You need to get up early tomorrow and we'll pack some little suitcases for you," Pam told her children and then she looked at Deborah and rolled her eyes.

Henry and Pam and the children all shook Deborah's hand and then left. Deborah had forgotten that Vincent and Sabrina were still standing close by. Sabrina looked slightly awkward but Vincent was grinning. Then before Deborah could say anything Vincent spoke first.

"Miss Deborah, is there something appropriate I can do for you?" he asked.

"No" she firmly replied.

"Well, is there something inappropriate I can do for you?" he then asked while pulling the most dead-pan expression he could muster. He saw his comment caught her off-guard, like a boxer landing a lucky punch. He saw her pause, she looked slightly unsteady on her feet and he thought she might almost be about to faint. Then she quickly re-gained her composure and looking Vincent straight in the eye gave him a stern look before speaking.

"Perhaps some other time because I have my hands full right now, so yours aren't going to be. Now please let me to get on with my work, the survival of the people here may turn out to be dependent on it" and having said that she walked to her Land Rover and drove away.

Vincent waited until she had started to drive away and then he roared with laughter.

"Vincent, that wasn't very nice of you. Why can't you simply be more patient, we're going to be stuck here forever and before you even think of saying anything to me the answer is NO. Can't you see she has a huge responsibility and even if she was ready for a relationship, she could hardly start one now, could she?" Sabrina told Vincent before glaring at him and walking away.

Deborah sat in her Land Rover and held her head in her hands and then thinking better of it decided to drive away and get inside her office as quickly as possible. Once she was inside, she sat down. She thought she coped with young Elizabeth's question quite well but Vincent's comments had shaken her. Her biggest regret though was how she'd handled it. She ought to have been able to laugh it off and send him away with a 'flea in his ear'. Instead, she'd taken the bait and been almost curt in her reply, in fact she had been curt. She'd have to say sorry to him now being so rude, so was on the backfoot again. Perhaps it would be best to simply be honest with him and ask him to be patient with her. On the other hand, that might raise his expectations and lead him to be impatient. What a fucking mess she'd gotten herself into. First calling him darling and now this.

She didn't know what plans Vincent had for that afternoon which also highlighted to her that she wasn't really managing him. She was just thinking about what to do next when there was a knock on her office door.

"Yes, come on in" she announced to the visitor. When the door opened, she was crestfallen to see that it was Vincent.

"Afternoon Maam" Vincent greeted her in more than his usual volume and with more of a military edge to it than usual, complete with his stamping to attention. "Please accept my apologies maam for my comments earlier which I now see were unhelpful and unwelcome." He told her.

"Please stand easy Vincent. I accept your apology and offer you mine. I'm not really my usual self at the moment and I guess I'm tired and lacking a sense of humour, so I was rude to you when I ought not to have been. We have some tough days, if not weeks or even months ahead so we both need to be professional for the sake of the people here. Well, I know we can be professional what I mean is we need to be focused on the job and nothing else. I also have my own personal challenges to work through and I can't promise you anything other than a job and a roof over your head." Then having said a lot more than she planned she gave Vincent a half smile. It was an 'I'm sorry' smile but a smile nonetheless.

"Thank you Maam." Vincent replied before coming to attention and smartly leaving her office.

Sabrina had organised the bunker tour for key personnel later the same day and Deborah was waiting for them when they arrived and greeted them.

"Ok everyone, we're having a tour of the bunker now so we've a chance to get familiar with it before we start running the island from it tomorrow and with everyone else moving in sometime afterwards. There are four main parts as follows: operations, medical, living and recreation but the bunker isn't laid out in that order. I've been in a few military bunkers ranging from decommissioned Second World War to active airfield and command centres in the UK and Gibraltar. No two are laid out the same but this is similar to some in having a central tunnel with everything off one side and each side room connected by access doors only used in an emergency, for if the central tunnel is compromised. There are two levels but the lower level is much smaller and has equipment plant rooms and storage rooms only. The bunker was built deep to provide protection from a direct hit rather than protection against nuclear fallout, though it provides the latter as a by-product from being deep."

"We are passing through the outer blast doors here. Next, we'll pass through the airlock doors which ensure the bunker remains at positive air pressure, providing protection from chemical or gas attacks. A filtered air pump system provides the positive pressure. There's a decontamination facility here and then another set of doors that lead into the bunker proper."

"Ok, here is the main Ops Centre. All these sub-offices around it on three sides are related to communications and stuff past and present conducted on the island, some of which are a mystery to me. At the far end of the bunker is an alternate Ops Centre called 'The Altar' which can replicate what's done here but is much smaller and cramped."

"Ok Doc, this is the medical facility and it has not one but two medical theatres and I guess room for a smaller ad-hoc one to be created if required. There are also several quarantine rooms, an x-ray machine and a CT scanner. Try not to swear when you see that scanner because it surely would have been invaluable for the diagnosis of your last serious case you sent to the UK." Deborah told him.

"Confession time for me Deborah. Will let me take that last serious case down here, in absolute secrecy at two in the morning. His rule breaking undoubtedly saved their life though caused no small degree of confusion in the UK who were staggered at the accuracy and detail of my diagnosis" Doc Caskey told her. Deborah raised her eyebrows in surprise "Really! Well, I guess you can tell us about what else we have here" she told him.

"You name it and its's here. A fully equipped and functional hospital with everything ever found in any hospital or surgery. You could quarantine or treat a space shuttle crew here or every crew member from a large military warship. There's a special medical elevator you may not have seen with its own discrete entrance and exit that's never been used. Certainly, I didn't use it on my visit but Will said, if necessary, I could have. Virtually all of the equipment is American because they paid for this part of the facility out of a NASA budget relating to Wideawake Airfield being a backup landing site for the shuttle. Hal told me the cost was lost somewhere in the NASA site building costs. Our only problem, Deborah, is that we'll never have the trained staff to use some of the facilities even if we needed to, though I doubt we will. Also, I'm a doctor not a surgeon." The doctor told his surprised colleagues.

Deborah then ushered them out of the medical section and they walked in silence down the bunker corridor until Deborah stopped and opened a door. They followed her into a large room which was clearly sleeping accommodation in narrow bunk beds that were three high. "In my previous jobs we always called sleeping accommodation rooms like this 'the submarine'. Triple deck bunkbeds, none of which have ever been used. Each one has a number on it and there's a total of a hundred and fifty in here and fifty next door. If two hundred sounds on the small side, the normal practice would have been to hot bunk with three people allocated to a bunk, with each person allowed eight hours occupation. The total figure for inhabitants on the island is well below a hundred so we can give every man and every woman their own dedicated bunk, the woman in the smaller dorm. There's also a senior officers' dormitory and a few other dorms which we can allocate on a need's basis. Doc, you can decide if you want to sleep in the medical facility rather than the senior officers' dorm or a room and let me know later."

She then led them to the next section announcing "This is the kitchen and dining area and back there, are the food storage cupboards. All the meals are cooked in microwave ovens or served cold. There are some refrigeration facilities though the milk's all produced from a powdered product as is the squash which we're all familiar with. The food is a broad mixture of British and American service issue and if you've never tasted it before, and I have, it's ok. Let's move on to the next room."

"This is the recreation area and it's designed for use by about two hundred people, while two hundred sleep and two hundred work. There are three large cinema rooms, a small gym, a snooker table, pool table and table tennis table and an open lounge area with a snack and hot drinks and soft drinks bar, the latter being powdered squash. There's also a small library in that corner which is print copy books only. We need a volunteer to check if the cinema has VHS players rather than DVD players and whether or not there's a reasonable stock of suitable films. Frank, do you think you can check this out and supply DVDs and players from the BX?" she asked.

"Yes Deborah, I'll do that tomorrow" he replied.

"I almost forgot, there's a small chapel that will seat about twenty or so people at a time. So that's about it, let's go back to the Ops room and have a chat. Frank what do you think and what can you tell me?" Deborah asked him when everyone was in the Ops room.

"Well Deborah, I already knew most of what was in the bunker and what it can do and stuff like that. I just never knew where the bunker was and no-one was going to tell me. Yes, we can run everything American from here and that includes everything we provide for you guys. I don't know about your listening stuff but I'd expect you can. We can run this place on the islands' power only switching over, or automatically switching over, to bunker power if necessary. I've also been in a few bunkers in my time and this looks pretty much standard for us apart from the hospital which is more extensive that anything I've seen before and there are some parts which don't look familiar to me which I guess are the British parts." Frank told her.

Deborah looked at Frank and she gained the impression there was something he wasn't telling her but couldn't understand why he might be holding something back. She'd have to remember to ask him in private. "Thanks Frank."

"Brad – what do you think?" Deborah asked.

"No problems. Assuming everything works we can have radar for planes and surface vessels and sonar for submarines, working as soon as we move in. If it doesn't work, we ought to be able to get it working within half a day or a lot less. I'd like to know where the cable risers are in case there's a cable break. I already know some of the route because I found some mystery outlets on my end that no-one would ever talk about so I figured there was some sort of secret bunker back-up. I've been training Lisa, my wife, how to operate the sets for some time now as I figured a time would come when we'd need to operate a shift system with less staff than we're used to." He replied.

"Your turn Alan?" Deborah said.

"Well, I've always suspected somewhere like this must exist and it's exactly what I expected to see. I'm not certain my kit will share the same cable risers as Brad's Radar and Sonar but, like him, I need to know where they are." He replied.

"It just so happens I do know the answers to both of your questions and we have a copy of the plans stored in the plant room I can show you tomorrow. I also think you will find there are no breaks in any cables and that everything works." Brian told everyone before adding "sorry not to have mentioned this before now, Deborah. When Will first appointed you, I figured you had enough to be going on with, and then so did I, and things just got busier. So, I got on with the cable checks at night, or rather the early hours of the morning" he told her.

"Vincent, do you have questions for me?" she asked.

"Not really, bunkers have never been my scene. There's unlikely to be much for our Defence Force to do so I suggest they double up with the Shelter Marshals or become the Marshals themselves" he replied.

"Reverend Bond, you're next and last" Deborah said.

"Jesus said 'So the last will be first, and the first will be last', so I don't mind being last. I'm what you might call a 'common or garden' vicar rather than an armed forces chaplain and it seems I'm the only person here who's only knowledge of a bunker is limited to a place where coal would be stored. Nonetheless I've found it very interesting. My thoughts, some of which are questions, relate to the occupants who will have no specific operational role or task to undertake. Perhaps you've heard that saying 'the devil makes work for idle hands'? I think it is important for everyone that there are no hands that are idle. People can become anxious and restless when they have nothing to occupy them and at time of a global crisis that may well end most of the life on this planet as we know it, being cooped up in this bunker may be injurious to them and perhaps others. Also, many of the people that will live down here for the duration of the emergency are not like city dwellers or office and factory workers used to being in close proximity to other people. They are people that prefer a good measure of solitude, the wind and sun on their heads and bodies and space to wander around where there is never likely to be a crowd. Lastly, this bunker will not be their home." Then the Reverend Bond paused before speaking once more and smiling. "Oh, and everyone calls me Simon, but if you prefer a little formality, you can call me the Reverend Simon or Vicar."

There were a few moments silence as those present realised that the vicar had raised some important issues which they'd simply overlooked. Except that is for Sabrina who felt vindicated in justifying Simon's presence at the tour of the bunker.

"Ok Vicar, you've given us a lot to think about and if you've got some solutions or possible solutions, please let myself or Sabrina know. Ok everyone that's the end of the tour. Tomorrow morning Vincent, or Sabrina or myself will open up the bunker and will be here during the day to admit you and your colleagues. We'll undertake the roles of Shelter Marshals until we get some volunteers to undertake those roles. I'm expecting this to be a mosquito free environment so all you need to bring is your pyjamas, clothes and personal effects like a book to read or music to listen to or whatever. There is a small laundry facility in the plant room and running it might well be another job for a volunteer. I'm guessing a number of questions will arise over the next day or so and I'll be grateful if you can put a suggested solution against them as well. Right, let's go back up" Deborah said.

Once everyone had gone on ahead, Deborah locked the bunker, knowing that the last time she locked it the world would be a different place but that hopefully Ascension Island would remain much the same. She drove the short distance back to her home and realised that she needed to check her own 'grab bag' which hadn't been used for a number of years and that she also needed a larger bag of clothing. Then feeling tired she decided to skip having anything to eat and went to bed early.

Uninvited guests

It was past Midnight when Deborah was woken up by her radio.

"Sorry to disturb you Miss Deborah. We have four planes on the radar, fast but subsonic and heading exactly for us. They aren't acknowledging any radio contact. They are flying an odd formation with two aircraft moving out in wide sweeps with the other two distant from each other. I'd guess one is a tanker. I'd guess the other two are some sort of escort, most likely fighters for the other aircraft. Whoever they are I'm guessing it's very important and it's un-planned," the duty radar controller informed her.

Deborah wasn't in a deep sleep and was able to follow what the radar controller had told her. The only thing she wasn't sure of was what time it was and she could find that out in a moment. She looked at her watch – just past midnight.

"That's ok you were right to wake me and tell me. Do you think it's part of the American's Pandemic evacuation?"

"No, that should all have been completed the day before and besides they flew direct to America. This is something different. This is miles and miles out of their way. I'm guessing they wanted to take a strange route to avoid interception. I don't think they'll stay. I think they'll just want fuel; they'll know we have some."

"You said they had a tanker" Deborah said

"I think they have a tanker but if they are going the long way home, they'll want fuel for that too and there's a risk they might lose the tanker and their escorts, so they'll still want enough for themselves. It's also possible only the escorts can air to air refuel."

"So, who or what's on the planes?"

"Well, it's not Airforce One and just about everyone, everywhere but here has been locked down in their bunkers for some time now so it's not royalty or politicians or generals. It's something quite different and perhaps unplanned. It's also a day if not two days late for the final American evacuation of Britain. I guess they will break radio silence about twenty minutes out when no-one other than ourselves can hear them, and we might find out a bit more."

"Ok, I'll be in the Air Traffic tower in about ten minutes." Deborah told him. She was quickly dressed and briskly drove the short distance to the airfield air traffic tower. As she parked her Land Rover she yawned and thought that she could have done without this.

It was only the second time she'd visited the air traffic building and she didn't remember the faces or names of the personnel working there but clearly, they knew who she was.

"Morning Miss Deborah I'm Jim Harvey and this is my colleague, Rick Buck. I think we met once before when you first arrived and Will gave you the grand tour." He told her with a smile.

"Morning guys, thanks for the call and the re-introduction. Is there an update?" she asked them.

"No Miss Deborah, it will be maybe another five to ten minutes before we can expect them to contact us. Would you like something to drink, we have some hot coffee?" one of them asked her.

Coffee instead of tea reminded her that radar was run by the Americans. "Yes please, with cream if you have it and no sugar." She replied. While one of the men fetched her the coffee, the other showed her a radar screen with the four blips on it. They watched it in silence and then the radio burst into life!

"Wideawake control request priority landing, two aircraft with quick turn round over." Said an anonymous American accented voice.

"This is Wideawake control. Unidentified aircraft request you identify yourself and state your purpose over." Jim, the radar controller replied.

"Wideawake our purpose is refuelling over." Came the reply.

Deborah, Jim and Rick looked at each other before Jim spoke "This is irregular and they have ignored our request to identify themselves. I can repeat my request if you want me to, or you are at liberty to do so yourself if you want to add some authority. I suggest you deny their request and call their bluff." Jim advised.

"Unidentified aircraft This is the Commanding Officer, Wideawake. Request denied and any attempt to land will be considered hostile intent over." Deborah told them without batting an eyelid.

There was a lengthy pause before her transmission received a reply. "Person claiming to the Commanding Officer Wideawake, be advised we do not believe you are the USAF Commanding Officer. Request we speak to, err, Colonel Hal Elliot."

"Unidentified aircraft, be advised he is no longer in command and the command has been passed to myself. I repeat your request to land is denied and any attempt to land will be considered hostile intent over" Deborah replied. Deborah looked at Jim and Rick who nodded almost in unison with Jim giving her a thumbs up sign.

Several minutes then passed before the unidentified aircraft made a further transmission which was in stark contrast to their previous ones and by a fresh voice. "Wideawake this is USAF Colonel Bill Yeager we are a covert mercy flight with tanker and fighter escort and if you want to deny us landing rights, we suggest you break out your code books and contact the Pentagon, over."

Deborah frowned and turned to Jim asking him "Jim why haven't the Pentagon contacted us? Can we contact them from here?"

"Miss Deborah, everyone is getting ready for war. Even if we sent a flash signal these planes would be circling before we got a reply. They probably do only want fuel and we might as well let them land and have it. They know they are more vulnerable on the ground than in the air though it seems they intend to keep two aircraft, I'm guessing fighters, in the air so the risk is theirs rather than ours in letting them land. They might be lying but that colonel sounded pretty pissed with us rather than threatening and either he's a good actor or their story is genuine. They also asked for Hal by name, so some of the aircrew may have been through here before, whether last month, or last year. Besides if they wanted to land some sort of force, I'd guess they wouldn't have replied at all or pretended they had engine trouble or something." Jim replied.

"Unidentified aircraft permission to land granted but not permission to disembark due to quarantine, I say again permission to land granted but not permission to disembark due to quarantine." Deborah told them.

"Wideawake acknowledged." Came the reply.

"Jim, we don't have a full fire crew, do we?"

"No Miss Deborah, but we've been training volunteers for days and I rang them before I rang you so any time now, we'll have two fire trucks on the tarmac. Uhm, but not before someone lands because here they come!" Jim replied.

However, rather than a large aircraft landing a fighter aircraft overflew the runway at low level and high speed followed by a vertical climb out before circling the island. Its actions made a terrific noise and rattled the tower while the glow of the re-heat of its exhausts lit up the night sky. There was a short silence lasting several minutes then a large cargo aircraft appeared, which circled before landing.

Vincent woke up with a start. A plane was taking off. No, it had taken off. He then jumped out of his bed and hurriedly getting dressed his mind raced. It's a fucking plane, where'd it come from? I'll take the Land Rover and call out the defence volunteers, he thought. He picked up the phone and dialled the first number and as soon as it was answered he spoke quickly shouting "This is Vincent we've a potential emergency at the airhead, ring the call tree and I'll meet you all at the airhead." Then quickly putting the phone down he ran outside and was on his way. He hadn't driven this fast since his dash to Georgetown for the Spire Beach rescue and that was in daylight whereas now it was pitch dark. At one point he had to swerve around a couple of donkeys that refused to move from the road.

There it was again, circling the island, a military jet, hard to see but looked as if it had twin tail fins, hopefully an F18 and friendly? He skidded to a stop and then tripped over his own feet as he scrambled out of the Land Rover. He picked himself up in time to see a larger plane approach low and slow on final approach.

"Unidentified aircraft this is the Commanding Officer, Wideawake. You were not given permission for your fighter to overfly the runway, over. Request explain yourself."

"Wideawake, we don't need to explain ourselves. We are on final approach and you will refuel us, over."

"Well, are we going to switch off the runway lights and risk pissing them off and crashing, or let them land? I'm guessing they must have armed troops on the cargo plane to be so bold." Jim told her.

"Let them land." Deborah replied with a sigh. No sooner had the plane touched down which turned out to be a C-17 Globemaster III, than Deborah was surprised to see several vehicles including a Land Rover pursue it down the runway. As it slowed down and turned to leave the runway on the fast exit, the Land Rover blocked the exit and the jet stopped sharply in front of it.

"This is Vincent to Air Traffic. Did you authorise the flyby and the landing?" he said.

"Vincent this is Deborah we authorised the landing only and now they are playing tough with us and we're concerned they are going to disembark troops and breach our quarantine, any ideas?"

It took Vincent only a few seconds to respond. "Tell them they have two minutes to get that fighter and any other aircraft landed. Also tell them if we see any sign of a door opening on any aircraft, or any canopy raised, or any person moving towards me or any of our rapid response vehicles we'll shoot every tyre out on their plane and we don't have any spare tyres."

"Unidentified C17 aircraft, this is the Commanding Officer, Wideawake. Be advised you have two minutes to get both fighters and the tanker landed. Also, if we see any sign of a door opening on any aircraft, or any canopy raised, or any person moving towards any of our vehicles, we'll shoot every tyre out on the first plane that landed and we don't have any spare tyres. We also await your explanation for your flyby, over."

"Wideawake, this is USAF Colonel Bill Yeager. We'll do no such thing and you'll remove your vehicles immediately; this is a presidential approved covert mercy flight and I'll have your command authority rescinded in minutes if you don't comply."

Deborah could feel herself getting angry. She never allowed anyone to speak rudely to her, or shout at her or try and bully her. She turned to Jim and asked him "Jim can that thing take off with one of the front tyres deflated?"

"Maybe" he replied

"Vincent, put a hole in one, I repeat one and one only of the C17 aircraft's front landing gear's tyres".

Bang!

"It's done Maam." Vincent replied over the radio.

"Wideawake STOP and STOP right now." But before the caller could say anything else Deborah spoke loudly over what he was going to say.

"Unidentified C17 aircraft, this is the Commanding Officer Wideawake. Request you comply when I fucking tell you to or my rapid response force will empty their fucking weapons magazines into your fucking planes engine intakes. I am responsible for the safety of the people on this island and I WILL enforce my quarantine. If you don't like it suggest you get your fucking code books out and contact the fucking Pentagon or the fucking President and see if they can give you some fucking advice, over." There was then a very long silence before she received a reply.

"Wideawake we will comply, over."

As she was swearing loudly into the microphone to the USAF Colonel, Jim and Rick looked at each other in disbelief. They could neither believe that anyone would swear like that to a USAF Colonel or that Deborah was capable of such foul language. Well, the Colonel had really pressed her 'buttons' and got her fired up and it was something neither would ever forget.

A silent stillness hung over the air traffic control tower while Jim and Rick looked out of the windows of the air traffic control tower and waited, neither wanting to make eye contact with Deborah.

"Here they come, low and slow, two fighters, F18s, they have their gear down, yep there's the tanker, a KC135, behind them; he's on finals too" Jim announced.

Deborah paused for a moment and then calmly spoke into her radio. "Vincent, wait for three more planes to land. Then can you slowly reverse back from the fast exit and down the runway towards the pan and the first plane will follow you and if you can then get each of your other vehicles to do the same with the other three planes. Can you also all apply the safety catches to your weapons, we don't want any accidents or for their fighters to engage us on the ground. Acknowledge."

"Island Volunteer Defence Force acknowledged."

While Deborah had been speaking to Vincent the Colonel had been speaking to Rick on the radio and Rick turned to Deborah to relay what he'd been told.

"Miss Deborah, I have military flight plan data, crew details, a grovelling apology and a partial explanation. Do you want to hear it?" Rick asked.

"Yes please." She replied tersely.

"Ok, well they are REAL sorry for pissing you off, REAL anxious about that front tyre and REAL compliant for anything we want them to do. They claim to have the last recoverable survivors from England and an antidote to the pandemic virus, and they are desperate to land in the USA before there's a nuclear exchange which they think could be any day now. They hinted at the spread of the pandemic across the continental USA and want the antidote and the survivors in a classified site they won't divulge." He told her.

"A pity they didn't tell us that in the first place. Mmm. Tell them we will hot refuel them but also that we have now activated our air defence system and if their fighters do anything other than climb out and depart our airspace when they leave, we'll shoot them down at any distance they care to name. After you've told them that, see if you can get Frank or Alan or anyone else to switch on some electronic stuff at the Pyramid facility, that will be interesting for them." Deborah told him. She listened as he relayed the message and looked at her while nodding and smiling. However, Deborah, wasn't pleased with herself. She'd allowed herself to lose her cool and swear, more than once. She should have stayed calm or got Jim to relay the message omitting her swear words. She'd been unprofessional and it only made her more irritated. Well, it was done now and she couldn't change what she'd said.

The covert mercy flight

Colonel Bill Yeager paced up and down the C17 fuming with anger. He realised he wasn't going to get much calmer in a hurry and decided he wouldn't wait any longer before speaking to the F18 pilot who'd conducted the overflight of Wideawake airfield.

"I want the arsehole F18 pilot who conducted the unauthorised airfield flyby to identify themselves and their aircraft designation now." He demanded. He was however, greeted by a silence so he spoke again. "I want the F18 pilot who conducted the unauthorised flyby of Wideawake airfield that would ALSO like to receive fuel in-flight rather than ditch in

68

the South Atlantic on our way home to acknowledge my radio message now" and then he added "or I could advise Wideawake my safety and theirs is threatened by rogue pilots and request they shoot your tyres out and put a magazines worth of rounds down your plane's jet intakes."

"Sir, this is Major Blenkins, I was undertaking a tactical manoeuvre and evaluation of the threat sir and wanted to ensure Wideawake understood our firepower and importance sir." The Major told him confidently.

Colonel Yeager shouted his reply down the microphone and everyone on the C17 heard him "Blenkins you pogue, don't tell me you're a Major because as of now you're a Captain! Thanks to you our mission is in jeopardy and my C17 pilots have got to get this bird in the air with one front tyre flat. You will do what I tell you to and nothing else, is that clear?"

"Sir, yes sir." Blenkins replied having thought better of reminding the Colonel he had suggested they should have been less secretive and hostile in their initial radio communication. He knew the Colonel could deny him fuel and even pretend there was a malfunction on the tanker to make it legal and that would be that. He could threaten the C17 and the tanker but almost certainly the other F18 would engage him in combat and the guy was a hot shot who hated his guts anyway. The Colonel might even find a fresh fighter escort before his final refuelling so he was fucked and would just have to hope the Colonel's mood improved before they landed and he did get air to air refuelled. Then just to rub things in, the hotshot called him on the other radio channel and waved to him from inside his canopy.

"Say buddy, how about you follow my lead on departure or maybe you can go first and I can give you a critique of your technique" the hotshot told him.

Blenkins didn't reply verbally but simply showed the hot shot the finger.

The C17 captain wanted to wait for the Colonel to calm down before giving him an update but seeing that was unlikely, he decided not to wait any longer. "Sir we are detecting some strange electronic activity coming from the island."

"What sort of strange activity" Colonel Yeager barked at the captain.

"Strange sir, it's likely they aren't bluffing about having an air defence system. A lot of the stuff here was always highly classified and there were rumours they could do more than track ICBMs and the shuttle, and that they had a DEW."

It took the Colonel a couple of seconds before he remembered what a 'DEW' was. The letters stood for Directed Energy Weapon and was fancier than just a laser. It was a Navy or maybe Army weapon as far as he knew but Ascension would be an ideal place for testing one. Well, he'd lost once already to that blasted woman and wasn't going to risk losing to her again and losing the whole mission.

"Ok, John, tell those F18 assholes the jolly news. I'm going to see if the Padre can calm me down before I have an anger induced cardiac." Colonel Yeager replied and then proceeded to stamp towards the middle section of the C17.

"Deborah, I've got Hank on the landline and he's advised he's now intercepting all the visiting aircraft's communications. He says the Colonel just 'chewed out' the F18 pilot whose flyby wasn't authorised and he's restored discipline by threatening the F18 pilot in a couple of different ways. They've also picked up whatever Pyramid is doing and they're convinced we're not bluffing about our air defence system. That's all there is for now but he'll continue to monitor and let us know if he hears anything of interest to us." Rick told her, grinning.

"Thanks Rick" she replied. She then watched someone get of out the fire truck and marshal the C17 to a refuelling hydrant where someone else was ready to make the refuelling connection. Next, they marshalled the tanker to another hydrant and they were likewise connected. She noted no connections were made to the fighters. She decided to maintain radio silence during refuelling after which Rick informed her the refuelling was complete and the aircraft were requesting air traffic clearance to depart, which she gave verbal agreement to for Rick to pass on. She then watched the aircraft take off. First a fighter, then the C17, then the tanker then the second fighter. Once they were all airborne, they then they made a single broadcast.

"Wideawake thank you and hope to meet again one day in happier circumstances, over and out."

"That was strange" Rick said out loud to no-one in particular

"It certainly was. And if that's not a warning sign that it's time to occupy the bunker I don't know what is" Deborah replied. She then said her good byes, drove home, and grabbed a couple of hours sleep before getting up and arriving at work at her normal time. It wasn't long after before Vincent arrived and she beckoned him into her office.

"Morning Vincent. Thank you very much for your help this morning and the help of your volunteers, you all did an exceptional job. Just one thing I want to ask, what gave you the idea about the warning message and then following it by shooting a plane tyre?" Deborah asked him.

Vincent looked slightly uncomfortable about what Deborah thought was a simple question. She pondered that perhaps it wasn't his idea but a procedure he'd been trained in, though she'd never come across it before.

"Maam Deborah, I prefer not to say maam." He replied.

Deborah was surprised at his response which while wasn't what she expected, was honest when he could have made up some sort of lie.

"Oh, well it worked well and we're very grateful to you all the same. How are things going for your move into the bunker?"

"Maam, you didn't mention it on your tour but one room we didn't enter looked to be an armoury rather than just a storeroom. As soon as you open the bunker, I'd like to check it out." He told her.

"Yes of course, I'm driving down now, would you like to follow me" she asked to which Vincent nodded a reply.

The bunker

Throughout the day various people arrived at the bunker carrying a diverse selection of bags containing a mixture of personal possessions, daily essentials and small pieces of stationery including pens and paper. There was a large whiteboard just inside the entrance and Sabrina used some adhesive gridding tape to mark it out, after which she wrote various pieces of information on it.

The operations room was fully occupied first and once each team had everything working to their satisfaction, they drew up a shift roster and pinned it onto a notice board. The shifts were a mixture of eight hours on and sixteen off, and twelve hours on and twelve hours off.

The bunker turned out to be the best place to wait for the beginning of the war not just because it provided protection, but rather because it had amazing connections to just about everything worldwide. Deborah supposed those connections would fail quite quickly once the war began and after that they'd be on their own. She supposed they'd obviously be pockets of survivors around the world but Ascension had nothing much to offer them and that's supposing they'd even heard of it. Nor would there be any point in any of them leaving to seek out other survivors, well not for a decade at least, she supposed.

She found a couple of the wives were willing to undertake administrative support duties and type up situation reports which were a summary of what was happening around the world. The volunteer shelter marshals and their deputies also moved in to get setup and stay. Everything was working as Deborah had envisaged and with everyone now spending their first night in the bunker, sooner than planned, in the morning the rest of the island would be moving in to join them.

Chapter Six – Life in the Bunker

Deborah and her key team of Sabrina, Henry and Vincent personally welcomed everyone that entered the bunker. Vincent was impressed that Sabrina and Henry had produced not just a list of everyone on the island but what their job and place of work was and what they'd need to be doing. The shelter marshals showed the men and the women to their respective dorms and then gave small groups of them guided tours of the bunker and explained the emergency evacuation procedures and how and when they'd be eating, when they could get washing done and things like that. They had also been given a welcome note and instructions the day before with guidance on what might be useful to bring and what not to bother bringing.

With the last person accounted for Deborah announced "Well, everyone's in and I've closed the blast doors. Everything is running ok, and all the posts are manned. I've posted all the shift rosters whether eight hours on and sixteen off or twelve hours on and twelve hours off. The bunk numbers occupied by everyone have also been produced so if anyone needs to fetch an off-shift person they can do so without disturbing the whole dorm. I'm expecting that at least to begin with there won't be much to do on shift and everyone will be instructed to be flexible in that they can go and watch a film or read a book if they want to. At some point we can expect the internet to go down, for good most likely, but while it works it can be accessed."

"Henry, I'm giving you the whole of the senior officer's dormitory for your wife and family. Sabrina, Vincent and myself all have one each of the other single officer rooms which leaves two unused rooms which we can worry about what to do with later. Doc and his wife are sleeping in the medical facility. Myself and Vincent are taking the first shift and will finish at midnight and we'll start the next shift at midday. A three-shift roster would have been preferable but this should work ok for sleeping but if it doesn't after a few days we can think about possible alternatives. We can also be flexible, and between ourselves, if there is absolutely nothing happening one person can 'stand-down' the other for a couple of hours or so. Lastly if whoever is on shift sees a burst of activity or has any concern, they can wake the other person on shift" Deborah briefed the on-shift team.

Someone was waiting to speak to Deborah, and once she'd finished speaking to her key team, the person patiently waiting for her introduced themselves as the duty shelter marshal, and advised that the bunker was now at a positive air pressure, the water tanks were full and they were running on the island's power supply (which had been switched over to automatic operation) rather than the bunker's.

For the first couple of hours in the bunker there was almost a party atmosphere, on account of everyone on the island being in one place at one time, and catching up with old news and being able to talk for as long as they liked. Gradually however, the cheerful mood faded as the world news reports became increasingly grim.

As overall commander Deborah did a full tour of the bunker as soon as she'd completed a shift handover with Sabrina and been briefed by Vincent of the key points of his handover with Henry. She was no stranger to this type of operation though the key difference was that this was real, not an exercise, and that she had overall command and that meant overall responsibility. Her first visit was to the tracking room where anything that could be tracked by radar or sonar would be. Next the radio room, where any message worth intercepting would be and she'd be passed transcripts. After that she went to the medical team which was the one team that were mostly fairly new, being comprised of those people who'd volunteered to undertake medical training along with the Doc and his wife. For the most part their normal duties weren't required for the bunker and they were a mixture of wives, workers from the farm, other maintenance workers and at least one fisherman. It was Doc Caskey's idea to form this volunteer group and he'd come up with the idea after Deborah had created the volunteer defence force. Assuming the war took place and ended with most of the world destroyed, the volunteer medical force would be able to provide a sudden boost of manpower for the doctor and his nurse, whether caused by some sort of mass fatality or outbreak of natural or other illness.

Deborah would also drop in on the groups that Sabrina had suggested were formed, which were rolling programmes of education briefings on various aspect of island infrastructure, ranging from the power station, through to the de-salination plant and the farm. It was a good idea because it spread knowledge throughout the community and helped increase resilience. Deborah pondered that on a submarine everyone was trained to do every job, or at least that what's she'd heard. While a cook or chef had their obvious primary task, in an emergency they might be called upon to do just about anything else. Lastly, but by no means least, there was the survivalist team. For as long as the internet worked, they were searching for every article or book or video clip they could download on how to survive outside modern society. They were looking for everything they could find from how to make your own soap to animal husbandry. Every piece of information was catalogued and cross referenced and then uploaded to a dedicated file server housed in the bunker. In due course some of it would be printed in hard copy for the eventual day when the last computer died.

Vincent noticed the more time he spent on shift with Deborah the more relaxed and familiar she became with him. Occasionally when nothing much was happening and they'd both 'toured' the bunker and spoken to just about everyone else, she'd talk to him like an old friend. At first, she talked about the island but then now and again she'd talk about other places, she'd worked, like Gibraltar.

"Have you spent much time in bunkers?" Deborah asked Vincent.

"No Maam." He replied, being unable to think of anything else to say.

"I have, but always on training exercises. I remember this one day I was the Intelligence Officer on an Air Force Exercise and locked down in an above ground hardened and pressurised facility. We had to wear NBC suits but didn't need to mask up except when there was an air raid, unlike the poor sods outside, who once it was NBC Black had to stay masked up until Endex. I'm not sure what your respirators were like but while ours had a drinking straw thing you could fix to your plastic water bottle you could hardly put it in a mug of tea. So, for the duration of an air raid when you were masked up you simply went thirsty or drank plastic tasting water. Of course, no-one knew when they'd be an air raid so you just had to take your chances. Except on this one exercise, I remember the Ops Clerks had been tipped off when an air raid was due. I think they must have had some reciprocal arrangement with the Ops Clerks at other stations for when their squadrons would be doing the attacking. I got on ok with them and things were relaxed between us when no other officers were about and they told me when the first raid would take place. I had enough time to go to the toilet, have a quick wash, as well as make and drink a mug of tea. I'd just finished it when we had 'air attack red'. I was standing there masked up and smug when this miserable sergeant announced in that muffled voice caused by talking in a respirator 'What a bastard, I'd just made myself a fooking cup of tea and now I can't fooking drink it'. I just smiled and shrugged my shoulders and thought if you hadn't been such an arse someone might have given you the nod." Then having finished her story she laughed at the memory of it and Vincent laughed with her.

Vincent began to rack his brains for a funny military service story he could relate but none came to mind before Deborah had another to share.

"Talking of talking in a respirator I remember this time when I had to leave the Ops shelter to go to a Hardened Aircraft Shelter – a HAS. I can't remember whether I was ordered to go or volunteered so as to get a change of scenery. I was all masked up and I couldn't understand why it was taking so long for someone to let me into the HAS. At first, I thought they were making me wait because I was Army, but I found out the real reason once I was inside. It seems that they were all cheating and not even in NBC suits let alone wearing respirators so one of them had to put everything on before they could let me in. Rather than give them a bollicking I took my mask off and boots off and put my feet up for half an hour or so. They were so relieved they gave me tea and biscuits. The funny thing though was that written on a large piece of cardboard, that looked as if had been freshly ripped off a box, was written in thick black marker pen 'put your respirator on before talking over the intercom' which they'd perched on top of the intercom itself. You had to give them marks for ingenuity." Then Deborah laughed again and smiled warmly at Vincent.

Vincent wasn't feeling particularly cheerful and didn't manage to reciprocate with a warm smile. He was slightly taken back when Deborah gently touched his arm and asked "Is everything ok Vincent?"

"Not really, can I take a short break?" he asked. Vincent was struggling and he knew he was close to being in real trouble and much as he didn't want to ask, he expected the only person that could help him was the vicar. He managed to find him in the bunker's chapel and it seemed like some sort of meeting or service had just finished.

Simon saw Vincent arrive and he could immediately see that he looked extremely uncomfortable. He was expecting that Vincent had some bad news to relay to him but was instead caught off-guard by Vincent's simple request.

"Vicar, I'm in trouble and I need you to pray for me right now please. I'm close to having a panic attack. Very occasionally when I least want to, I suffer from claustrophobia and I want you to pray for it to go away please" Vincent told him.

Simon knew who Vincent was and he felt certain that Vincent had over the years much blood on his hands, yet he didn't think any of it was innocent blood. He thoughts turned to King David who God loved very much but would not let him build the original temple in Jerusalem because of the blood on his hands, odd that given he fought for the Lord from the time when he slayed Goliath, and went on to lead the army. "Yes of course I can. Do you mind if someone joins us in prayer?" he asked.

"No vicar." Was Vincent's terse reply.

Simon managed to catch someone's eye just before they left and beckoned him over and introduced him to Vincent as 'Johnny'. He then paused for a moment and then said "Sometimes Vincent, I will pray in a foreign language as well as English, it's quite usual for me, is that ok?"

"Yes vicar." Vincent replied.

Simon and Johnny then put their hands just above Vincent's head, almost hovering them over him. They then prayed for Vincent in a mixture of languages he didn't recognise and also English. He also felt a lot of static electricity over his head and imagined his hair might be sticking up. Then he relaxed and felt at peace and his panic attack was over.

"Err thanks very much. I feel ok now so I guess I'd better return to my job" Vincent told them before shaking each of their hands and leaving. Vincent returned back to the control room and sat back down with Deborah as if nothing had happened. Not much new happened on their shift other than it was obvious the pandemic was no longer under any kind of control and tensions were rising. At the end of the shift each of them said 'good night' to the other and went to their room.

Vincent slept well and woke up to the sound of his alarm clock. However, he checked the time on his watch, and smiled because he really liked it. This was one Frank had given him and it really was light as a feather but not too 'showy'. He also liked the midday to midnight shift pattern which seemed to agree with him. He'd have liked it more if he could have been outside at night, sleeping under the stars or something like that and made a mental note to do this once this was all over and he'd left the bunker.

It was straight after that thought that he felt a slight pang of guilt. Here he was in comparative if not complete safety, simply waiting for the world to end so he could get back on with his life. He supposed those people that has died in the pandemic would have been the lucky ones, followed by anyone else who had a quick death. For anyone with radiation sickness from the inevitable nuclear fallout, death would be slow and unpleasant. Still, there was nothing he could do to help them now and he let the guilt pass and went to take a late breakfast.

After breakfast Vincent didn't have much to do so he had a wander around the bunker and searched out every member of his volunteer force that was either on duty, or resting, and checked they were ok, which they were. The mood in the bunker was more sombre now he thought. He supposed people realised that things weren't improving and they'd be here for a while longer. Although he'd not long had breakfast, he decided to have an early midday meal so that once he started his shift, he could concentrate on anything he needed to do without having to worry about when he was going to get his next meal. After that he took a mug of tea with him and went to the control room.

"Morning maam" he said.

"Morning Vincent," Deborah replied "I arrived slightly earlier and had an early de-brief from Henry and Sabrina so they could have a slightly earlier finish. There wasn't much to say, things haven't changed very much. The pandemic now appears to have wiped out most if not all civilised life as we knew it and there have been no breakthroughs in vaccine development," she told him.

Not much else happened for the next few hours other than it seemed like forces hostile to NATO were getting ready to make a move. Then something unexpected happened. The Brent phone rang and both Vincent and Deborah looked at it. Vincent had been told it was a secure phone of an old type but still in widespread use, especially where the local usage meant its replacement couldn't be justified because of the cost. The digital display indicated the caller's location and it meant nothing to Vincent. He looked at Deborah and saw that she scowled before picking up the receiver. Vincent had never seen her scowl before and it seemed out of character for her.

Deborah looked at the display on the Brent and she recognised it immediately because it was one of the places she'd worked previously and her lasting memories of it were bad. That place was Corsham, England, and she guessed the call was being made from somewhere within the massive bunker complex there. She picked up the receiver and decided to speak immediately though she was tempted to wait and make the caller speak first.

"Commander in Chief Combined Forces Ascension Island. Caller identify yourself." Deborah snapped into the phone in a manner that made Vincent automatically sit to attention.

"Lieutenant Jane Briggs speaking, maam. Is it possible to speak to Miss Deborah Black, Maam?" the caller replied meekly.

Vincent watched Deborah's demeanour change to one of what looked like controlled anger and she appeared to mutter something under her breath before speaking.

"I am Miss Black and I am the Commander in Chief Combined Forces Ascension Island. What do you want, Lieutenant Briggs?" Deborah snappily replied in a raised voice.

"Maam, I'm ringing to say sorry to you for all the wrong I did you. I can't change the past and I can't make good what I did and so I'm doing the only thing I can do and that's to be sorry and to say sorry." Lieutenant Briggs told Deborah.

Deborah paused. There was a time, not that long ago when she'd have liked to have wrung Jane Briggs neck. There was also a time when, had the occasion arisen, she'd have seen to it that Jane Briggs might have had an unpleasant accident, probably a terminal one. However, she thought that Ascension Island had healed her of some of those unpleasant thoughts and the memories that produced them but now she was on the end of phone listening to Jane Briggs saying sorry and realised that, rather than having dealt with her unpleasant past, she's simply buried it. Corsham was a massive bunker and the occupants would most likely survive whatever happened to England but they'd have to come out one day and they might not come out too much worth surviving for.

Deborah let out a long sigh, unaware of either Vincent's close scrutiny of her expressions, or that he was near enough to overhear both sides of the conversation. "Ok Jane, call me Deborah and get on with saying sorry so I can rebury the past, though God alone knows why you feel a need to bother now, it never bothered you at the time," she told her.

"Thank you, Deborah. I'm so grateful to you for listening. You always were a kinder person than I was. After you left, I made sure the cruel nickname I made up for you followed you to Spyglass at Gib' and I'm sorry for that. I'm sorry I was jealous of you and Duncan and what you had together. I'm sorry Duncan died in that accident. I'm sorry I was a mean bitch to you and was a thorn in your side whenever I could be. I'm sorry I was your enemy when I should have been your friend. Duncan was my big brother and I loved him too and it hurt me too when he died. There's one other thing I want to tell you. God does indeed know why I'm ringing you because not that long ago I found Jesus. Sorry if that sounds twee. God has forgiven me and I hope you'll be able to as well, then you can forget about me forever," Jane told her and then started sobbing.

Vincent would rather have not overheard any of this conversation and he felt extremely awkward. He thought about leaving but didn't think that would be a good idea. He saw Deborah's expression change once more, calmer now but sad.

"I forgive you Jane. Also, if you survive everything that most likely will happen, try and get here if you can. I have to go now, goodbye Jane." Then Deborah put the receiver down and looked at Vincent before speaking to him. "Vincent, I believe I have to take what is called 'a moment'. I'll be back shortly."

Vincent nodded and then looked away in case Deborah was crying and didn't want him to see her crying. What the fuck was all that, it seemed pretty intense. What was finding Jesus supposed to mean, wasn't he supposed to have risen from the grave and then go to heaven, it was how this island got its name? Who had Duncan been? Well, now didn't seem to be the time to ask those questions, not of Deborah anyway.

Vincent was interrupted in his thoughts by Deborah returning quicker than he'd expected and she looked intently at him and began to speak.

"Vincent, that was my past calling. A long time ago I worked at one of the sensitive units at Ministry of Defence Corsham in England. It's an above ground facility but is also built above the biggest bunker in the United Kingdom, probably hundreds of times bigger than this place. I worked with the young woman who rang just now, Lieutenant Jane Briggs. At a mess function I met her brother, Duncan. We fell in love with each other and were engaged to be married. Not long after that he died in a motorcycle accident. It was a very difficult time for me as you might imagine. The worst part though was the strange and unpleasant behaviour of his sister, Jane. She nicknamed me the 'Ice Maiden' and was incredibly cruel and horrid. Eventually I was given a special transfer to Gibraltar and she was subject to some kind of formal disciplinary action. Gibraltar never really worked for me and I secured this post here despite it being a retrograde move from a career perspective. Being here proved to be healing for me, or at least I thought so. I suppose that call was like the final scab on a wound falling off and leaving fresh and slightly sensitive new and pink skin exposed. So, Vincent, though I haven't asked you before, I am now, be patient and gentle with me for a while please."

"Yes of course Maam" he replied though he didn't believe there had been a time when he hadn't been patient and gentle with her, had he?

Neither of them said much for the rest of that shift and Vincent was glad when Henry and Sabrina appeared for their handover and the start of their shift. While Vincent hadn't spent any time in hardened facilities, shelters, he had paid close attention to Deborah's briefing and he sought out the Shelter Marshal.

"Is there enough water for me to have a shower?" he asked the duty Shelter Marshal.

"Yes, Vincent, we've discovered that unless there is an actual attack, we can top up the bunker's tanks from the Island's supply, so there's plenty of water." The Shelter Marshal told him.

Vincent thanked him and grabbing his towel and wash kit had a long refreshing shower and then went straight to bed. Vincent's sleep wasn't restful and at one point he woke from a recurring nightmare he suffered from infrequently. He'd survived a nuclear apocalypse and was part of a small gang of other survivors searching derelict streets and buildings. Most of the time he was wearing a gas mask and there was a lot of gunfire and at least once he saw what was left of someone he'd killed in combat. He woke up with a start and decided he might as well get up now, rather than have any more nightmares.

After eating and doing an earlier version of his usual tour of the bunker he went to the control and found that he'd arrived before Deborah. She arrived shortly after his arrival and they both handed over from Henry and Sabrina. The shift was a busy one because there were a lot of radio intercepts that were handed to them and they were mostly reports of Soviet advances into Europe in strength, despite weakened numbers due to the pandemic. About the same time, they learned that the Chinese had invaded Taiwan with quite small numbers of troops. So, the fighting had started in earnest, yet diplomatic efforts were still ongoing to prevent escalation and put in place a cease-fire. Just before midnight Sabrina and Henry appeared and were briefed by Deborah, after which Deborah and Vincent retired to their respective rooms.

"Did you think they both looked haggard, Henry? Sabrina asked him.

"Yes" he replied and adding "none of this news sounds good, in fact it all sounds bad. I'm guessing whoever has the heaviest losses will be the first to fire nukes on the other. Besides, the pandemic has massively reduced everyone's conventional forces" He replied.

During Henry and Sabrina's shift they learned that NATO forces were quickly stretched in Europe while American and Australian forces were likewise stretched in the Far East. During the early hours of the morning several countries appeared to exploit those situations by border incursions. As the morning wore on the initial rapid gains and advances of the Soviets into European NATO countries were halted and the Soviets began to be slowly pushed back. The radio interception team were overwhelmed with traffic and they'd had to prioritise what to intercept and what to no longer bother to intercept, which limited how much they could understand.

On Deborah and Vincent's shift they realised that, although fighting had broken out, that wasn't really the start of the war because it now seemed that it had started biologically - germ warfare. 'When were the first germs released and who released them?' was one coded communication that was intercepted. Further communications were intercepted that suggested a hardening attitude to the Soviets and Chinese from the Western powers due to anecdotal evidence that the pandemic hadn't been an accident, but a Soviet-Chinese pact were behind deliberate germ warfare, with the objective of gaining control of the world's oil in the Middle East and for the Pandemic to spread from Latin America through Mexica to the USA and from the African continent to NATO countries in Europe. The Australasian continent had contained the Pandemic, at least initially. However, without clear evidence a Soviet-Chinese pact were behind it, the Pandemic had left every other country on the 'back foot'. There was an expectation that a full ground assault would take place on more than one front and it happened in the Far East when Chinese forces attacked their old foe Japan. There were other conflicting reports that suggested both the Chinese and Russians were now subject to huge losses of life due to the pandemic, either because it had mutated or their own vaccines had proven to be less effective than they should have been or because they themselves had been subject to a germ warfare counter-attack.

Once their shift was over both Vincent and Deborah went to their respective rooms. Deborah was worried because the live events played out through the radio intercepts were remarkably similar to the exercise scenarios she'd worked through in the past. Before ending her shift, she'd left instructions to be woken if there were any sudden developments. Sure enough, in the early hours of the morning Sabrina had come to wake her and she quickly pulled on her clothes. She decided she ought to wake Vincent up, not so much so he could witness the end of the world as they all knew it but in case of a missile attack on the island, for which she'd need his leadership to complement hers.

Vincent thought he heard someone mention his name. Then he felt a hand touching him, then it stroked his arm and held it. He realised someone was trying to wake him up. He looked up and turned on the bedside light, it was Deborah. As he gradually emerged from his deep slumber, he realised his luck hadn't changed but rather it was the call of duty.

"Quickly, Vincent, I think there's about to be a huge increase in offensive action by both sides," Deborah whispered to him.

Vincent jumped out of bed and heard Deborah supress a small squeal. He jumped back into bed and rummaged around on the floor to find his boxer shorts and once he put them on under the covers, he jumped back out of bed, but Deborah had already left.

As Vincent ran down the corridor, still getting dressed, he was aware of a few others doing the same thing and all heading for the control room. Once he was in the room it was pretty much standing room only. The only person who was talking was Rick. He was the lead operator for the American radar and telemetry sites whose purpose was for radar and telemetry tracking functions for rocket launches and the movement of the International Space Station. He, however, had managed to adapt them to monitor all Inter Continental Ballistic Missiles (ICBMs). Apparently, the facility to track ICBMs was some sort of secondary programming that existed but hadn't been previously used on the Ascension Island system. He announced, "There's been a huge missile launch from China and the Soviets, the height and trajectories are diverse, a lot heading for mainland USA. They are ICBMs so bound to have nuclear warheads. America has now launched. Looks to be some Submarine launches. Pakistan has launched, India has replied, several launches in the middle east, don't look to be ICBMS. North

Korea have a couple of launches, what must be sub launches have replied. There are several NATO countries that have launched including the British. There are some odd sub launches to some targets."

Rick then shook his head "There's too many now to monitor and my system has 'hung', I didn't see any heading our way, neither was anything launched from anywhere near us." He looked at his watch while everyone in the room was silent before speaking again. "They'll be landing anything up to half an hour from now. God save us from this madness."

In the mostly silent room Vincent asked Deborah in a whispered tone "How many missiles will have been launched?"

"It's hard to say, the total number in existence is over a thousand, maybe one thousand three hundred, it depends if everyone has launched everything they have. Most or all will have multiple warheads so the destructive force is enormous and there are other nuclear weapons as well, including those dropped by long range bombers." She replied in a whisper.

There was a strange atmosphere in the control room. Aside from the occasional whisper, no-one spoke but everyone looked up the clock or at their own wrist watch. After more than thirty minutes had passed there was a realisation that, while Ascension Island hadn't felt as much as a tremor, much of the most densely inhabited parts of the world would have been destroyed by now.

Chapter Seven – 11 Nov, Mostly silence

The silence stifled the thoughts of everyone. It was the cruellest irony that it was on November Eleven, Remembrance Day, the first and most likely the last ever global nuclear exchange had finished almost as quickly as it had started. Every major civilisation and city, large town and small town alike, had either been destroyed or were beginning to feel the effects of high levels of nuclear radiation. This wasn't like Neville Shute's novel 'On the beach'. They were a long way from everywhere and it was highly improbable nothing other than light radiation levels would reach them. There would be some contamination, but it ought to be easily survivable. Would there be a nuclear winter? No-one knew, and if there was, could they survive it?

It was Sabrina who broke the silence and it was with a prayer. When she had finished everyone said "Amen" in unison, even Deborah.

Sabrina was surprised at herself. Why on earth had she said that prayer? She never said prayers out loud on her own, let alone with a group of people. She supposed it had been buried in her sub-conscious and found its way out at this poignant moment. She was relieved no-one had minded or were shocked, but had simply said 'amen' at the end of it. She looked up and saw Simon giving her a serious but kind smile. Sabrina realised that Simon should have been the person to say a prayer but didn't seem to mind that she had done so.

Deborah sat in silence and tried to collect her thoughts. Millions of people had just died and millions more would die a more painful death in the days ahead, some might take weeks or even months to die. They would only have each other to help them. The planet would slowly recover but the human population would take over a thousand years to reach pre-apocalypse numbers. Yes, it wasn't a war it was an apocalypse.

Over the next few hours various news reached them from diverse sources. They could and did listen into civilian and military radio networks around the globe, though, whereas before the strikes there was too much traffic to monitor, now there was considerably less. Some of it, though, was useless to them because they didn't have anyone that could understand and interpret the language being spoken. Some military communications were no longer accessible because it seemed more frequent changes of encryption codes had been made than had been planned for by their respective military commands. Other military channels were wholly and unexpectedly silent for reasons not clear to them, perhaps linked to rapid changes of encryption 'key' suggesting communications compromise had forced silences.

They did learn that Argentina had launched a large-scale conventional attack on the Falkland Islands which had been successfully repulsed. Then shortly after that Buenos Aires had been destroyed by a nuclear strike which may have been submarine launched but which no nation claimed responsibility for. It wasn't certain Britain had launched the nuclear missile because of the risk of the fallout reaching the Falkland Islands though it seemed the wind was unfavourable to that happening. The islands themselves were ravaged by the pandemic though there were thought to be large numbers of survivors.

Those continents escaping nuclear strikes had already been devastated by the pandemic but which was now believed to have been caused by germ warfare of Soviet or Chinese origin, but not delivered by their hand. They already knew attempts to contain it had failed, compounded by gradual increase of nuclear fallout. They already knew that St Helena had fallen victim to the Pandemic which was sad for the islanders, being their nearest neighbour, and a place where they knew many of their friends had recently returned to. They also knew the African continent had already been devasted by the pandemic and survivors were thought to exist only in the remotest parts.

They waited for two further days after the apocalypse before Deborah decided they needed to undertake a visual check outside the bunker. Vincent was first to volunteer to do this and Henry had volunteered to go with him, but Deborah had told them she couldn't spare her best two men and that neither could go. At this point Simon stepped forward, announcing "I'll go because if I don't come back God will raise up some else to do his work here in this place." Deborah agreed he could go not so much because she agreed with him but because she didn't want to debate for hours the merits of who could go and why and so on and besides, he seemed the least useful person they had to her thinking and she could afford to lose him.

So, the Rev Simon Bond accompanied by one of the members of his congregation, Johnny, emerged from the bunker, being very prepared to meet their maker. They were also very prepared in every other sense because they'd been forced to wear full Nuclear, Biological and Chemical (NBC) suits, including gas masks, which Vincent had informed them were respirators. They'd also been given a hand-held two-way radio and some sort of meter to check for radiation, though the bunker gauges weren't measuring any external radiation.

Simon pressed the talk button on the radio as soon as he was outside the bunker. "Everything looks the same as how we left it. We are walking to the Land Rover now. Well, it started first time and we are now driving slowly to Georgetown. Everything seems normal. There's a donkey and there's another. It's even quieter than usual. There's no reading of radiation. We're at the quayside now and it also looks the same as when we left it. We can see a few birds flying about, it's possible the noise of our arrival disturbed them. It's very hot in this suit and the sweat from my face is running down inside the mask and collecting in a puddle at the bottom. Do we have to continue to stay masked up?"

Deborah looked at Vincent and he instinctively replied "With no reading of radiation and birds flying about I can't imagine there's any risk, besides, we can quarantine them when they get back if necessary" he told her.

"This is Deborah. You can remove your masks and suits if you are satisfied it's safe to do so and from what you've seen so far everything seems normal. However, we may need to put you in quarantine when you get back even after a full decontamination, if you've removed your suits and masks."

"Ok Deborah we are talking off the masks and suits" Simon told her.

"I've just had a thought, Vincent." Deborah said and added. "What if they see something later on, like dead birds or something and they simply don't tell us because they don't want to face quarantine or whatever?"

Vincent thought for a split second before replying "If we can't trust the vicar and one of his flock to tell the truth we're screwed as a community. Besides, they were prepared to give up their lives to go and check things out so I doubt quarantine will bother them" he replied.

No sooner had he spoken those words Deborah realised she'd made a serious error of judgement. She felt a tremor of fear run through her whole body. These people trusted her and needed her to lead them through all kinds of problems no-one could imagine. She couldn't afford to make mistakes, especially not serious ones, especially not errors of judgement. She felt a hand on her arm and she saw it was Vincent and he was looking at her, and he looked concerned.

"Is everything ok Deborah" Vincent almost whispered in her ear.

"Yes Vincent. It's just that I realised the Vicar might just turn out to be one of the useful people on the island and I was prepared to cast him aside as useless. What a foolish misjudgement." Deborah told him. Vincent just shrugged his shoulders in reply.

They stayed in the bunker for a full week after that because they wanted to be certain no late attack occurred and that nuclear fallout wasn't heading in their direction. Eventually with everyone in the bunker getting restless, Deborah agreed it was time to leave. She formally stood down the bunker staff and shook everyone's hand as they left until only herself and Vincent remained.

"Ok Vincent we are going to be last out" she told him as she gestured to him to leave and when he did, she followed him outside and closed and locked the doors behind them.

They were both glad they had their sunglasses to hand because while the bunker was well lit, it wasn't as bright as daylight on a clear day on the island, and it was a gloriously clear day. Vincent looked at Deborah and he wanted to hold her hand and walk together as a couple but she seemed to sense this and moved slightly away from him. Neither of them spoke.

Chapter Eight – The planning meeting

The day after getting out of the bunker Deborah called a meeting for the following day. Not much seemed to have changed during the time they were in it but there were tell-tale signs that it had. There was no communication from the outside world and there were no radio messages. There was the occasional short military communication intercepted but they were sporadic and in code. There were no planned arrivals or departures by air or by sea. There were no deliveries of anything. She'd called the meeting for eleven in the morning to give herself a bit of extra time to check through what she wanted to say.

"Ok, we're it. Thanks for coming to the meeting. I want to ease some concerns both short term and long term and put in place some plans that will do more than just ensure our survival, but actually make our life here pleasant. Feel free to interrupt me whenever you want, though I'd prefer if you waited till the end of my talk. Drinking water is one of our key resources and currently we get it from the English Bay power station reverse osmosis plant, what has sometimes been called the de-salination plant. It won't run indefinitely though might hold out for years if not decades, so long as we have fuel for it, and we do have lots of fuel. Of course, life existed here before the plant and I plan to reinstate the 200-year-old water supply the Marines used. The heritage project at Dampier's Drip and the water catchment wasn't quite all it appeared to be and is fully functional. We also have enough cast iron pipe and plastic pipe if we need it, to replace all the original pipes and connect the heritage tanks to some of our modern tanks, though at a push we could even use St George's water tank. We'll need some volunteers to not only undertake the work but assist with the planning." Deborah looked around after she had finished speaking and there seemed to be a mixture of relief and amazement on the Islanders' faces and she continued with her talk.

"We have lots of electricity generated by five diesel generators and five wind turbines. It's probable we'll get fifteen to twenty years out of the wind turbines and perhaps more years than that from the diesel generators if we conserve their running time and fuel consumption – we probably have enough fuel to run them until they reach the end of their lives – they'll last longer the less we use them. We have some solar panels of which some are quite old, but we may be able to de-commission and store those panels currently on unoccupied homes. We have a fair number of new panels for our solar farm and we can get 25 years or longer out of them, maybe twice that albeit at a reduced output. We aren't going to starve, but when the

Weetabix and packet foods run out or go way past best use by dates, our diets will have to change. We can fish for more than all of our needs, but sooner rather than later we won't even be able to bake bread and our packet potato will run out. However, Green Mountain farm should more than manage to support all of us. It's also more than just a heritage project and will be growing more fresh fruit and vegetables than was done in the past by using some state-of-the-art equipment that was purchased a while ago. For the farm to work it will also still require a few more of us to become farmers. I'm satisfied that the produce from the farm will help us eat a balanced diet. Of course, the farm doesn't need to increase its output overnight and our stock of tinned and packet food will last us several years. There are a number of cottages on Green Mountain that were also renovated under the guise of being a heritage project. They can be available if anyone wants to live in them who also wants to become a farm worker but my preference is that we keep them as holiday homes so that every now and then we can have a change of temperature and live in them for a weekend or a week."

"No looting please, just ask. Our old friends, neighbours and maybe in the isolated instance, enemy, have left and are unlikely to return even if they are still alive, which I also think is most unlikely. So, if you want any of the property of someone who has left let me know and I'll keep a record until such time there's no longer any point in keeping records. If more than one person wants the same house, car or whatever, my decision will be final, though I'm confident there is more than enough of everything to go around. We might need to think about all living a bit near each other at some point but we can worry about that later, along with whether or not we have enough electricity to keep our mobile phone network running."

"No hoarding please. There are all kinds of things that we will either run out of or it will go out of date so far as to be unusable. We do have a large stock of toiletries but they will run out eventually, as will cosmetics. The good news for the ladies is that you can use pumice stones for removal of hair in places you didn't want it to grow, and pumice stone is one thing we'll never run out of!"

"At some point we'll have to see if we can make our own soap, shampoo and toothpaste. We'll run out of flour and it's unlikely we'll be able to grow enough grain to produce a regular supply but we might manage some now and again. We have a doctor and a dentist but no optician and even if we had an optician, there's no means for us to make lenses."

"Don't throw anything away, especially clothing and footwear. I don't think we will run out of new clothes for a while but once we do, we may need to patch, mend or recreate clothing from items we would have once thrown away."

"Before Christmas, we'll have an open shop at the American BX and take what we need rather than let everything turn to dust. There are also some storehouses I need to open and have a look inside of and hopefully find things of use to us."

"Are we vulnerable to attack? Yes, we are very vulnerable if attacked but also very unlikely to be attacked. We're unlikely to get any visitors and have no military value other than we have a long runway and lots of aviation fuel. Our greatest strength and weakness are the same – we are a long way from anywhere. Possibly a long-term threat might be from a submarine, or pirates, again something to worry about later. Also, we aren't the only survivors in the world, there will be small and large groups across the world. Over time they will be vulnerable to the long-term effects of radiation swept around the world and many will die. That brings me to my last point. From time to time, we might need to spend time in the bunker, whenever there is a high risk of airborne radiation reaching us. We have a warning system in place to let us know when that threat is high."

"One of the biggest things I want us to achieve is to be self-sufficient in energy generation. What that means is we can have enough electricity to live reasonably civilised lives just using the power generated from the sun or the wind. Reasonably civilised means we can continue to run our land line telephone network, though we might cut off some whole sections – we're not sure about that at present."

"There're some things we are going to switch-off and effectively mothball though we can't envisage ever re-commissioning them. Rick is leading on this as the foremost US electronics expert. What this achieves for us is a simple reduction on how much electricity the island consumes and in turn saves us fuel and the life of anything that generates electricity. The 'golf balls' US radar and telemetry, and everything that goes with them, are the first big things Rick will be turning off."

"That's about it for now. Our lives here will continue albeit not quite the same as before but it will be bearable. If there are any questions feel free to ask now or at any time. Perhaps more importantly we'll need ideas of how to do things. Ok, thanks." Deborah told them

Once the meeting had finished and everyone had left, some after asking questions, Deborah looked at Vincent. He looked fairly fed-up and didn't take much notice of her looking at him, though she guessed he was aware of it.

"Is there anything I can do for you Vincent?" she asked him, without really thinking what she was saying.

"You know there is, but why bother asking when you know you aren't going to." He replied. Then without waiting for a reply he walked away. What to do now he thought? There was a time when he might have got drunk but the thought of having his head down a toilet bowl throwing up for a couple of days didn't appeal to him. He'd like to get away from it all for a few days but there was no obvious place he could escape to. He could go for a hike for several days but he'd need to be able to access drinking water and that would be difficult and he couldn't carry more than he'd need for half a day. Parking outside his house, he opened the door and locked it behind him. He then pulled the plug on the phone and ran himself a cool bath. He lay in the bath thinking, but since no obvious ideas came to mind, he decided he might as well have an early night. When he woke up in the morning, he decided he wasn't going to bother going to work. He lay in bed for a while before getting up and making himself a mug of tea. He supposed he could take up where he left off and go for a 'Letterbox' walk. On the other hand, he didn't want to meet anyone. Then he had an idea. If he drove his vehicle somewhere and hid it and then walked back home anyone that passed his home would assume, he was out somewhere because his vehicle was missing.

Vincent also decided that while he'd almost reached a point of acceptance about his circumstances, he certainly wasn't happy about those circumstances. He supposed he'd need to think some more and put a plan of action together to cheer himself up, when there was a knock at his door. It was an insistent knock and he supposed he might as well answer it. Outside were Brad, Simon the vicar, Frank, and Alan.

"Wanna go fishing?" Brad asked and added "Or just carry on eating canned food?"

Vincent was surprised by his group of visitors. He couldn't recall ever having had a group of friendly visitors ever turn up outside anywhere he had ever lived before to ask him to go on a leisure activity.

"Yeah, but I don't have a rod or any gear or anything" he replied thinking that even when he was at sea, he'd never joined any of the other members of the crew that would occasionally fish.

"We have a bunch of gear and a cool box with some beer and sodas. So just bring yourself." Brad replied smiling.

It wasn't long before they were at the quayside in Georgetown. Vincent could see the launch was there waiting for them along with Arnold who gave them a cheery wave. He could see the launch was already loaded up with rods and cool boxes. He also noticed for the first time that the launch had a name 'The Ascension Frigate'. His spirit lifted as he boarded the boat and realised, he had some friends and, while fishing might be routine to them it would be something of an adventure for him. Life could be both good and interesting without Deborah. Arnold started the engine and after letting it warm up for a couple of minutes, gently eased the launch away from the quayside and put out to sea.

"Thanks for inviting me guys, not sure why you did but I'm grateful." Vincent told the group.

"Well, Vincent, we've been fishing together for a while now and it just seemed the right thing to us to see if you'd like to be one of our regular party. Of course, a time will come when the beer and sodas will run out. A time will even come when we'll have to use a rowing boat because for whatever reason the launch can no longer be used, but the fish will still be here. I forgot to mention, this isn't ordinary fishing, this is what is called big-game fishing, pretty much the fishing for the very wealthy. We might catch Yellow-fin Tuna, Wahoo if we're lucky, or possibly some kind of shark. We can feast on something this evening and put the rest in a freezer," Brad told him.

With the island still in reasonably near sight, and specifically Clarence Bay, the launch slowed down and Alan sat in a seat at the back of the boat that looked like any other seat until Vincent realised it was a special fishing seat. Alan was strapped into the seat and the rod was strapped onto him. Some bait was applied to a hook and the line cast. Then the boat slowly passaged through the ocean with the bait dragging on the line behind it. Then there was a sudden burst of action as a fish took the bait. Vincent found watching the whole lengthy process fascinating and was amazed at the size of the yellow fin Tuna that was landed. Brad was next and also caught a tuna but a smaller one while Simon caught nothing in his whole hour in the seat. Simon did get teased a bit for this and it took Vincent a while to make the connection between Simon being a vicar and his namesake in the bible being a fisherman.

"Your turn now Vincent." Brad announced and promptly helped him into the seat which he was told was called the 'fighting chair', albeit not quite as special as your average millionaire's big game fisherman might have used any more than their boat was. It was near the end of his turn in the chair when a large fish took the bait and Vincent realised why it was called a fighting chair. It took a lot of time and encouragement but eventually Vincent landed what turned out to be a large Tiger Shark. He got teased a bit for having 'beginners' luck' but he didn't mind. It was late afternoon by now and the fishing party decided to head back for Georgetown.

"Well, Vincent, we, and probably half if not all of Georgetown, are going to have grilled fish for our supper, and then put what's left of the fish in a deep freezer. Would you like to choose what we are going to eat?" Brad asked him.

"It's been a long time since I last ate shark so I'd really like to eat that now, is that ok?" Vincent asked.

"Absolutely, besides you caught it so you'll get the double blessing of eating what you caught, - c'mon let's get these fish landed." Brad replied.

There was a small crowd of helpers at the quayside and more women than men and Vincent guessed some of them were the wives of his fisherman friends who he vaguely recalled being introduced to in the bunker. Vincent told them he'd prepare the fish and he impressed them with his expert knife work and preparation and while he was doing this a barbeque had been lit and soon a whole bunch of shark steaks were being grilled. It was at this moment that Vincent, hearing a chance remark, realised it must be Saturday. So much for planning to bunk off work for the day he didn't have to work on the weekend! He enjoyed the evening and the shark steaks which were delicious and he felt good, cheerful even.

Garden Cottage

Late on Friday afternoon Deborah decided she wanted to get away for the weekend and decided she'd go to Garden Cottage on Green Mountain. She let Sabrina know where she was going and after making a couple of detours to: get stocked up with food and drink, take some books to read and pack some changes of clothing, drove up to the Cottage.

Deborah quickly unloaded her Land Rover and transferred everything into the cottage. It was some months since she'd last been here but it was just as she expected and just as she'd left it. It was much cooler here than in Georgetown and as she'd done on her last visit, she lit a small fire from pieces of wood she'd collected, not just for the warmth it would generate, but simply so she could watch the flames of the fire consume the wood. She boiled a kettle on a gas ring and made herself a mug of hot chocolate and slowly sipped it. She found that her thoughts constantly drifted between Duncan and Vincent. She knew she had to let go of one and embrace the other, not so much as replacing one with the other but to make a fresh start. She'd come to the island to make that fresh start but she'd clung onto some of her past and she hadn't been able to let it go. There would be time to think tomorrow and Sunday and after a quick wash with a flannel she went to bed early in peace and quiet and alone.

It was dark when Deborah woke up and she decided to get out of bed without caring what time of the night, or hopefully morning, it was. She was soon washed and dressed and put a few things in a small rucksack. She was going to walk along Cronk's Path to North East Cottage and then back via Rupert's Path. The heritage guide leaflet told her it would take about two hours but she planned to take most of the day. Then on Sunday she would walk Elliot's Path and drive back to Georgetown.

The sun was just coming up when Deborah closed the cottage door behind her and as it did, she reflected that living on the equator with near equal day and night all year round was a mixed blessing. There were of course no miserable short dark days of winter but then neither were there those glorious long light summer evenings. Then with that thought she set off along Cronk's path, named after the Farm Superintendent or Head Gardener Hedley Cronk, who created it in 1920. She wondered whether he did all the work creating the path himself, or had some of the farm workers assist him, or if in fact the farm workers did all the hard work while he simply directed them.

As she walked along, she saw quite a lot of land crabs and wondered whether anyone had every tried to eat one in recent years and if they had, what they had tasted like? The only time she'd ever eaten crab meat was as a young child on a family holiday to Cromer on the East Coast of England.

There were lots of ginger plants on the mountain and she saw lots of them on the walk. She paused now and again when she came across one of the endangered species of plant and wondered how they would survive now there was no longer a dedicated conservation team on the island. She would have to see if anyone would form and lead a group of volunteers to keep the paths clear as well as nurture the endangered species.

Weather Post

When Vincent woke up on the Sunday morning, he decided that he'd like to go on another letterbox walk and chose 'Weather Post'. He could see that it wasn't too far from the old NASA site and so drove to the site and parked his Land Rover there and then proceeded on foot.

Vincent looked around the old NASA site after he had parked up and wondered what it would have been like in its heyday. It had been used to communicate with satellites, the moon landings and then the space shuttle before being closed down. After leaving it, he consulted his map and began to follow an old dirt road that once led to something called a collimation tower which he understood to be something to do with calibrating equipment. It was a steady climb up to Weather Post. Once at the top he wrote his name in the visitor's book and had a look back through all the previous entries out of interest. He thought the name of the site unusual because it was originally a look out post and except when covered by low cloud offered good views across that side of the island including Boatswain Bird Island. It was also well above Cricket Valley. Now that was an interesting place, he thought to himself, Cricket Valley. There was no letterbox in the valley, it was difficult to get to and he hadn't found anyone who had been there, though there were rumours there were scorpions there. It might make an interesting venue for a day's expedition one day. After eating some food he'd brought with him, some cloud rolled in and he decided to make his way back down to the old NASA site.

Back to Work

Some weeks later, while in his office, Vincent knew he didn't need to think too hard about what his job would demand from him post nuclear apocalypse and pandemic. The threats would be from the sea and were more likely to be pirates than a hostile warship. He'd already spent some time documenting a detailed training programme for the island's Volunteer Defence Force. While the island's radar was working, which it was likely to be for some years, that would provide early warning but after that he'd had have to consider whether or not some duty watch system would need to be put in place. He wondered whether over the years the risk would increase or decrease. He decided that as machinery wore out and fuel supplies became harder to access, the risk should decrease. He'd read in a book about the island that no pirate ship had successfully attacked the island in the past but rather had passed by without incident. He thought it was a great pity there was no way to reverse the deactivation of HMS Hood's old guns.

He took a moment to look around to check if Deborah had turned up but she hadn't, just as well really. He'd taken to avoiding her whenever possible and while the island was small so was the population and it was easy to make yourself scarce. He'd been training the volunteer defence force twice a week in skills he'd hoped they'd never need. He'd also began to teach them outdoor survival skills and occasionally he'd got them to camp on a remote part of Green Mountain. Once or twice, they'd caught a rabbit and after skinning and cooking it, they'd eaten it. He also had an idea for target practice he'd talk to Arnold about. In fact, he might as well wander over to the quayside to see if he could find him right now.

After a short search he found Arnold in one of the dockside buildings.

"Morning Arnold, I've a couple of things I need doing that might interest you."

"Morning Vincent, things are a bit quiet so I am interested, tell me what you need?" he replied.

"What I want is some sort of moving target for the defence volunteers to practice shooting at. I had in mind an old oil drum or anything that floats with targets mounted on it that could be towed on a very long line across the bay, left to right and right to left. It doesn't matter if it doesn't tow very well and jumps about, that will just add to the challenge." He told him.

Arnold smiled. "Yes, I can make something that might keep me busy for several days." Then he laughed and asked "You paying me in cash for this job mister?"

Vincent laughed and they shook hands and Arnold set about drawing up some sketches of what might float. Eventually he decided he could use an old fifty-gallon oil drum. He welded a large flat keel on it to stop it spinning round when being towed and welded some light metal framework on what would be its topside that could be used to mount a piece of board with targets pasted onto it. Lastly, he bolted and welded a couple of towing eyes to the drum, at different heights. The following day, and having thought a bit more, he was concerned the drum might be top heavy or if shot below what would be its water line, it might sink.

After having a look around his workshop he decided to simply bolt a section of flat scrap metal bar either side of the keel to make it sit lower in the water. Then he fetched his foam gun and fitted a can of the intumescent grade foam and emptied the whole can inside the drum and then a second can for good measure, and with the drum upright so it could vent air out of its top as the foam expanded, he made himself a cup of tea. After drinking the tea, he could see foam oozing out of the top of the drum and the drum itself looked to have expanded a little and was now not just round but bulging round.

Leaving the drum, he cut some large rectangular boards which he checked would slot into the metal guides of the target holder.

On the third day he trimmed the expanding foam and attached a length of rope to the middle position towing eye. Then he used his barrel wheel trolley to wheel the barrel to the quayside and found someone willing and able to work the dockside crane to lower the drum into the water. It floated as planned and he had it lifted back out of the water so he could take it back to his workshop and paint it.

Vincent waited a full week before returning to see Arnold and he was really impressed with Arnold's work. "Great work buddy. Can we give it a test Saturday? Do you fancy towing it behind the Ascension Frigate?"

Arnold laughed before replying "You paying any danger money for this job mister?"

"There's no money and no danger!" Vincent told him and as they laughed together, he thanked him once more. He then used Arnold's workshop phone to ring the volunteer force call tree to tell them to be at English Bay Beach at first light Saturday. He'd need to ensure they had plenty of ammunition and he'd also need to make sure the rest of the Island were alerted to their being live firing in the bay. Vincent realised that it would take a lot of time to keep checking the target to see how accurate the firing was and hit upon the idea of painting the bullet tips with different coloured paints that would leave corresponding different coloured marks on impacting the target, and in this he had Arnold help him.

On Saturday morning Vincent realised that as well as defence volunteers there were a number of spectators. Doc Caskey had decided he'd have his medical volunteers practice casualty evacuation and first aid for gunshot wounds, with the noise from the live firing providing noise and tension to make their practice both more realistic and difficult.

It took a while to get everything set up including a suitable firing position on the beach and, safety lookouts at each end of the beach. So, it was late morning before Arnold made the first practice pass with no firing. Vincent had wanted this practice run to check the rope on the target was long enough and for Arnold to scare away any turtles.

"Morning team. Today we're not just shooting at a target but we're going to practice shooting at a moving target, at sea. We're doing this because the most likely attack on the island will be a small boat or boats at sea and hitting them before they can land on the island is our best defence. I have a list of your names and the colour of the ammunition allotted to you. You will each have two firing practices: the first when the target moves left to right and the second when it returns and moves right to left. You can shoot prone or standing up or a mixture of both. You have a single magazine and you can choose to use all or some of it on each pass but if you use it all on the first pass you don't get a second magazine. Note, you will not be allowed to put your weapon into your shoulder until I give you the command to. That's not to make things difficult for you, rather it's to make sure Arnold and the Ascension Frigate can't possibly be hit by accident. Also, there will be someone standing close to your left and right sides. They are there to prevent the amount of movement you can make each side and thereby limit your firing arc such that the angle isn't so great that there is a risk of hitting Arnold and the Ascension Frigate. I'll go first. Are there any questions?" Vincent asked and there being none, he radioed Arnold to advise him he could start the first pass.

Following his own safety rule, he didn't put his rifle into his shoulder until Arnold had passed in front of him. Then he saw the target to the right

98

and he did his best to track it at a constant speed before opening fire and making a slight adjustment for height before he ceased firing, as he'd reached the end of the arc. He could hear some whispering behind him and guessed that at least one of his team were using a scope or binoculars to see how he was doing but even that wasn't an easy task. He could then see the boat turn and was making a return pass. He thought he did better the second time though was a bit low to begin with and thought he'd put at least one round into the barrel.

Vincent swapped places with the person behind him and they then waited for the target to pass by and they began their target practice. And so, shooting practice continued until everyone had taken a turn and Vincent radioed Arnold that he could return to the harbour. Once he was at the harbour and the boat moored, he grinned at Vincent as they pulled in the target which took quite a while. "Thanks Arnold, I think the team have something for you, come and join them" he told him.

The defence volunteers welcomed Arnold and then one of them presented him with a baseball cap on which had embroidered on it: 'Captain' along with gold decorative leaves. He grinned and shook all their hands and they all had a lunch and soft drinks together. While they were occupied Vincent went and had a look at the target on the barrel. He could see that he managed to hit the target a few times and the barrel, as had others. He could see that some of his team hadn't managed many hits and some had only hit the barrel but one person had out shot him, which impressed him.

"Captain Arnold, are you ready for the second practice of the day?" Vincent asked him.

Arnold smiled before replying "Thanks for this baseball cap Vincent, I really appreciate it and yes I'm ready. Same as before or have you got something else in mind?"

"You guessed it. If you can safely be slightly further out to sea, that would be good" and he patted him on the back.

The afternoon practice was conducted much the same as the morning and Vincent felt a bit happier with his shooting than he had earlier. He watched his team and they also looked to have shot a bit better as well. Once the shooting was finished, the target was removed from the water and lowered onto the quayside and Vincent, with Arnold's help, counted and recorded the total number of hits on both the target and the drum itself. Vincent laughed out loud when he realised that Naomi had outshot him and not that much further down in the merit order, was Hannah. The target itself was still usable and clearly Arnold had done a good job in making it.

Vincent called everyone together for a debrief. "Ok, firstly, special thanks to Arnold, not just for towing the target today and giving up his Saturday, but also for spending time last week making it. We appreciate it and I have an idea how I can show you that thanks next week. I know you've presented Arnold with a small gift and I have one to present as well, only it's for one of us. This is a marksmen's embroidered badge and the best shot of the day gets presented with it. There are two snags and one is that the best shot isn't me and the other is that the best marksman is actually a markswoman. Naomi, please step forward and receive this award."

There was a big cheer from everyone and Naomi stepped forward to receive her badge. She then looked back at her husband who nodded at her unspoken question, and she then kissed Vincent on the cheek before stepping back turning around and holding up the badge, to another loud cheer. After that, Vincent said them that everyone had hit the target and the barrel, and he was very impressed with them all. He then invited them to ask him how they'd done, which one by one they did.

After they'd tidied up and it was just Vincent and Arnold together, Vincent spoke to him. "If you wanted to, Arnold, we could spend some time on the RHIB and I could show you some tactical manoeuvring."

Arnold smiled and said "Vincent you are a good friend and good to me and I'd like that very much, and thank for you giving me this job." Then they shook hands and Vincent drove home.

While that was the end of the first live firing practice, it wasn't a one off, and Arnold and Vincent worked together over many weeks to create a programme that included smaller targets, eventually towed by the RHIB at a faster speed than the Ascension Frigate was capable of. Arnold also created a smoke generator for each boat and sometimes they fitted a small smoke generator to the target to make things more interesting for the volunteers.

Chapter Nine – Flora, Fauna and History and Legacies

Despite most life on earth having been destroyed by a nuclear apocalypse, life on the island seemed almost normal, albeit quieter than in the past. Deborah pondered the fact that weekdays now had the stillness of weekends. Every day was as quiet as a Sunday, whether you had to work or not. While neither a naturalist or botanist, Deborah loved to explore the diverse flora and fauna on the island. Of course, hardly any of the plants were indigenous species, most had been introduced here and it made the island an amazing place. It was also what made Green Mountain Green.

Island life had quite quickly settled back into a modified version of its old routine. The population was about a tenth of what it had been pre-apocalypse and there were still adjustments to be made by everyone, with some things no longer requiring to be done and others still needing be done but now by someone else. The islanders were currently experiencing something of a time when everything was plentiful, but they were aware that when some things ran out, they couldn't be replaced. The farm workers were doing well but had a lot of work ahead of them. The planning work to lay the four-inch diameter cast iron pipes for the water supply was keeping some islanders busy but progress was slow and the work, once started, would be heavy. Deborah pondered how much harder it must have been for the marines, without any machinery to assist them.

She was thinking those thoughts while sitting next to one of the pair of muzzle-loading twenty-four-pound cannons, at the remains of Fort Bedford on Cross Hill. More recent breech loading guns were nearby, the old guns from HMS Hood removed in Malta and then sent here. But she preferred to be with the 1849 era canons, even though they were rusty rather than painted. The 1800s were the formative years of the island, the time when it changed appearance the most. The second world war brought the next biggest change with the building of the airstrip. The Cold War had also brought changes, with the creation of an American tracking station in 1956, along with improvements to the island's roads and a few years later the building of the Nike Zeus test facility, for anti-ballistic missile measurement with the "Golf Ball" radar antenna on Cat Hill. That was followed in 1966 when Cable & Wireless British built an earth station 'dish' as a direct data and voice link (via satellite) between the various Ascension sites and mission control Houston, America, as part of their Apollo moon programme, and about the same time the building of the NASA site and the road to it. In the early 1980s the Falklands conflict brought further change, especially to the airhead, with much improved aircraft handling facilities and the new domestic site at Travellers' Hill and yet another aerial 'farm'. Now with the global nuclear war, the third world war and the pandemic, there was unlikely to be any dramatic changes to the island, other than perhaps slow and gradual decline. She didn't really care that the island would slowly decline because it was the manmade structures that would decline rather than the wildlife itself. She'd never imagined things would turn out like this. She'd fallen in love with the island and on occasion resigned herself to having to leave one day, when her job ended because of her age or because it was no longer needed. Tourism plans for the island had never really succeeded, which she regretted, because it might readily have brought in enough money to restore the heritage of the island and given it some of the character of Gibraltar, or Valetta, Malta. Yes, it was the British Navy and warfare that was the common denominator of all three but most likely now only Ascension would survive. Well Gibraltar and Malta might survive but it was unlikely the population of either would survive nuclear radiation, though she was aware of the military facilities deep within the Rock of Gibraltar because she'd worked there for a while. She sighed.

She'd been invited to a barbeque at Comfortless Cove and she decided that, for a change, she'd be sociable and go. It was a short drive, as most places were on the island, but certainly too long to walk to in a reasonable length of time. She got in her Land Rover and pondered that if they ran out of spare parts for all their vehicles, life would be more difficult. Still this one, while second-hand; was in a near new condition. It was a rash purchase Will had made about a year ago that made no sense. He'd also ordered a large number of spare parts for this vehicle and the other one that arrived the same time. She'd queried this with him because it was a lot of money and there were enough spares, brake parts, wheels with tyres on, and stuff that was mystery to her, to last a lifetime. He'd, uncharacteristically for him, avoided eye contact when replying; just as well because his reply about rationalising official vehicles on the island made no sense. He'd seemed embarrassed about this whole incident and she'd never raised it again, assuming he'd made a mistake and didn't want to own up to it. Both vehicles were diesels and he'd ended the conversation with some sort of throw-away remark, that if the island ever ran out of petrol or diesel, they could add oil to aviation fuel at a push.

Deborah stood hard on the brakes and stopped the Land Rover. He hadn't made a mistake at all. He'd planned ahead for the war, which he suspected would happen but wasn't telling anyone. She sat dumbfounded for a moment. It seemed that Will was more fore-sighted than she was. It all made sense now, all those spare parts that would last decades. He'd even made sure the wheels with the tyres on were carefully stored in an especially dark part of the warehouse, something about protecting the rubber from ultra violet radiation from the sun. She was interrupted in these thoughts by the noise of a vehicle stopping behind her.

"Everything ok Miss Deborah?" asked a man who had a strong St Helenian accent that it turned out was Henry, her Chief of Police.

"Yes Henry, I had a sudden thought and decided to stop and ponder it rather than carry on driving and have an accident" she told him.

He nodded and smiled and then asked "Are you going to the barbeque?"

"Yes, and I better get a move on before all the Wahoo is gone" she told him. In fact, she was sure if there was going to be any Wahoo, and there usually was, someone would save her a bit. She liked Henry and his family and just before the war, she'd recalled when she'd had to apply a fair bit of pressure to him to get him to move into Will's house, the Residency. It was the most prestigious house on the Island and well furnished. It was too big for her and since Henry had a family, the only young family, she felt it right he moved into it. He was also the senior policeman on the island. No-one had minded him moving in and most of the islanders were content to remain in their own homes though out of convenience, some now lived at more than one house to reduce travelling.

She parked her Land Rover and grabbed her picnic basket from the back of it. She didn't visit Comfortless Cove very often. It was a rocky cove with a sandy beach and a permanent barbeque facility. She knew it as the place early telegraph cables were laid to, or was it from, the island. It's history, though, was older than that and just above the cove there was a cemetery and it had been linked to the quarantine sites for visiting ships carrying yellow fever. Unlike English Bay beach there were no large waves or breakers and it was as nice a place as any to have a swim and relax. However, it was also a popular place to swim and relax and she generally preferred something quieter.

Everyone greeted her warmly and one of two of the bolder ones gave her a hug. She was hungry and had a wander over to the barbeque to see what was on it.

"Don't worry Miss Deborah, we made sure some Wahoo would be left for you," an older man whose name was Alf told her. She beamed him a big smile in reply. She had only been big game fishing once and she hadn't found it very appealing. She also didn't know much about big game fish other than what they tasted like. She had eaten Shark for the first time when she'd first arrived on the Island and quite liked it, but Wahoo was her favourite fish. It was a big, but fast, fish. Apparently, it could swim faster than most speed boats could travel, at up to 60 mph despite weighing in about the same as an average man. The meat was pure white when cooked and tasted delicious. It had never been a common fish to catch but not a rare one either and, from time to time, someone caught one. It was her favourite food on the island.

Vincent of course wasn't here because he knew she would be here. She felt regret that she hadn't moved on from where they left off in the bunker. In truth she'd given him mixed messages or rather clear messages of 'yes' and then 'no'. She'd treated him badly yet not once had he complained. He was, of course, highly pissed off with her and in small ways he expressed this, some deliberately and others perhaps subconsciously. It was just as well he wasn't interested in Sabrina. She assumed Sabrina wasn't interested in him or perhaps she was just waiting and biding her time, respectfully waiting for her friend to make up her mind, for once and all. The island never used to be like this because in the past men had generally outnumbered women. However, Deborah knew the circumstances of everyone on the island and only three people were without a partner, in fact a spouse, and they were herself, Sabrina and Vincent.

While she tucked into the Wahoo, she pondered what she could do to retrieve the situation. She realised she was at fault and that whenever she'd managed to let go of the past and get close to Vincent she'd got scared. She knew she was kidding herself that she'd manage to break free of the chains of her past, and by the time she did, she'd probably have lost Vincent for ever. At the thought of this she sighed and Henry noticed it but then pretended he hadn't and looked away.

The rest of the barbeque passed without incident or observation and Deborah even enjoyed a short swim before thanking everyone for a lovely day

Hal's Legacy

One of Deborah's more pressing tasks when she was back at work on Monday morning was to discover what surprises Hal had left in the main US Air force warehouse. It was a task she wanted to have undertaken a while ago but was always too busy to manage until now. Once she had let herself in, she found the whole warehouse's contents was a survivalist's dream. The warehouse was divided into quite separate areas with each area containing different types of things.

There were indeed many surprises: a seed bank, small domestic size windmill generators, bicycles, small wind pumps, a couple of substantial rowing boats, all kinds of hand tools, a lot of steel girders, in all sorts of sizes, termite or white ant proofing the future, she supposed, were just some of things she found. It also seemed that most of the items were designed to operate without power, or to create it.

Hal's legacy wasn't just a storehouse and while Deborah hadn't given the American armoury a thought, other than that Vincent could take responsibility for it, he had taken an interest in paying a visit to it. It was about the same size as the British one but stocked completely differently. Vincent didn't believe in co-incidence or happy accidents and looking around the American armoury, he guessed there had been agreement the Americans would stock heavier weapons than the British and only a few rifles and not pistols.

There were a large number of the obsolete anti-tank M47 Javelin man portable guided missile and several heavy machine guns. He supposed the M47s could be used against a ship if you could get close enough and doubted anyone would seek to land tanks on the island. Almost certainly that's why they were here because from memory they'd be easy to use and were pretty much point, shoot and keep on pointing. He'd never used one personally but knew of them and they'd be interesting for his volunteers to have a practice with. He supposed they were practically giving these away and while a Stinger missile would have been his preference, it made sense to leave these here.

The heavy machine guns were fifty calibre M2s and an old favourite of the Americans and a lot of other countries. They would be ideal against boats or even helicopters in the right position. He'd need to decide who to train to use them because he'd only set up a couple of positions for them.

After turning off the lights and locking the armoury back up Vincent hoped the day would never come when any of this stuff would need to be deployed, let alone used. But if the day did come his team would be proficient in using them.

Long Beach

As Deborah drove back to her home, she saw the sun setting over Long Beach and realised that, by now, some Turtle eggs might be hatching. She'd lost track of how long it was since her turtle had laid her eggs but thought those might have hatched by now, but there should be others hatching. After she'd eaten her evening meal, she showered, tidied up and headed for Long Beach. She walked slowly up and down the beach for hours. Looking and listening and shining her torch across the sandy beach but saw nothing. Eventually, it was the very early hours of the morning and she'd still seen nothing and, feeling tired, was half inclined to sleep on the beach but it was also only a short walk back to hcr home. She got home tired and disappointed and went to sleep straightaway.

Chapter Ten – A Post apocalypse Christmas

Henry had not long finished work and also not long finished eating his dinner with his family, when he became aware of some whispering and nudging between his children. His wife looked at the children and she then looked at her husband. This was his cue to pose the question "Is there something one of you would like to ask me?"

The children looked at each other and then turning to look at Henry spoke in unison "Father Christmas will still be coming this year, won't he?"

"Err, I guess so" Henry replied with a sinking feeling. He had forgotten all about Christmas.

"What does your dad know? Father Christmas always comes to bring presents to good children so if you are good, he will bring you presents" Pam, Henry's wife, confidently told them. The children seemed satisfied by this second confirmation and then made themselves scarce.

Henry knew that in his household it was his job not only to pay for and buy Christmas presents but to choose them as well. While there was still some time left before Christmas, it was something that had to be planned for well in advance, as the lead times for ordering anything were usually quite long. He also knew he hadn't began planning early enough and nothing he'd ordered had arrived. He supposed these were things he could worry about tomorrow because there was not much he could do tonight, apart from make a lot of phone calls which he didn't plan on doing.

The next day Henry did his customary mid-morning tour of the main island areas and Frank waved him down for a chat and invited for a coffee.

"What's on your mind Henry, you look pretty glum?" Frank asked him.

"Christmas, that's what's on my mind Frank." He replied.

"Christmas, I'd forgotten about it, I guess it's only a few days away." Frank said.

"Yes, I'd forgotten about it as well but my kids hadn't and I never ordered anything to come on the last boat before there were no more boats." Henry told him.

"I think there is still some children's stuff in the BX and you have the only children on the island, so why don't we pop over at lunchtime for some Christmas shopping?" Frank suggested.

Lunchtime arrived and Henry met Frank at the BX, and after letting him in, closed and locked the door behind him. "Follow me to where I think there are some children's' toys, a load of those little plastic building blocks that you can make all sorts of stuff out of, Lego; I think that's what it's called. You might want to pick up something for yourself because Deborah told me she is planning to have an open shopping day before Christmas," Frank said.

Henry was relieved to find there were enough children's toys for him to take enough to satisfy his children on Christmas morning and at Frank's insistence he took a couple of things that he could give to his wife as well.

"Frank, if you grow yourself a beard you really will be Father Christmas rather than just act the part." Henry told him as he patted him on the back to thank him, before getting back to work.

Rev Simon sat at his desk and sought spiritual wisdom in prayer about what to do about Christmas. Christmas was for the most part the hijack of an English pagan festival, yet so successful everyone had long since forgotten that, and it had become as Christian as Christian things could be. Yet how could you have a major celebration at a time when most of the planet's civilisation had died, and for many, gone to a lost eternity? He was both God's representative and leader on the island and there would need to be a Christmas Day service, which was awkward enough anyway since it had never snowed on Ascension Island and was never likely to. Then he had an idea. He could link the hope the islanders had for the future with the hope that the birth of Jesus brought to the world. He could even make it evangelical by linking the fact that the island had saved them and that Jesus would save them. The celebration was that of 'hope'. Yes, that would work and he began to put together his Christmas message with enthusiasm.

Vincent was aware that it was soon going to be Christmas. He hadn't bothered doing much at Christmas for many years and wasn't planning on doing much this year either. Henry had invited him for a Christmas Day meal but seemed a bit cagey on who else might attend, and Vincent asked him outright if he'd invited Deborah, and Henry somewhat sheepishly admitted he had and that she'd accepted. He explained quite politely that he had no social interaction with Deborah and so he'd not be attending but was grateful for the invitation. He supposed that while Henry was a good policeman and fast becoming a good friend, he was a crap 'match-maker' and 'fixer'.

Deborah opened the envelope that had been hand delivered to her at her office and found it was an invitation to a Christmas Eve carol service and midnight mass. It took her a split second to realise that since she was now the Administrator it was her duty to attend. She didn't want to attend, she didn't want to hear about God and Jesus, and she didn't want to celebrate anything, especially Christmas. She did however, feel a strong sense of obligation and so she would go. She knew where the church was, you could hardly miss it, but she'd never been inside it all the time she'd been on the island. Well, there was a first time for everything. She was going to have to celebrate Christmas anyway because Henry and Pam had invited her to Christmas dinner at 'The Residence' and having leant on him to get him to move in there, she could hardly not agree to have dinner with them. Deborah supposed she had something of a 'humbug' and 'Scrooge' attitude to Christmas but recalled 'Scrooge' had a dramatic change of character in the story and everything had a happy ending. Well, the world hadn't had a happy ending, or perhaps it had? Once everything had settled down from the global exchange of nuclear weapons and the lives lost by the pandemic, global warming would be reversed. The wildlife of the world would slowly recover and surely thrive? The remnants of mankind would have more to worry about than fashion, fads and consumerism. In a sense Ascension Island would be something of an oasis and she liked the idea of that. So, she'd do her civic duty for this lovely island and the inhabitants that were her friends and go to the service. She might even dress up and actually wear a dress and heels and put her pistol in her handbag.

"Sabrina, I think since it's nearly Christmas we ought to open the BX up to everyone on the island, so everyone can take some things from it for Christmas. It might seem a bit old-fashioned to have ladies first but someone has to go first and I wanted the ladies to shop separately from the men, so as well as pick something for themselves, they could pick something for their husbands for Christmas if they wanted to. The men can also pick something for themselves and something for their wives and if they end up having chosen for themselves the same things their wives chose for them, and vice versa, it won't matter. What do you think, nine to ten in the morning for the ladies and eleven to twelve in the morning for the men?" Deborah asked her.

Having agreed it was a good idea Sabrina publicised it using a mixture of communication media, having agreed everything first with Frank. What became known as the Christmas Shopping Day was very popular despite the weather being wet but warm rather than hot. There'd been more wet weather than usual for the time of year but no-one complained and the island was likewise greener than usual within a few days. Deborah and Sabrina supervised the shopping, being the only two people on the island without a partner, apart from Vincent who said he'd prefer to be doing something else that day. Everyone's shopping was very restrained and most had to be encouraged to take more items than they'd originally planned and the BX still wasn't even close to being cleared out.

Soon the war and the pandemic seemed to have been forgotten and everyone was focused on making a big effort for Christmas, including planning Christmas Day meals. It was shortly after the fishing trip that the

Rev Simon had invited Vincent to join himself his wife and a couple of other friends for Christmas Day dinner. Vincent decided that he'd spent more than enough Christmas's on his own, and that it was time for a change. Besides, it might be the last chance he'd get to have turkey on Christmas Day even if it was out of a tin, though he supposed it might be frozen. He also decided that he might as well also go to church. He knew he didn't believe properly but he was very grateful for the prayers in the bunker which had worked. He learned there was a Christmas Eve service and a Christmas Day service and decided he'd rather go to the evening service and get it out of the way and then he could lounge around all of Christmas morning if he wanted to, before getting up for dinner. He decided he'd wear long trousers and wear a shirt and tie and look respectable. He'd found a shoulder holster for the Browning and while it would be uncomfortable under a shirt, he'd look sort of respectable. Or maybe he'd look like a mob boss rather than a gangster?

It was Christmas Eve and it was so long since Vincent had been to a church service that he'd forgotten that you needed to turn up early if you wanted a seat at the back, especially at Christmas. He hadn't turned up early and when he arrived, he found the church looked quite full; probably most of the island were there. There was nothing for it then to walk further towards the front of the church and look for a seat. Several people smiled at him and one or two shook his hands. As he got nearer the front of the church, he could see what must surely be the last spare seat, next to some woman in a lovely dress on the very front row. It was at that point that Vincent realised that the woman was Deborah. Vincent realised that he was trapped, well not quite trapped, a hasty retreat was always an option but not one he was going to embark on. As he took his seat Deborah turned to see who was about to sit next to her and when she saw it was Vincent, she gave him a glowing smile.

"Hello Vincent, how lovely to see you" she said.

"Yeah. Right." Vincent replied in a low grunt.

Deborah realised that Vincent hadn't only not planned their encounter but wasn't pleased about it either. That was hardly her fault. Well actually it was her fault and she was sorry for it for both of them. She decided the best thing would be to concentrate on the service and pretend Vincent wasn't there. Unfortunately, she found her thoughts drifted and she thought back to when they were in the bunker where, in the unlikeliest circumstances, she'd allowed herself to get close to him before she'd beat a hasty retreat. It was that retreat that she supposed had upset him because she had led him on and then slammed the door, without a good reason either. Someone had once told her that even God couldn't change the past and she certainly couldn't.

By reading the words on the piece of paper and singing the hymns Vincent had managed to avoid any further eye contact with Deborah. Holding the piece of paper at all times meant his hands were also fully occupied. The praying part was even easier, as he followed his childhood practice of hands together and eyes closed. The talk was interesting and everything seemed to be going ok and Vincent was beginning to feel Christmassy and have a hope for a better future, which he knew wasn't hard for him; given his chequered past. Then the Rev Simon explained they were going to make peace with each other and God, and Vincent initially thought this was an excellent idea and unaware it was part of most, if not all Sunday services, as well as this one. The Rev Simon explained you greeted the people around you, everyone in the church if you really wanted to, and said 'the peace of the Lord be with you' then you greeted them with a handshake or a hug. 'Fuck' thought Vincent and then wondered if God knew what you were thinking and disapproved of such a thought in his church.

Vincent looked to his right and realised afresh, his seat was on the end of a row and the person on the opposite side of the aisle was already working his way to their right. No, there was nothing he could do apart from greet Deborah. He turned to his left and found she was already waiting for him. They made eye contact and Vincent thought she looked sad. She seemed like she might want to hug him so he put his hand out a bit sharpish, so she'd shake it. She didn't as much shake it as hold it and gazed upon him. The moment passed as everyone had finished making their peace and practically last of all, first Deborah then Vincent said the words of the peace.

Next everyone took their turn to go to the front of the church to receive what Simon explained was Holy Communion, or bread and wine, or alternatively receive a blessing. Vincent had a vague awareness there was some sort of church process to have been through, to take bread and wine and he knew he certainly hadn't been through it, but decided he needed all the blessing he could get and went forward, with Deborah close behind him. After receiving his blessing and once he had sat back down at his seat, he chose to watch everyone else take their turn. He was surprised he recognised so many people and was glad he had come to the service, but nonetheless when the service was finished, he managed to get to the door before anyone else and give Deborah the slip, though he wasn't sure he actually needed to. He was soon in his Land Rover and driving slowly back to his home in Two Boats. It was of course not only the early hours of the morning, but Christmas Day. Happy Christmas to me, thought Vincent when he got home. He wanted to reflect on what sort of year it had been but fell asleep almost as soon as he lay on his bed.

Christmas Day

"When do you think Vincent and Deborah will get together, perhaps we should have asked her to join us as well?" Elizabeth asked her husband while they were preparing for Christmas dinner.

"I think you will find it will be in the Lord's timing, which could be anytime and probably when least expected, but not a moment too soon nor a moment too late. And since they are both making strenuous efforts to avoid each other we wouldn't have succeeded in having them both join us. I don't think he would have sat next to her in church if it wasn't for the fact it was the only spare seat left and there was no obvious way for him to leave the church without being seen, or even stopped on the way out."

"Did you invite her for Christmas?" Elizabeth asked.

"Yes, but she had already agreed to have dinner at Henry's" he replied.

It was later than usual when Vincent woke up. He looked at his watch and smiled, it was a very nice watch and this one, the yellow faced one, was his favourite. He got up, made himself a mug of tea and thought about getting ready for Christmas Day dinner with Simon and Elizabeth Bond. He didn't know whether they had picked up anything from the BX for themselves but he had picked up something for them, a pair of Omega wristwatches, automatic and self-winding that should last them a lifetime. He'd also found a couple of bottles of some sort of non-alcoholic sparking fruit drink.

Simon and Elizabeth made Vincent very welcome for Christmas dinner with them and they'd even managed to find some Christmas crackers. Vincent pondered whether it might be possible to make the snapping part of the Cracker out of cordite. Elizabeth was a good cook and while Vincent tended to view eating as a necessity rather than a pleasure, he enjoyed his meal.

After lunch Simon produced a board game called Monopoly, which Vincent had heard of but never actually played. Most of the games he'd played had been with a deck of cards and he was rarely successful. After the game finished it was time for tea and after that Vincent made his excuses so he could leave early, thanking them for a lovely day and then walking along the beach before driving home.

Deborah was out of bed later than she'd planned for on Christmas day. She guessed that the Pollack's would have been up early on account of having small children. Sabrina was having her Christmas dinner with Luke and Rebecca Caskey, and Deborah would be joining them for a Christmas tea. She hadn't been able to find out what Vincent was doing or where he was going for Christmas Day. Her diverse enquiries had drawn polite replies but no forthcoming information. She guessed he wasn't spending it on his own and the certainty was that he wasn't spending it with the Pollacks. Henry had sheepishly confessed that he'd invited him but he'd declined.

She checked she'd got all the presents she needed to take with her. It seemed like an age ago when she'd ordered them all last summer. She'd had expensive suits made for both Henry and Luke and some nice things for their wives. Presents for Henry's children had proved a challenge because the things that children appeared to like seemed to change as quickly as they grew taller. In the end she'd settled on some nice glove puppets and a lot of colouring books and artists materials, ranging from pencils to paints.

On Deborah's drive to the residency, she saw a small group of donkeys and wondered what would become of them. She'd like to have fed them but knew of problems in the past with the occasional donkey that had become too dependant on human handouts. She'd had a lovely Christmas dinner with the Pollack family and they'd managed to decorate some rooms of the house and even had a huge artificial Christmas tree. It worked out convenient for her to be able to leave early and drive to the Caskey's' for Christmas tea and catch up with Sabrina as well. It was a struggle to eat a big tea but she supposed she could always not bother to eat much for the next couple of days.

Eventually Christmas day was over and it hadn't seemed massively different from other years, perhaps that was because she hadn't lost the family ties that others recently had, hers being lost long ago. She wondered how Vincent had spent his day and then wished she hadn't.

New Year's Eve
Deborah woke up and realised it was New Year's Eve. She'd already declared New Year's Eve and New Year's Day National holidays so nobody would be at work. Unlike more normal years, there was no single large party planned on the island this year. The mood was still quite subdued and Christmas had been quiet. Nobody was going to make a long-distance phone call to the UK, USA, St Helena or anywhere else. She had been invited to several small evening meals and Luke and his wife had told her it would do her good to relax and unwind. She'd agreed with them but decided she'd rather be on her own. She hadn't really given the day much thought, or how much had changed, yet not really changed in the last couple

of months. Then she realised that she could spend most of the day on Long Beach to see if any of the turtle's eggs might hatch. It was bad news if they hatched in the daytime, but sometimes they did, and so she took a large bucket so, if necessary, she could rescue them and release them once it was dark. It would be peaceful on the beach and she had nothing to lose. After spending most of the day on the beach on her own and having seen nothing, she returned home before it was dark and not in the best of moods, she spoke loudly to herself. "Deborah Black, it's time you let go of the past and shacked up with Vincent before some other woman arrives on the island and you end up more of a lonely woman than you already are." She also knew she needed a bit more time to move on and while it was a bit cranky for her to talk to herself, she also realised she was at least talking about it and supposed before long she might even manage to talk to someone else about it.

New Year's Day

A happy New Year to me, Deborah thought as she woke up and after lying in bed for ages, she got up had a shower and lounged around all day until she was restless. She was still disappointed not to have seen any baby turtles and then decided she'd go to the beach again, tonight. There was a risk she'd still not see any and would end up even more disappointed, but she guessed she was not only used to disappointment, but would be able to cope with it.

Vincent punched his attacker in the face and spun around to slash the other with his knife. He breathed hard through his respirator. He looked back and blew Deborah a kiss and ran for all he was worth. He felt a pain in his leg. He picked up a machine gun and put down some heavy fire and shouted to his team to move fast. It was no good, his pursuers were gaining on him, so he turned round and gunned them down. He'd not been in this part of the ruined city before and it was dangerous. He looked at his dosimeter and the radiation levels were dangerously high. They'd need to find a vehicle soon or else they wouldn't escape. He felt hot and uncomfortable and anxious, he looked around once more, then he seemed to be caught up in a net and then something hard hit him.

Vincent woke up and found he was on the floor. He realised he'd had a nightmare and must have fallen out of the bed. He was wet with sweat. The mosquito net was tangled up around him. This wasn't the start of the new year he'd been hoping for. He looked at his watch and smiled, it was a lovely watch, light as a feather and glowed in the dark, it was the blue one.

Chapter Eleven – An unexpected arrival

It was early January and so less than a couple of months since the apocalypse and pandemic, yet most days Deborah wondered whether it was time to switch off the islands' radar and sonar and save both fuel and generator life, in generating electricity to run them. She was working in her office when her radio sprang into life and vindicated her decision to keep them switched on.

"Deborah, we've spotted something in the distance in the South East. It's very slow moving and looks to be several small vessels rather than a single large one." The anonymous voice told Deborah.

"Ok thanks, can you get someone to get the RHIB launched" she replied. Deborah had still been avoiding Vincent and he'd still been avoiding her. Each knew what the other was working on and there was quite a lot of work to be done, mostly long-term planning and putting in place various systems and procedures and soon they'd be working together on the water pipe project. However, they rarely spoke to each other but Deborah would have to speak to him now so she called him on his radio, from hers.

"Vincent, it's Deborah. We've some possible visitors on the horizon. Can you get your volunteer defence force armed with live ammunition and at the quayside? I want whatever is heading our way intercepted by the RHIB before they get too close. I'd also like someone to follow up in the launch, armed as well if that's possible." Deborah told him.

"Sure thing, maam, if you can get the RIHB in the water and the engines running, it will save us time" he replied, as casually as he could manage.

Deborah was slightly surprised at Vincent's last message; he surely couldn't get his armed volunteers at the Quayside in less time than it would take to launch the RHIB. In any event after contacting Arnold, asking him to launch the RHIB, she picked up her radio, her megaphone and her emergency 'grab bag' and jogged to the quayside. She could see that Arnold and couple of men she didn't immediately recognise were busy getting the RHIB into the water. She managed to catch Arnold's eye and rather than wave she motioned a swirling finger to indicate she wanted the engine's started and the propellers turning. By the time she had reached the quay she heard the gentle splosh of the RHIB making contact with the water and then after a couple of coughs, she heard the first and then the second engine start.

"Thanks Jon," she told one of the men she now recognised as Jon, who handed her a life jacket or was it a buoyancy aid, no time to ask now. Jon then passed her a large dry bag and once she'd put everything in it, he then passed it to down to Arnold. Deborah then heard a bit of commotion and saw several vehicles race to the edge of the quayside, having raised a large cloud of dust. She recognised Vincent who was shouting at several men and at least two women, who jumped out of the vehicles and before she had time to collect her thoughts, they had formed a tight group fanning out from Vincent with weapons pointing in all directions. Where the fuck had they got some of the weapons from; apart from a heavy machine gun, they had some sort of hand-held rocket or missile launcher.

"Morning Maam, the Island Defence Volunteer Force at your service" Vincent told her. Then in response to her surprised look and unasked question he added "American armoury Maam."

Deborah held up her hand and put her radio to her ear. "Ok, got it." She said and then turned to Vincent and the defence volunteers. "There's a group of small vessels, heading for the island from the South East, so I'm guessing they might even have come from St Helena. As far as we know St Helena was wiped out from the pandemic so we might have several corpses or people very sick. I want us to intercept the vessels and see what we've got. If anyone is alive, they're bound to want to land here and if so, we'll need to have no contact with them. Doc and his volunteer medics will handle them, being suited to full chemical warfare standards and waiting to quarantine them in the hospital by the time we get back. Our potential visitors might be armed, desperate and dangerous so we won't rush to get too close, though I can't imagine they'll outgun yourselves" she told him.

Vincent nodded and turned to face his team. "Ok team, Naomi will be second in command to myself with the call sign Marine Two in the launch. We'll put a heavy machine gun and a couple of M47s in it with Dominic and Steve. Arnold will pilot it. The rest of us will take the RHIB and will stow everything apart from the Pistols, which we'll wear under our life jackets and try and keep them dry. Our Call sign will be Marine One. We'll do a fast intercept and then once we are several hundred yards away, we'll slow to an idle and get our weapons out and do a slow broad sweeping circle of them. If they fire upon us, let them have it without waiting for any order to open fire from me, but be prepared to hang on tight, as I'll make a maximum speed departure and zig zag. The launch should stay behind us at all times unless we're obviously in trouble and then act and engage as they see fit. Is everyone clear?" Vincent told them.

"YES VINCENT" they all shouted in unison.

Vincent then looked at Deborah and she looked back at him. She could see he was deadly serious which made him look more handsome than ever. She wanted to sigh but supressed it. "Ok Vincent, you haven't asked for overall command and control but you seem to already have it. I'll act as your number three if you need me to. If there's nothing else we need to do, let's leave now." She told him.

Vincent boarded the RHIB and Arnold and Vincent exchanged a handshake and a pat on the back and Arnold then helped everyone on board with Deborah last of all before getting off and then boarding the Ascension Frigate launch.

Vincent looked back down the RHIB and checked everyone and everything looked reasonably secure. Then looking ahead, he steadily increased the power of the twin outboards before looking back. He saw the launch was now following them and he then put the throttles on the stops and the bow rose high and the RHIB jumped forward. It was soon in deeper water and was skimming the tops of the larger waves with a series of body jarring thuds. There was a radar set on the RHIB and Vincent set course for an intercept on the contact it displayed.

The yachts were not as near as they had expected and as they approached them Deborah pondered if a small group of yachts was called a fleet or a flotilla of yachts. Deciding on the latter she hailed them with her battery powered loud hailer as the RHIB slowly circled them. "Flotilla of Yachts, drop sail and wait for further instructions." there was no response so Deborah repeated the command. "Flotilla of yachts, drop sail and wait for further instructions."

Deborah looked at Vincent and he gave one of the women an instruction. The woman pointed what Deborah knew to be a British Forces issue sub-machine gun of a no longer used type, to the left of the small flotilla. She then fired a short burst before quickly pointing the gun to the right and firing another short burst. Deborah was surprised at how much noise the gunfire made and then she realised that whenever she'd been shooting on the range, she'd worn ear protection.

The response from the flotilla was dramatic with several figures emerging to wave white flags. Deborah hailed them again with the same message and this time all the yachts dropped their sails. Some of the yachts looked a bit tatty but all the masts were intact. She hailed them again. "You have entered the territorial waters of Ascension Island and I'm advising you that we are operating under martial law, and while you may land here you will first be subject to a strict medical quarantine. If you are in agreement, we will give you a gentle tow to our quay. You will need to form a tow line between yourselves." One of the yacht people shouted their agreement and a line was thrown to them.

Using the RHIB's radio which had a much longer range than her own handset she said "Doc, its Deborah. We're on our way back with some yacht people. Can you confirm you are suited up and ready to walk them to the quarantine ward of the hospital and then lock them in?" she said.

"Yes boss, that's exactly what we will be doing and we're dripping wet inside these blasted suits already. If you can let them know where they are going and that their quarantine will be for fourteen days that would be good." The Doc told her. Deborah announced that information by the loud hailer to the yacht people, who acknowledged with several nods.

Once at the quayside the yacht people, who Deborah observed looked thin and generally unhealthy, and included some children, were one by one helped up the quay steps. As they looked back Deborah advised them, again by loud hailer, their yachts would be safely moored and no-one would touch them.

Training

It was a few days later when Vincent and the volunteers met again for their weekly training meeting. "Thanks for turning out once more. That was a slick operation intercepting that flotilla of yachts, and while they gave us no trouble, they might have done. So, what's next?"

"Any fighting force needs to be kept fit and competitive and I suppose you all know about the bi-annual Dew Pond run and some of you may have run in it before. I'll be running it for the first time and I'd like us to enter two teams. This week and next I thought we might spend our training time on a run rather than weapons and tactical training but if you can find the energy, we can do both – run with weapons. I know the runners amongst you will be training anyway but I want us to train together now and again. For our first run we'll run from One boat to the Red Lion. My experience has been that if you are running or training with someone else you each push yourself a little harder," he told them. "Ok, let's drive up to One Boat, park up and go for a run."

Quarantined

"We are safe now and we can rest" Paul said.

"But are we safe, we've been locked up like convicts?" The admiral said.

"No, we haven't father, they explained we had to be quarantined in case we had the virus?" Jo replied. The Admiral walked off in a huff. Jo looked at her mother, the Admiral's wife but didn't say anything. This was the fourth day since they had been in quarantine and rather than deteriorating and getting sicker than when they'd arrived, everyone was feeling a lot better and stronger.

"Well mate, what do you think?" Paul asked Jake.

"We're alive on something a bit like a desert island but without the coconut trees. The people seem ok and they've taken good care of us. They said from the beginning we don't have to stay but this place is miles from anywhere and I'll bet is reasonably self-sufficient. I mean, if it wasn't, they wouldn't be looking after us like this, unless they were cannibals." He replied and laughed. They then saw the admiral look in their direction and frown at them. "I'll tell you what though, he's becoming a pain in the arse. I know he helped us and we wouldn't have got here without him but we helped him in return, gave space on our boat for him and everything. We also beat off that attack on the other island" Jake added.

"Well let's make sure we don't end up living next door to him." Paul replied laughing.

Jeff smiled at Paul and Jake. He was glad he'd met them and he'd found that their wives and the children were all very kind. He'd overhead the children talking about the beach they'd seen and they hoped they'd be able to make a lot of sand castles. He did talk to some of the others in the group but he still felt lonely. He wasn't the only single person, because Jo was also single but she was also with her parents. He was then the only person without any family in the group and, on occasion, like now, he felt lonely. He was pleased he was feeling stronger but he knew he was still sleeping a lot and he often felt tired. He wasn't in a rush to escape the quarantine, to him it wasn't that much different from being on a yacht and he'd become accustomed to that. No, he'd survived one adventure and was in no hurry to embark on another.

Doc Caskey had just finished his morning visit of the yacht people and removed his protective clothing. He was pleased they were looking a lot better. He'd given each of them a thorough examination and weighed them. There was no sign of them getting ill. On the other hand, it was perfectly plausible that the virus might manifest itself once they got healthy. Nature could be cruel like that. So, however well they looked, a fourteen-day quarantine was a fourteen-day quarantine. A pity that old guy was so miserable, a trouble maker if ever he saw one.

Quarantine ends

For the next fortnight Deborah was fully occupied with managing the islands' resources, and even without having to place orders, or look at flight and shipping schedules, or respond to messages from the UK, she was busy. She was still avoiding contact with Vincent and she felt some shame at doing so. The doc had been in daily contact with her and apart from some initial concerns about the condition of the yacht people they were now looking healthier every day and seemed sure to be ready to leave quarantine on time. Just at that moment her desk phone rang.

"Morning Boss, its Doc, times up and they can all come out. I trust you have a welcome message for them and stuff like that?" he said.

"Yes Doc, and Sabrina has prepared homes for them at Two Boats, and I'll be welcoming them at the hospital." She replied

"What about Vincent?" Doc asked.

"What about him?" Deborah asked.

Doc sighed before speaking "He is the operational head of your armed forces and I suggest it might be a good idea for him to be present, along with the police to make sure they understand how things work here. Also, there's one old guy who's been a bit bolshie."

"Yes, I see what you mean now, I'll make sure he's with the welcome party. See you in a few minutes."

Deborah picked up her things and having asked Sabrina to come with her and rather than radio to ask Vincent to accompany them, she asked Sabrina if she knew where he was.

"He's already outside the hospital waiting for us," Sabrina replied with the faintest trace of a smile.

As they walked to the hospital, Vincent came to attention without making any eye contact with either Deborah or Sabrina and followed them into the hospital. Doc had the yacht people assembled as a group and behind him were two policemen, one of which was Chris.

Deborah smiled at the group of yacht people and began her welcome speech. "Good morning and welcome once more to Ascension Island. I want to explain to you all how things work here and how you'll need to fit in, assuming you want to stay." But she didn't get much further with her welcome speech before the oldest man in the group interrupted her.

"Do you know who I am? I haven't sailed half way across the Atlantic for some jumped up woman to tell me what to do." He said in a loud angry voice. Then before Deborah had chance to reply, the man lunged at Deborah and knocked her over. However, before Deborah had even finished sliding across the floor, or the man had made another move, Vincent had leapt forward, spun the man around and had slammed his pistol in the back of the man's head jerking it forward as he did so, following through with a knee to the man's back which saw the man land on the floor. Then there was then a loud mechanical clack-clack noise as he cocked the mechanism of his Browning pistol, so it was ready to fire.

"Don't move or you're a fucking dead nobody, and I don't care how much mess your fucking head makes in our hospital" Vincent shouted and added "no-one else move neither."

The man stayed frozen on the floor, breathing heavily, and Deborah picked herself up. Without even beckoning to them, one of the policemen stepped forward and cuffed the man. Vincent stepped back and watched the policemen lead him away. Deborah was shaken. She began to think and supposed he would be locked in a police cell and Henry would ask her what to do with him later, but her thoughts were violently interrupted by a deafening loud bang which made everyone in the hospital jump except for Vincent. He'd fired his pistol, aiming it at the floor. He then quickly manoeuvred himself in front of Deborah and with his arms locked, held the pistol in an aimed position sweeping slowly from left to right and back again in front of the yacht people. Deborah could smell the smoke from the freshly fired pistol and saw some smoke spiralling slowly from its barrel.

"Miss Black has absolute authority here, and if necessary, I will help her to enforce it. You can either stay and be grateful or get back on your shitty yachts and fuck off." Vincent shouted while staring angrily at the yacht people. An older woman fainted and a couple of the yacht people helped her to a nearby chair. A couple of children started crying. Then a younger woman slowly stepped forward with her hands held open-palmed above her head and spoke to Vincent.

"Sir, please excuse my father. I'm sure he never meant to hurt Miss Black or seek to usurp or challenge her authority. He's a retired Admiral who sometimes forgets he's retired. We had a traumatic sea journey getting here. None of us knew what to expect when we reached this island, not even being sure we would reach here safely, or at all, and he didn't deal with the quarantine well. My name is Jo Cockburn." The woman said in a nervous voice. Her parents had actually named her Josephine but from a young age she refused to answer to anything other than 'Jo'.
Vincent, still holding his pistol aimed at the yacht people, turned his head around to look at Deborah who nodded in reply to his unspoken question. He then put his pistol back in the holster.

Deborah really wanted some time to think but realised there wasn't going to be any. "Ok Jo. Your father is under arrest and he'll be kept in the police cells until I decide whether or not he is to be charged and punished for assault. We don't summarily execute people for assault but we can keep him imprisoned indefinitely. He'll be able to have visitors in due course, drop by the administrator's office and we will arrange something."

Deborah was interrupted at this point by the sound of a woman loudly crying before asking between sobs, "Have they shot him, is he dead?"

Jo turned towards the woman, who'd evidently was the woman who had fainted and had now revived, and put an arm around her before speaking.

121

"No Mother, they just fired a warning shot. He's been arrested and taken away by a policeman. I'm very angry with him because he was very stupid and got us all off to a very bad start."

Deborah decided she might as well carry on with her welcome speech, but she'd firm it up as she went along. "Ok. We might as well carry on talking here and now and have some introductions. I'm in charge. I hold the positions of Civil Administrator as well as Military Commanding Officer for both the United Kingdom and United States of America. Lieutenant Vincent Irving is the head of our defence force. You can all stay, subject to our law and authority. Alternatively, you are free to leave and we will replenish your vessels with fuel, water, food and medical supplies. You're the only people from anywhere to arrive here since just before the war started. You don't need to make a decision now and you can change your mind and leave anytime you want. Here are some details of some houses you can live in along with sets of keys. They've been unoccupied for some time but I've had them checked out for you and provisioned them with some food and drink that will keep you going for a few days. You'll be driven there by Miss Sabrina Triumph and some islanders. I'll send someone to see you in a day or so but if, before then, you want to find me, or one of my staff, then go to the Administrator's Office here in Georgetown." Then having finished what she had to say she left, followed by Vincent. Deborah realised she was badly shaken and she wanted to get away from the yacht people. She wanted to be in a more friendly place.

Vincent could feel the warmth of his freshly fired Browning pistol even through the holster. He knew he shouldn't have fired it because it wasn't what servicemen did, let alone an officer, but rather more the act of a gangster, enforcer, bodyguard or mercenary. In his anger at seeing the man strike Deborah he'd let his old life rise to the fore and it had betrayed him. He was also reminded of some other things he'd done that he regretted and that he thought he'd forgotten about forever. It was all too late to pretend it hadn't happened and it was unlikely anyone would be able to extract the bullet from the hospital's floor in a hurry either. He followed Deborah outside until she'd stopped walking.

"You ok Deborah?" Vincent asked looking at her, noting her complexion was on the pale side.

"Yes and no. Can you take me to Fort Bedford?" then seeing the mild look of puzzlement on his face added "The hill, Cross Hill, outside town with the old cannons on them." Vincent nodded and once they were in his Land Rover he drove slowly to Ford Bedford. Once he had parked up, Deborah was out of the vehicle before him, and she walked to the cannons and stood by them. He followed her and stood behind her, to let her collect her thoughts.

Deborah turned to look at Vincent and he could see that she had started to cry and then before he had chance to say anything, she had put her arms around him and was sobbing and embracing him. He could feel her warm and lithe body pressed tight into his. He could feel her breathing, rapid at first then more slowly. He'd never seen her like this before and he thought it would be ok to put his arms around her, since she had hers around him.

"These aren't tears Vincent, my darling, this is melted ice, the melting of the ice maiden. Of course, I'm not a maiden, sorry. I'm ready now, to be yours for ever, if you still want me. Sorry it's taken me so long." Then she stepped back, but as she did so she caught hold of his hands and clasped them tightly with her own. Then in one sweeping swift movement, she pulled him to her and kissed him firmly on the lips, while moving his hands onto the cheeks of her firm bottom. Then as quickly as everything had happened, she stepped back once more, but this time gazed upon him.

Vincent was dumb struck, speechless, in mild shock. He was still thinking about what had happened with the 'Yachties' and he hadn't really thought why Deborah had wanted to come here. Her unforeseen passion had really taken him by surprise. It was for him a very lovely surprise, the like of which he didn't think he'd had since opening his Christmas presents when he was a small child. A tear ran down his cheek and then another. He was going to wipe them away but Deborah had produced a small handkerchief and wiped them away for him. He was just about to try and say something when Deborah spoke first.

"Vincent Irving, I want to spend the rest of my life with you, share every intimacy I can offer you, and be with you always, if you'll have me" she told him.

"Yes Deborah, yes to everything." he haltingly replied.

She kissed him once more before speaking. "Let's take the rest of the day off and go up Green Mountain, to the Dewpond, I don't think you've been all the way to the top and I haven't for ages. We can just be together and talk or be silent, would you like to go?"

Vincent was still shocked and words weren't coming to him easily but he managed to reply "yes, I'd love to."

"I'll just tell Sabrina and then we can leave" she told him, to which he nodded in reply. She then drove them both back to Georgetown in Vincent's Land Rover and after finding and speaking to Sabrina got back into the driving seat, which wasn't unusual because she knew her way around better than Vincent did, though sometimes in the past he'd driven and she was the passenger. What was unusual this time though was that almost as soon as they had fastened their seat belts Deborah reached out for Vincent's hand and placed it on her thigh. This is odd, in a pleasant way, Vincent thought, as they drove out of Georgetown. He knew the way but was surprised when at One Boat she turned onto a dirt road that ran across Donkey Plain. He'd been shown this way but it was very dusty and bumpy and he'd never used it other than the first time he was shown it. Despite needing a high degree of steering input Deborah managed to take one hand off the steering wheel to momentarily stroke his neck. Then she turned and smiled at him with the most wonderful smile anyone had ever given him. At the end of the Donkey Plain dirt road the mountain could be seen clearly ahead. Vincent then realised that they'd most likely pass-through Travellers Hill before starting on the mountain road itself. There wasn't much difference in the time or distance travelled going this way but this route was less populated and avoided driving through Two Boats where the Yacht people were going to and who might have caught them up. The Land Rover was soon slowing down and now in first gear. Deborah then stopped and moved the gearbox into low ratios and set off again, managing a quick change into second gear, low ratio.

"I'll park at the Red Lion and grab something to drink before we start the climb on foot" Deborah told him smiling.

Vincent couldn't get over the change in Deborah. It was if she was a different person. He realised he knew very little about the Red Lion but did know it wasn't the name of a pub but the name of the farm and perhaps the most important place on the island that would ensure the long-term survival of the islanders. They got out of the Land Rover and were walking hand in hand as if they'd been doing so for decades rather than minutes, when they met the farm manager, Richard. Vincent observed that he looked completely 'gob-smacked'.

"Good morning Richard. Yes, your eyes aren't deceiving you. The ice maiden has melted and fallen in love with Vincent Irving, and you are the very first person to know this. None of this was planned, including our being here and we wondered if you've any bottled water you can let us have, for our climb to the Dewpond." Deborah told him smiling.

Richard had always liked Miss Deborah because she was extremely efficient in her job and was a woman of her word. Sometime after she had just arrived on the island and before the apocalypse, she'd visited him and explained that while she admitted she didn't have as much of a grasp of the farm as she'd like, she thought it was extremely important to the long-term future of the island and not just as heritage project but as a working farm again. She'd then got him to write out a long wish list of everything he might wish for to use to develop the farm. Then, after he'd produced the list, she asked a series of questions and made him add extra items. He thought it was very peculiar at the time and never dreamt in a thousand years much would come of it but then on the penultimate ship before the apocalypse, every single item had been delivered to him, mostly in a larger quantity as well. He was worried for her that she'd been foolish and would lose her job for wasting public money, but then the apocalypse happened and he realised she was very wise indeed, and with great foresight. Her actions might not just have saved the islanders from future hardships but might even have done so for generations to come. He'd never liked her nickname of the 'ice-maiden' and didn't think it originated on the island, though he heard she could seem to be aloof and cold in character, and shunned men. Well maybe she'd had a troubled past, certainly she looked very happy now and he was pleased for her.

"I think I might manage something better than bottled water, wait a moment." he told them. When he returned, he had a handful of canned drinks that were in fact cans of 'Mountain Dew'. "Here, take these, there aren't many left now but this seems like an occasion to cherish and celebrate our Mountain with a Mountain drink." He told her. He wasn't quite prepared however, for her to kiss him on the cheek and give him a small hug before thanking him and waving goodbye. Vincent shook his hand and then Richard watched them walking away, seemingly without a care in the world.

Deborah didn't talk so much during their walk to the top of green mountain, as provide a guided tour commentary, being a mixture of history, botanical facts and things of interest generally. She walked hand in hand with Vincent, except for those places where the track was too narrow to do so. "If you wanted, we can look for a place to live together in Georgetown, there are several empty houses that are very pleasant that no-one else has moved into. Would you like to?" she asked.

"Yes Deborah." was about all Vincent could manage.

"There, you see that little plant, it's one of the rare ones, it's an original native species. When Joseph Hooker, the botanist, began his big planting experiment that made green mountain green and trapped the clouds to dramatically increase the water supply, it was little plants like this one that suffered." She told him. "The whole of the mountain once looked completely different from how it does now. If you look up ahead you can see the start of the Bamboo Forest which goes to the top and all around the dewpond. I believe it was planted in the 1870s. Can you imagine a time when thin bamboo canes were cut for schools to strike school children across the hand or the backside? I don't suppose you've ever visited the

Royal Botanical Gardens at Kew in London, or even London, I did once. Joseph was the director there, succeeding his father, William Hooker" Deborah told him then she finished talking and simply gazed and smiled at Vincent.

Vincent wasn't wholly sure he wasn't dreaming. Perhaps he'd had an accident and was unconscious in the hospital. Deborah didn't really seem like she was the same person to him, but he could tell she was, and that all he'd seen of her before were simply glimpses of who she really was. She was leading him up a steep and muddy climb now and then all of a sudden, they were in a large clearing, with what looked to be a large round fish pond in front of them.

Deborah began to talk again, "Here, look at this green plant, I believe it's another one of the original plants found on the island. I'm sure there's a much larger area of it somewhere else. Don't the water lilies look pretty, how strange to find them here on the top of an old volcano on a volcanic island. The ferns all around the edge of the pond look lovely as well. I'd forgotten how pretty everything was." She paused, not so much to catch her breath, but to softly kiss him on the lips and then she smiled again.

No sooner had she turned away to lead him on the narrow path around the pond, Vincent shook his head to make sure he was really awake.

"Here it is my darling, the letterbox." Deborah told him and she opened the box and took out the book and the pen and passed it to Vincent.

Vincent opened the book and before he wrote his name decided to read the entry before him and was surprised. It wasn't that unusual for someone to leave a message in the letterbox for the next visitors to read. This message had been written by Simon and Elizabeth Bond and simply said 'A rich blessing in Jesus' name to the next couple who visit the Dewpond's Letterbox. Vincent didn't fully understand what a blessing was meant to be but if it meant being very happy then he was blessed. He signed his name but wasn't able to think of a message and passed the book to Deborah and she simply signed it and passed it back to him.

"We have a decision to make now. We can cross the other side of the pond where there isn't actually a path so 'off-piste' you might say or we can go back the way we came." She told him.

Vincent didn't really know what 'off-pissed' meant but wasn't about to say so, instead replying "Let's cross to the other side." So, once clear of the bamboo forest they found themselves on the other side of the mountain with some spectacular views. It was mostly light vegetation and eventually they found themselves on a path which Deborah confidently informed Vincent was 'Elliot's Path'.

"Another decision. We can go left or right but both ways will take us through some tunnels and both are about the same length" Deborah announced, rather than posed as a question.

Vincent was gradually getting over the surprises of the day and he recollected his early days on the Island when Henry had taken him around this very path. "Let's turn right and then when we get to the Marine Barracks; we could take a walk around Bishop's Path and finish at Bell's Cottage" he told her.

It was a pleasant walk and, in several places, they saw land crabs and Deborah explained that one group of shipwrecked sailors had eaten land crabs but she didn't know of anyone living that had tried to eat one. She told him she supposed they would taste similar to sea crabs but couldn't be certain and wasn't interested in finding out either. She told him that while they were land crabs, they were born in the sea because the female crabs had to migrate all the way down to the shore to release their eggs and then come all the way back here again. She explained she wasn't sure but thought it might take them about five or six weeks or longer to make the round trip. Vincent found all this information very interesting and he began to realise that Deborah actually didn't just love him but also loved the island and everything about it.

It wasn't long before they had passed through long and short tunnels and were at the old Marines' Barracks. Deborah knew that, since the apocalypse, a lot of work had been undertaken to them; she'd read updates and seen photos Sabrina had given her, but this was the first time she'd seen them since the work on them began. It was of course a heritage project she'd initiated but, well, one she'd lost interest in, compared to what she thought were more important things.

They entered the building and immediately Deborah noticed how warm it was. She remembered being told that the original floor had been lifted and substantial insulation laid and the floor placed back on top of it. The interior walls looked modern and flat and she knew this was because the walls had been insulated before being dry lined. There were electrical heaters powered by solar panels for the coldest and wettest days, at other times they simply weren't needed. It was a lovely large building and would have made an excellent conservation building with living accommodation.

"Did you know the other barracks built around the same time is what we now call the Exiles Club that took three years for them to build. Years later a second storey was added but those termites, the white ants, have caused a lot of damage so they can't be used now. It's the conservation project that never got completed, that I regret not getting completed, the most.

"Ok my darling let's set out for Bell's cottage via Bishops Path and we can stop at the scenic view for something to eat." Deborah next told Vincent while gently swinging their arms since they were hand in hand.

"Yeah, sure thing" Vincent replied. He'd been a lot of things to many people, including several women but he couldn't recall ever being a darling, a lover yes, but not a darling. He found it slightly unsettling though not annoying or unpleasant. He supposed he was spoken for now, and for keeps, for life. As they set out on the short walk around Bishops Path to Bell's cottage, he wondered how Deborah had managed to suppress all these intense feelings for him and then he remembered when she hadn't, before the apocalypse, when he'd had his accident. It was a pleasant walk with lovely views, and when they got to the scenic view, they stopped and had a light snack and drank some of the Mountain Dew drink. Deborah didn't speak but simply hung onto Vincent.

After they'd set out again, it wasn't long before they arrived at Bell's cottage. Deborah explained how history had come a full circle for the cottage from being a residence to a holiday home to pigsties and now a holiday home again. It wasn't named after a ringing bell as it were, she told him but the name of a farm superintendent whose surname was Bell. It was once a popular holiday home because it had a bath and when she'd had it restored, she'd had a 1920s bath re-enamelled to given the whole place an authentic touch. Deborah then smiled at Vincent and with a sparkle in her eyes she asked him "Would you like me to arrange a weekend for us to stay there, we could have a bath together?"

Once again, Vincent wasn't really sure if he was dreaming all of this, having some sort of suppressed fantasy. He'd wake up in the hospital with a splitting headache and half his head blown off or something. Deborah saw the slightly puzzled expression on his face and kissed him before boldly announcing "You don't have to be gallant or anything, the taps are on the side so no-one has them digging into their back or clonks their head on them." Then she laughed and Vincent laughed with her because he didn't know what else to do.

Vincent liked the look of the cottage but he looked at his watch, he was wearing the green one. They needed to be thinking about getting back so there wasn't going to be time to look around the cottage, or for Deborah to run an impromptu bath. They walked in silence back to the Red Lion and where the Land Rover was parked. Vincent decided he'd drive and as he carefully negotiated the hairpin bends of the mountain road, he realised he'd need to drop Deborah off in Georgetown and then drive back to Two Boats, or something like that. It was just turning dark when he parked his Land

Rover outside Deborah's house. She leant across the gearstick and passionately kissed Vincent before speaking.

"Who could have ever imagined a day like this? There are some things that shouldn't be rushed, so I have to go now and I look forward to being with you tomorrow." And with that she waved him goodbye. Deborah looked across town to the Administrator's building and saw there were some lights on, and had a wander over to it. She was surprised to find that everything was unlocked and she realised that maybe she hadn't been clear to Sabrina, that she wouldn't be coming back. In fact, the events of the morning seemed like a lifetime ago. She made sure everything was put away and locked up behind her.

Vincent drove slowly back to his home still mystified by the day's events but feeling happier and more cheerful than he could ever remember, and hoped it would last.

Chapter Twelve – The Yacht people

It didn't take Henry long to reach his Police Station and Chris was waiting for him. He related to Henry exactly what he had seen happen, reading from his notebook. Hmmm, this wasn't the first 'customer' for their cells but he might turn out to be the person who'd spend the longest amount of time in one. He was relieved nobody seemed to be hurt and then he caught sight of the back of the man's head. "Call the Doc. Tell him what's happened, if he doesn't already know and tell him we'd like a bruise on the back of the prisoner's head looked at." Chris nodded and went to his office to make the call. Henry was cross because it seemed like everything bad about the world, or what was left of it, was now on his island and had already caused trouble, and to one of his dearest friends.

The Yacht people were gathered together and were silent and subdued as Sabrina handed them each a key and politely informed them, "At least for now these are the keys for the houses you can live in. They have been stocked with some groceries, such as we have, and an information leaflet has also been left there as well as a map of the island. Myself and other islanders have volunteered to drive you to those houses and one vehicle, with a full tank of fuel will be left for you. At some point, we should be able to find you additional vehicles. Follow me please."

Just then Deborah appeared and Sabrina thought she looked as if she might have been crying but she sounded very content and relaxed when she spoke. "I'm taking the rest of the day off Sabrina. Vincent will be with me and we going to go to the dewpond. If there's any more trouble, which I doubt, let the police deal with it. I'll see you tomorrow, usual time." Then she was gone and Sabrina was back on her own with the Yacht People and she didn't have time to wonder why Deborah and Vincent would be together.

Aside from the man in the police cells, his wife and daughter, the group consisted of nine other people comprising several couples, including some with children and one striking young man whose name was Jeff. He didn't so much as catch Sabrina's eye, as she caught his. He managed to manoeuvre himself to the front of the queue both to get a better look at Sabrina and attempt to speak to her. He'd spotted she wasn't wearing any rings on her wedding finger on either hand. It would just about be his luck, if she was already shacked up to someone else. She had a kind, if somewhat melancholy face, but who didn't have a melancholic face after what had just happened? He was a bit shy when it came to women and this one looked to be a few years older than him, maybe even ten years older, awkward.

Jeff being first in the queue found he was directed by the woman in charge to the most distant vehicle and not the one Sabrina was going to drive which it now seemed might be the last one. He supposed that since the group had got off to a bad start it wouldn't matter that much if he ended up by annoying the islanders some more. So, instead of going to the vehicle he'd been directed to, he managed to slip back behind the last person and re-joined the queue.

"Oh. So, we meet again." Sabrina told the young man, before pausing for thought. She looked at him and it seemed to her that he had the expression of a lost puppy. "Well, if it's your intention to travel with me, you appear to have succeeded. Sit in the front and then you can tell me your name" she told him as they drove out of Georgetown. Sabrina felt flattered that the young man was so keen to spend time with her and barely managed to avoid being flustered by his attention.

Once they were on the move, he answered Sabrina's question. "Jeff, my name's Jeff Learoyd. Umm, I'm not like the err, others. Err, I'm a real sailor and worked for some of the group and kind of met the others along the way. What's your name Miss?" Jeff asked, trying not to sound too excited.

Sabrina decided to rashly abandon her normal 'play hard to get' attitude and get right down to it, since she found him appealing and he might turn out to be the last available man she'd ever meet. "My name is Sabrina. I'm twenty-nine years old and I have a thirty-eight-inch double dee chest and I'm available for the right man." Then she looked at Jeff. She hadn't realised it was possible for anyone to go quite so red in the face as fast as he had. She then realised her own cheeks were now also going very red. She slowed down, waved the other vehicles past and stopped. "I'm so very sorry Jeff. That was extremely rude mannered of me and it made me sound cheap or desperate or both and I've embarrassed you, not to mention myself" she told him adding "I don't know why on earth I said that, it's not like me at all."

Jeff tried to recover his composure and hoped he hadn't fallen into the hands, or was it the bust, of a man-eater, though she didn't look like one. Fuck knows what he'd do if he had, and she was, death by smothering most likely. "Err. Well, err. Well, I've got a forty-inch chest but I'm not quite twenty-nine years old and I'd be available for a kind woman who was patient and not a man-eater." He informed her, candidly without managing to smile.

Sabrina felt her hot flush was passing, thank goodness. "Thank you. I believe I am kind and patient albeit an extremely foolish woman sometimes as you've just seen. Let's get going again, and get you settled" she told him. For the rest of the short drive to Two Boats Sabrina didn't so much as make small talk but point out local landmarks and impart parts of Island history relevant to their journey. "If you look to you left, Jeff, you can see what looks to a pile of paint. It's called the Lizard and people used to paint it as a kind of superstition when they were leaving the island if they never wanted to return. You see that upright boat – it's called One Boat. We are going to Two Boats which was named after two halves of a naval rowing boat that were set upright to provide a shelter from the heat for the driver of horses when giving the horses a rest before they had to ascend the mountain, I believe. The boats are still there today, though they might not be the original ones" she told him.

She glanced across at him and he seemed more relaxed now than earlier, or bored or maybe tired, but nonetheless she still felt annoyed with herself and still embarrassed for having made such a fool of herself, she should have stuck to her normal attitude with men because while it never worked very well or as planned, at least she never felt embarrassed, foolish or cheap afterwards. They arrived at Two Boats and Sabrina pulled up outside one of the slightly less-appealing properties. She realised she'd deliberately chosen less-appealing properties for all the Yacht people. Once more she felt embarrassed. She snapped out of these thoughts because she realised the young man, Jeff, was staring at her. However, unlike most men, at least in her experience, he wasn't staring at her boobs, he was staring at her face and was looking into her eyes.

"I'm a bit lost for words Sabrina and I'd invite you in for coffee but there might not be any, or any milk or sugar either." he told her.

"I happen to know there is tea, coffee, milk and sugar, and I'm thirsty," she told him passing him the door key.

"Ok, come in for a tea or coffee, but I'm still a bit lost for words so perhaps you can do the talking" Jeff told Sabrina as he unlocked the door. The house was quite nice inside and he felt at home at once. Sabrina had gone past him, through to what he discovered was the kitchen, and was sitting on a sofa in the lounge. It only took him a few moments to find milk; well milk made from powdered milk, coffee and sugar, in little sachets, and a couple of mugs. The kettle was soon boiled and he made coffee for two, even finding a small jug for the milk, which he brought through on a tray offering it to Sabrina, which she took from him with a kind smile.

Sabrina decided she ought to do most of the talking and see if that would help Jeff. She could tell him some more about the island as a starting point. "Well Jeff, everything is free for now, while it lasts and no-one has to go to work because they aren't going to be paid. However, there is work to be done and, over time, things will get harder but not unbearably so, at least I hope not. The island's most valuable commodity is drinking water and we'll always have enough while the population is at this level, or even double. Yours is the first group of people to arrive after the apocalypse and others might or might not arrive, which we can cope with. The island has a long history of: warfare, defence, epidemics and change. The people here have always survived and so has most of the wildlife. It's remote but pleasant enough. Several hundred people left before the apocalypse and will never return. That's how this house became vacant, and there are others still empty. I'm sorry I've been doing all the talking. Is there something you need? Is there something I can get you? Would you like to tell me about how you got here?" Sabrina asked him.

"Thank you, Sabrina," Jeff replied, being slightly more relaxed now an immediate threat of being smothered appeared to have passed. "I'm more of a keen amateur sailor rather than a yachtie - I'm not rich, and only owned a dinghy rather than a yacht. I sailed British coastal waters rather than the oceans, though in the past few weeks, or is it months, I guess I've now sailed halfway across the world."

"Things weren't looking good for Europe and on impulse I thought I'd be safer as far away as I could get. So, one day I packed some stuff into my van and told everyone I was going on a sailing holiday. I said goodbye to my mates because I couldn't persuade any of them to come with me. I can't blame them because, unlike me, they were tied down with family, or girlfriends, or whatever. I knew I was taking a big risk but I didn't care. I'd planned to drive through France and Spain and get to Africa where I figured I'd be safe from a Nuclear War and it was before the pandemic had started. I didn't really have much of a plan and when I got to Southampton everything changed. I met these two blokes who said they wanted someone to help them crew a yacht and was I interested. I told them I would be interested, except my sailing experience was limited to coastal waters and I only held a Royal Yachting Association Coastal Skipper certificate of competence, so I couldn't really help them. They told me they liked my honesty and they'd pay me in gold sovereigns, so I could leave them whenever we made port and I wouldn't have to worry about foreign currency or anything. I was a bit suspicious of them at first but accidentally noticed they had fairly rough hands, the sort that worked for a living.

"They explained they had their wives with them and two children and it turned out their yacht was a big one, it's the biggest one in the flotilla. I think they simply bought it half an hour before I met them! The weather wasn't great when we left and it turned out between us, we only just had enough experience to get us to Jersey and that's where we met the Admiral.

He said he would help us if we'd help him. He needed space for more people than he had on his yacht. He told us our best chance was to sail for Saint Helena and see out the war there. It was a small self-sufficient island and out of the way. He told us there would be strength in numbers and as well as his boat there were several other smaller ones and he could help us by providing some experienced crew members. So, we set sail on the beginning of our nightmare.

"We made reasonable progress at first around the coast of France and Spain and that's when we first heard about the pandemic in China becoming much more serious. We then went to the Canary Islands, rather than the coast of Africa because the Admiral said there was less chance of the pandemic spreading there as quickly as it would through Africa. We didn't stay there but just collected provisions and sailed on to Cape Verde. At Cape Verde it was the eve of the war and we ran into trouble, when there was an attempt to prevent us from leaving and to rob us. My original two guys saved the day when they produced a bunch of shotguns and we had a pitched battle; late at night. One of the small yachts was set alight but we all escaped, though it's likely several of our attackers were badly injured or killed in the fight. The Admiral said afterwards that the shotguns were Purdy's and Hollands' and the two pairs probably cost more than his yacht did!

"Some-time after that the war broke out in full fury, though we saw nothing of it. We only heard about it over the radios. Then we were caught in a huge storm in the Atlantic and were blown off course. It was days before we were clear of the storm and we had been scattered. We made radio contact with the Admiral who had found two out of the three other smaller yachts. We regrouped well clear of the coast of Africa, Angola maybe, and found wreckage but no survivors from the missing yacht. We were low on food and water but the Admiral was confident we could reach St Helena safely. Along the way we caught a few fish and tightened our belts.

"Everyone was jubilant when we saw St Helena but couldn't raise anyone on the radio until we got quite close. Then, we received an automated message telling us the island was in the grip of the pandemic and not to make land. The Admiral explained that our next best alternative was here, Ascension Island. He explained he was worried it may have been a military target because it had a big airfield runway and some sort of tracking stations. Or the population might all have been wiped out by the pandemic or worse still in the grip of it. The other alternative would be Africa, which we knew, from radio messages, was previously in the grip of the pandemic.

We were low on water and food and there was a chance we might not make it at all but simply die mid-Atlantic, but everyone agreed we'd try to get here. After a while we got increasingly weak and tired and the Admiral wasn't strong enough to lead us. My original two guys decided to rope the yachts together and only sail the lead yacht, theirs. It would be slow progress but it meant we could concentrate on crewing one boat, rather than all four. Every day we travelled a shorter distance and we slept more than we stayed awake. Then one day your boats appeared and you know the rest.

"I feel sorry for the Admiral because without him none us would have made it. What do you think will happen to him? Is there anything I can do to help him?" Jeff asked Sabrina.

Sabrina was fascinated with Jeff's story and guessed, having been at sea that long, there must be a lot more details to it which she hoped to hear about one day. But she was interrupted in her thoughts, as Jeff having finished talking, had now started to cry and she could see small rivers of tears running down his face.

Jeff hadn't wanted to cry but relating the story of the traumatic escape, from the end of the civilised world as he knew it, had caught up with him. He managed to speak before looking at Sabrina and said "I never thought I'd make it."

Sabrina didn't think she had ever seen a man cry before and as soon as he'd finished speaking and they made eye contact, she leant across him and, giving him a big hug, drew him to herself, taking care not to bury his head in her chest. The moment quickly passed and Jeff recovered his composure as if nothing had happened. Sabrina felt she needed to say something and didn't really feel there was time to think about what to say, so said the first thing that came into her head. "If you wanted, I could find you a place in Georgetown and then we'd be neighbours, if you wanted to be neighbours that is?" Sabrina asked him.

"Where's Georgetown?" he replied.

"Sorry, I keep forgetting you've only just arrived on the island. Georgetown is the main town, it's where we drove you from earlier today. It's where I work. Perhaps I can show you around the island; we can take my car." She suggested.

"I feel really tired Sabrina, I know it's not really time for bed but I'm ready for it. You don't mind if I turn-in, early, do you?" he asked.

Sabrina didn't mind as much as she was disappointed. She had taken an instant liking to Jeff and found his story fascinating. She wanted to be able to find him a useful job and make him feel welcome, introduce him to her friends, see if he would come to church with her and a hundred other things. She also admitted to herself that she was desperate to be with a man, and he'd been interested in her when they first met, and she wanted to believe in love at first sight whether it was a rubbish notion or not. "No, of course not, if you're tired you must rest. You go and lie down and sleep and I'll wash up for you." She replied and watched Jeff go into the bedroom, without so much as kissing her goodnight or good afternoon.

After washing up the mugs and tidying things away, Sabrina sat down on the sofa in what was now Jeff's house. She wanted to be with him and hoped he might wake up and she could cook him dinner and listen to him talk again. However, when she peeped into the bedroom, he looked fast asleep. She'd been rash and foolish already today and agonised whether what she wanted to do now was of the same ilk, or actually a positive move. In the end, she decided she couldn't help herself and removing her socks, shorts and top, crept into the bedroom, underneath the mosquito net and lay on the bed next to Jeff in just her bra and knickers. She felt at peace once she done this and her only regret was that she was wearing her every day underwear and not her special stuff.

Jeff woke up and wondered where he was, and then he remembered he was on Ascension Island in a house he'd been given the use of, after being let out after two weeks quarantine in the island's hospital. Then he remembered having coffee with the lovely Sabrina and then as he sat up in bed, he saw she was lying there, in just her underwear, on his bed, fast asleep, next to him. He had been very tired yesterday and didn't remember her coming to bed with him. He thought she'd said something about tidying up. He didn't mind and she was very pretty. Just as well really because it seemed like she wasn't going to take no for answer for anything and he couldn't imagine giving her the slip in a big city, let alone this small island. Looking at her lying there in her bra with an impressive cleavage, it did seem that she would present a serious smothering risk and he realised it would be a long time before he would have enough courage to tell her that he was a 'leg man'. Her legs were ok, he'd noticed them earlier, though what he found most appealing about her though was that she had lovely soft brown eyes and a kind and pretty face. It was dark outside and since he still felt tired, he decided that he would go back to sleep and he did.

Sabrina woke up and realised that she was not on her own bed. She quickly realised that she'd been rash again and was lying on a bed with Jeff. He was fast asleep. Rather than embarrass him again with her foolish behaviour she decided if she was very quiet, she might be able to leave without him waking up and finding her lying next to him on his bed. She managed to get off the bed and find her clothes, shoes and socks, got dressed in the lounge and after leaving him a little note, quietly let herself out of the house. Getting into her car and grimacing at the noise starting it made, turned the headlights on and drove back to her home in Georgetown.

Jeff woke up again, and he could see it was still dark outside. He turned to look at Sabrina again and found he was now lying on his bed on his own. Perhaps he'd dreamt Sabrina spent the night with him. Well, looking at an alarm clock and seeing the time was six-thirty in the morning and feeling hungry, he decided he might as well get up. He got out of bed and turned the light on and was about to tidy the mosquito net up when he saw a very long dark hair on the bed. It was the same colour as Sabrina's hair, so clearly, she had been in his bed in the night. He sniffed the air and he could also smell a lingering perfume that certainly wasn't from him.

It had been a while since he'd last had a girlfriend. He liked to think he was discerning rather than choosy or picky. He quite liked Jo but she hadn't registered the slightest interest in him whatsoever. At the time he'd been slightly discouraged but it didn't bother him now. It then suddenly struck him that it was now light outside. He had noticed this during quarantine but he'd spent a lot of the time resting and sleeping so hadn't given it much thought. Someone, possibly the admiral, had explained Ascension Island was very close to the equator and sunrise and sunset was much quicker than it was in England.

Jeff wandered into the kitchen and found a small note had been left for him and this was what it said:

My Dear Jeff,

I hope you didn't find my attention smothering and sorry if you did. I hope we can become close friends. I have to go to work today but I can take a long lunch break or no lunch break and finish work early if you want to meet up. My office is very near to the beach where we can walk and talk but not swim. I work in the Administrators Office. I hope to see you soon.

Love from Sabrina

He smiled after reading her note and he then read it again and smiled again. He looked at his watch to see what time it was and realised he'd lost it, so didn't know what time it was and went back to the bedroom to the check the time on the alarm clock.

Chapter Thirteen – The Admiral

When Vincent arrived back at his home and had showered and cleaned up and grilled a shark steak, he felt tired and ready for an early night. He'd found the day emotionally draining and more than a bit confusing. As he removed his pistol from its holster, he noticed the barrel was dirty and when he checked the magazine, he found there was a round missing and, if he needed any confirmation that he hadn't been dreaming, that was it, but now it was time for real sweet dreams and he crashed out on his bed, under his mosquito net, leaving the pistol to be cleaned in the morning.

Deborah was up extra early and in work early but daydreaming about what a lovely day she'd spent with Vincent yesterday. How she'd finally broken free of her past and allowed herself to fall in love with someone who felt the same way about her, as she did about him. Then it suddenly dawned on her that the trigger point for this whole wondrous new life she was embarking on, was the Admiral's attack on her. She sat up sharply at her desk. He was still in the police cells. She decided to get on with some work and then wait for someone to ask to see him. The day passed quickly and Deborah realised that Vincent would be here soon and would be looking for houses with her and she hadn't sorted out the keys of the prospective properties. She hurriedly found the keys and popped them all into her handbag and then realised she'd still done nothing about the Admiral, nor had anyone asked about him, well not of her anyway. Mmm, he'll have to spent another night in the cells.

Vincent spent the morning preparing some practical exercises for his volunteers and it was late afternoon when he drove into Georgetown and parked some distance from the hospital so that he could hopefully enter it without anyone seeing him. "Afternoon Doc. I've um, come to say sorry about the damage to the hospital floor, that I did err, yesterday" Vincent told the doctor for what was uncharacteristically for him, an embarrassing moment.

Doc Caskey realised that Vincent had forgotten being told that Deborah was one of his and his wife's friends. He had a keen sense of humour, which he deemed essential to being a good doctor and while he wasn't at all pleased at what had happened to Deborah, he thought Vincent had acted very gallantly in standing forward to protect her from any further possible harm. Also, that he'd done a first-class job in regaining command and control of what might have been more than an ugly situation; it might have been harmful to the long-term survival of the island community. He'd missed all the action but he'd had it related to him several times by several different eye witnesses. Of course, he'd known all along there was more to Vincent than regular military training and yet it didn't seem like special forces training. He was also still amazed that Vincent had been able to extricate himself from the lava flow with such a badly gashed leg. Yes, there was a lot more to him then met even a searching eye, but nothing that worried him.

"Nothing to worry about Vincent, I'm a doctor not a policeman and there are only a couple of things that disappoint me. Firstly, there's a lost opportunity in me and you teaming up to rob the BX or something like that. I mean with everything free there can't be an armed robbery. Secondly, I was going to punish that dude that hit Deborah with a bunch of suppositories that would have made his shit look like garden twine for a month. But now he's not likely to need them, nor his wife either I guess. Still, it's an ill wind as they say in England. Not least I'm grateful you didn't blow his head off and make a mess that would have brought the flies in for days, and us scrubbing things clean to try and persuade them there's nothing for them to search for." Doc told him without smiling.

Vincent was relieved the Doc seemed so understanding and laid back. He seemed to be having some fun with him but Vincent always took a doctor seriously and made sure he never got on the wrong side of one. His best bet now was to make a quick exit, while the going was still good. "Thanks for being so understanding Doc. I have to dash now but if you ever need, err, a favour, let me know." Vincent told him while thinking he sounded like a hitman. Time now to pick up where he left off yesterday and hope Deborah hadn't reverted to previous form, though he doubted that was the case.

Vincent arrived at Deborah's office and knocked on the door. "Afternoon Miss, is this the Georgetown Estate agents? I'm looking for a very agreeable house to live in with the most beautiful woman on this island?" Vincent asked while doing his best to pull a serious face.

Deborah rushed forward to greet him and gave him a clinging embrace, before releasing him to kiss him passionately on the lips. "I think the most beautiful woman on the island is already spoken for so you'll have to make do with me." She told him. Then she quickly locked everything away, waved goodnight to Sabrina and walked arm in arm to the nearest residential area of Georgetown. She patiently walked from property to property and Vincent liked all of them but none especially, so she didn't even get to unlock any of them. She was beginning to feel slightly deflated, when Vincent spoke up and pointed to a house.

"What about that one? Is it empty?" he asked.

Deborah almost jumped for joy before spontaneously kissing him on the lips. "We live there, it's our home."

"Really, great, when can we move in?" he asked, slightly taken back once more by Deborah's surprise show of affection.

"Vincent Irving, you have chosen my home, the one I already live in, so all we have to do is move you in." She gleefully replied.

"Ok, I haven't got much, err stuff, I might need a couple of boxes." He told here. He didn't elaborate on the 'err' which was his realisation that he had twice as many watches as he was supposed to have. He'd have to keep one set permanently in his Land Rover or maybe keep a set at the American armoury or maybe his office or some other place. He supposed he'd need to tell her eventually or give them away.

Deborah went to her home and quickly re-appeared with a well-worn hard type of Samsonite suitcase. So, in a shorter time than either of them had imagined, within a couple of hours, they were living together as man and wife but without the paperwork.

Dad

"Josephine when are you going to ask about your father?" the admiral's wife asked, but there was no reply. She sighed and then asked "Jo, when are you going to ask about your father?"

"Mother, why don't you ask about him, after all you choose to be with him whereas I had no choice." Jo replied without looking up. "Perhaps he needs some more time to cool off in that police cell?" she added.

Sentencing

It was a few days after Vincent had moved in to live with her, when Deborah remembered the Admiral again. She was surprised no-one from his family had been to see her to ask what was to be done with him. He'd been in the police cells for a week now or was it a week and a day? In any event it was time to make a decision and to go and see him, so asking Sabrina to come with her, they walked to the police station.

Inside the station and outside the cells, Deborah was sorry to see the Admiral looking very dejected and yet when he saw them, he almost stood to attention but not in a proud way with his head held high, but more in a beaten down way to show his respect. At that instant she decided there wasn't much point keeping him in the cells any longer, nor any point in charging him with assault, after all a monetary fine, some sort of community service or further time in the police cells wouldn't help and wasn't needed.

As she drew near the cell door the Admiral started to speak. "Maam. I apologise for my shameful actions, not just a common assault, not just a common assault on the Commanding Officer and administrator, but the lowest thing of all, an assault on a woman by a man. I'm not going to ask for forgiveness because I don't deserve it, but a just punishment." After speaking he then looked forlornly downwards.

"Well, Admiral, I think you've been punished enough already and I'm not going to raise any charge against you. In a moment's time you'll be released and then perhaps we can sit down over a cup of tea and see how best we can retrieve your circumstance with a measure of dignity and move forward positively" Deborah told him. No sooner had she finished speaking the duty police officer appeared from behind her, unlocked the cell door and beckoned the Admiral to leave the cell.

The Admiral looked very surprised but still very downcast. The police officer watched him intently from a distance with one hand resting on his baton. He then walked a few steps away and stood opposite the police chief's desk, while Deborah sat in the Chief of Police's chair, she knew Henry wouldn't mind. "Pull up a seat beside me Admiral so we can talk as equals" she told him.

Having recovered his composure somewhat, the Admiral began to speak. "I can see, maam, that you are very gracious and kind. It would be a mistake for me to misinterpret kindness for weakness and I won't repeat my mistake. I realise now that I'm simply an old man whose past deeds are forgotten except by himself and those family members, whom he constantly reminds. From what I've overheard you aren't simply running this island by a quirk of fate, but you proactively and very effectively ensured it wouldn't just survive but might even thrive. I've met some tough ladies in my time but you might just be the first one I've ever met that had balls, if you get my meaning, which is complimentary. Neither you nor this island needs me. I'm old and no longer physically strong and I can't see I'll be anything other than a dragging anchor for you all." Then he looked downcast once more.

At that moment Henry, in his Chief of Police uniform, arrived and, smartly saluting Deborah, said nothing but presented a tray with two cups of tea, real sugar in a bowl, and milk in a jug, all in his best matching bone china.

"Thank you very much" she told him before he made a discreet absence. The arrival of the tea had given Deborah time to think. "Admiral, we have a lot of engineers here and several people with all kinds of practical ability, but aside from myself and my deputy we don't have anyone really interested in history, naval history or with impeccable English. The airfield might dominate the island but the history is naval, from the original guns from

HMS Hood to the first sailing ship that discovered the island, and the British ones that followed. I can and do issue administrative orders and publish updates and reports but no-one any longer reports the news of ordinary events, good news and what's actually happening on the island. What's more with no news from the rest of the world, there's something of a news vacuum. If you were interested you could be the head of the island news service and resurrect our paper 'The Islander' rather than be a head of communication, but you could be both if you wanted. If you are any good with a camera you could add photos as well. Perhaps a fortnightly update might work and could include a well written and researched part of the history of the island. It might not seem much at first but I'm confident it would be a key building block in maintaining morale and a respectable job for anyone who is, in truth, semi-retired. And, if that didn't keep you busy enough you could become head of island conservation as well. There's no pay of course but then there's nothing to purchase here. We have more than enough of everything for everyone, at least for now. If you aren't interested, I haven't got anyone else that could really do this and it might be a while before either of us could think or find anything else for you. You don't need to give me an answer now but think on it for a couple of days, have a wander around the island, soak in the history, and then let me know your decision."

The Admiral had to look down to wipe away a tear from his eyes before looking up. "I'll take the jobs Maam, all three of them, and do them well." He told her. Then he looked down again and shook his head before adding "I've disgraced myself and been foolish and rash, and everyone will know that."

"Oh, I don't think so Admiral, I expect you were suffering from sun-stroke with a degree of dehydration, being more susceptible due to your age, when the unfortunate incident of the other week occurred" Deborah told him.

"My dear maam, I'm not sure that's the truth" he replied in astonishment.

"Well, Admiral, I'm not sure either but neither of us is a doctor, so we're not lying. The island doctor wasn't present and if I suggest to him our trouble was due to your having had some sort of relapse and you might still need to have some extra tests for a couple of days, and you oblige him, and then he gives you some sort of extra treatment, salt tablets and extra fluid, everyone comes out with honour and some extra wisdom and experience. The doctor won't argue with me because he already partially blames himself for not realising how 'fired up' you were." Then, having finished, Deborah pulled her serious smile which she used to signal things were ok, but nothing to celebrate.

The admiral stood up and the duty police officer discreetly re-appeared. "May I make a fresh start and give you a small hug?" and added "I'm sure my wife won't begrudge me it" the Admiral asked.

"Yes of course Admiral and welcome to Ascension Island" she told him.

Then the admiral hugged Deborah and began to weep, for some time, on her shoulder leaving a large wet patch on her blouse. Next, he stepped back, saluted her and saluted the duty police officer and shook hands with Sabrina, and being directed to, stepped outside.

Sabrina had already arranged for the Admiral's wife and Jo to visit him after Deborah's visit and they were all very surprised to see him walk out of the police station.

"I hope you can both find it in your hearts to forgive this proud old fool and then accompany me to the hospital, where I think I need to be under medical supervision for a few days because I really don't feel quite myself." He told them.

Well, Deborah thought, that had all gone better than she'd expected, and her only worry now was what Vincent would think about the whole episode. She was still getting to know him and in lots of ways he was still a closed book to her. One of the mysteries was that he seemed very bashful about the whole incident and while practically everyone they met congratulated him on dealing with the Admiral, he seemed to want to forget about it. She supposed if she told him what she'd done and the Admiral would be no more trouble after a little more care in the hospital, voluntary this time, Vincent wouldn't mind.

Over their evening meal Deborah explained to Vincent what she done about the Admiral and he didn't say anything but simply nodded. As she'd explained all this to Vincent, he wasn't thinking about the Admiral at all. He wasn't even thinking about showering together, again. No, he was thinking how he'd explain to Deborah that she was giving him too much to eat, too often. So far, they hadn't had a cross word or misunderstanding, well no misunderstandings he was aware of.

Chapter Fourteen - The Dew Pond run and laying pipe

The date for the Dew Pond run had been set for the last Saturday in January, when the global crisis was in its infancy, and the date had never been changed. It was probably the most important sporting event in the island's calendar. It was an endurance run from Long beach to the Dew Pond at the top of Green Mountain. It wasn't a long run at about seven miles but was from sea level to the top of the mountain some two thousand eight hundred and seventeen feet. Deborah wasn't sure of the fastest time it had ever been run, but didn't think anyone had ever completed it under an hour. Her own time was a modest one hour and forty minutes so not even amongst the fastest ladies but was still respectable. Some people did the run for fun and others were more competitive, and others like Sabrina cheered people on. It had generally been accepted that it was the Administrator's job to be at the finish along with a couple of time keepers and while that had suited Will, it didn't suit her as she wanted to compete. She'd ask Sabrina to represent her and she knew she wouldn't mind.

"Morning Sabrina, I don't suppose you are competing in the Dew Pond run this year, are you?" Deborah asked politely.

"I never really fancied giving myself black eyes for two hours, Deborah, while dripping in sweat." Sabrina replied laughing.

Deborah smiled and laughed with her before asking "that's what I thought, so I wondered if you'd like to fully deputise for me and greet the runners at the top, and take charge of the timekeepers or maybe just timekeeper?"

"I'd love to. Would you like to have a look at the entry list?" she replied to which Deborah nodded in reply.

Sabrina showed her the entry lists. There was an individual list and a shorter team list for teams of three. There was a total of fifty entries which was more than half the population of the island and more than half were men. There were two entries for the Island Defence Volunteer Force, one for the police, one amusingly called 'The Yachties' and other teams that reflected small groups of friends. Deborah hadn't realised how seriously Vincent was about the event until they'd started living together. He'd explained he needed to eat less than she'd been cooking for him. Also, every evening he would go for a run and not come back until well over an hour later, sopping wet with sweat. He'd once wrung the sweat out of his running top into a mug just to see how much he was sweating. She'd found his demonstration disgusting and pondered how strange men were. She knew that Henry and his policemen were also training hard and they wanted to win the team prize. It was Vincent and 'The Yachties' that were the 'dark horses' because everyone else had run before and had a good idea of how quick or slow a time they could produce.

The day of the run had arrived and it was only just light when the runners had assembled on the beach. The tradition was that the runners had to have one hand in the sea at the start and then at the Dew Pond, dip the other hand in the pond itself. Deborah looked at Vincent and felt very proud of him. He was talking to all his team members and giving them words of encouragement while looking deadly serious. It was time to get ready now and she lined up on the beach with the other runners.

Vincent decided that if he finished in the top ten or even top five runners, he'd be happy. He expected to be competitive based on the amount of training he'd been doing and how much training he knew Henry and his sergeants had been doing. He'd done a few team runs as well and the other two runners in his Island Defence Volunteer Force 'A team' were quick and capable. He did particularly want to beat a couple of the Americans who he wasn't particularly keen on, one of whom he'd nick-named 'the skull'.

A starting pistol was fired and Vincent leapt forward with all the other runners. He settled into his stride and was somewhere near the front of the pack when they started the steep climb out of Georgetown and was disappointed that at least eight people went past him and with the few in front of him at the start, meant he might already be outside the top ten. Still, it was a long race and he was going to run it his way and didn't try to increase his pace, not being sure he could if he wanted to. One thing he knew was that he was no sprinter and he hated the start of any exercise. Out of Georgetown and on the gentle slope up to One Boat before starting on the mountain climb, he felt good and he even managed to increase his pace a little. He could see several runners ahead of him and one by one he passed them, not because he'd increased speed but because they had slowed down. He felt vindicated in sticking to his plan and began to enjoy his run. It was now getting very hot as he passed the One Boat shelter but this didn't trouble him and he knew it would get cooler as he began the ascent on the mountain road.

It never occurred to Vincent to look behind him to see if anyone was gaining on him, he just focused on each runner ahead of him, one at a time. Just as he started the mountain climb itself there on the first ramp was the American, he wanted to beat, who had stopped and looked exhausted. He hadn't been keeping a proper count of how many runners were in front of him but guessed he must be in the top ten if not the top five by now. He felt good and settled into a good rhythm on the climb and allowed himself a smile as he managed to get past his friend Henry about halfway up the climb.

There was a small crowd at the Red Lion and it was the first time he had seen anyone who was cheering the competitors. He could see Doc Caskey and as the Doc saw Vincent, he shouted at him.

"Vincent, you are third, come on, you can win this!'

Vincent was surprised he was doing so well and decided he could increase his speed a bit and did so and up ahead he could see the other two runners ahead of him, neither of which he recognised. He pressed on now as hard as he could and while he could feel his heart pounding, it was cooler now and he went absolutely as fast as he could manage. He passed the first runner in front of him and then the second. He still didn't look back and tried to maintain his pace. He was now on the last part of the climb to the dew pond and it was muddy in places before he reached the steps. He'd had to slow down a bit, to avoid slipping, but so would anyone else. At one point he could hear the panting breath of a runner behind him but they'd have to get alongside him before getting past and there was barely any room to do so. Once on the steps he powered on and suddenly there it was, the dew pond, and with a final push he gave it everything he had and then stopping and putting his hand in the pond, he almost fell in. He then moved forward to give room to the runners behind him.

"You're first Vincent" Sabrina told him and she'd have given him a hug except he looked pretty wet with sweat and she didn't want to look like a prize winner in a wet T shirt contest.

The time keeper gave Vincent his time and he shook hands with the runners that had come after him including Henry and cheered them all on, especially the guys in his team. Since there wasn't room for more than a dozen or so people at the top of the Dew Pond there was someone just below the final climb with a radio that radioed Sabrina and advised the first group of runners could come down and so they did. They were then able to cheer on the next group of runners before walking slowly down the twisty mountain road. Doc Caskey was now manning a drinking station at the Red Lion. He patted all the runners on the back and made sure they all took a long slow drink before leaving him, while telling them to drink lots more for the rest of the day.

Vincent had just reached the Red Lion when the first lady runners were appearing and Hannah from his volunteer force was the first of them. He cheered her on and ran with her for a while. Next there were a couple more ladies, some men and then he could see Deborah. He realised that he'd been so focused on his own training and that of his team, that not once had he gone out even for a jog with her. He watched her get close and he thought she looked absolutely knackered. Once she had reached him, he ran with her for a while but rather than cheer her, on he simply told her how much he loved her, then he said goodbye and stood still smiling, looking at her sweet cheeks slightly escaping from her running shorts.

Further down the mountain were the back markers of the run, who were mostly slightly overweight rather than old and some jogged then walked then jogged again. He encouraged them as did everyone else behind him because it would have been an achievement for anyone to even walk from Long Beach to the mountain in this tropical heat let along jog or run. He supposed that because it was taking them longer to complete the run, they'd spent more time in the heat of the day, as it warmed up very quickly. He unfurled the piece of paper with his time on it and saw written: one hour, ten minutes and fifty-one seconds and the word 'First'. He smiled because while he knew he hadn't set a record; it was a very respectable time and especially since he'd never thought of himself as a serious runner.

Guilty

It was Monday morning and Rev Simon was sat in the church office with a cup of tea, and was just wondering how much tea was left on the island, when Sabrina entered.

"Morning Simon, can I talk to you about something that's troubling me?" Sabrina asked

Simon was slightly surprised at Sabrina's question because for weeks she looked most untroubled and, in fact, looked the happiest he'd ever seen her. He knew she'd formed a relationship with Jeff, the young man who was one of the yacht people and they seemed to be made for each other and they both came to church. Simon didn't have time to run through a likely list of issues because Sabrina had already begun to speak.

"I feel troubled that I'm so happy. Myself and Jeff are madly in love with each other and it's hard to conceal our happiness from other people. Yet I'm conscious and Jeff is more so, that billions of people have died or might still be dying of hunger, disease or radiation poisoning. The civilisation that existed external to this island has gone forever. Yet the impact here is small, and the pace of change is also small." And then having finished speaking she looked at Simon.

"I understand, Sabrina. I was once in a position where something very sad had happened in my life. Then one day something good happened and I felt happy. Then I felt momentarily guilty because I wasn't sure I should be allowed to feel happiness again. For me the happiness was somewhat fleeting but eventually I moved on. At the present time our recent past is sad but we are part of the future of humanity, and perhaps no more so than you and Jeff. I think people will understand why you might be happy and if they don't, that's their problem to work through. I don't think you or anyone else should live a life of misery for being spared from the apocalypse, nor feel guilty about it. Perhaps as an island we ought to have some sort of special remembrance service so we can all start to focus on moving forward. Then later in the year we could have an annual remembrance. How does that sound to you Sabrina, perhaps I can discuss it with Deborah?"

"Thank you, Simon. So, it's ok for me to feel happy and I shouldn't feel guilty about feeling happy?" she asked.

"Yes Sabrina, as a Christian, having been forgiven all your sins you are guilt free. Besides, if God hadn't wanted you to be happy, he wouldn't have brought Jeff to the island, who is of course an answer to all our prayers, isn't he?"

"Yes Simon, that's right. Thank you very much for listening to me" she told him and then giving him a very brief hug, waved goodbye.

Once she was back at her office Sabrina had one unanswered question she'd hadn't put to Simon because it was a question only Deborah could answer, though it was almost the same question she'd asked him in respect of herself. "Deborah, I'm pleased you and Vincent are together and you are both very happy. I wondered though if you ever felt any guilt in being happy, since most of the rest of the world's population have died?"

"I don't feel any guilt about what's happened to the world because it wasn't my fault it happened. Nor could I have done anything to have prevented it. More than that though I don't feel any guilt because a lot of my life was hard, sad things happened to me when all around me good things happened to others. I take the simple view that a happy life and a lovely man were natural things that in my own life had been missing for a long time, and were overdue. However, I'm not going to take anything as my entitlement in life, or take Vincent for granted. Rather, I'm going to treasure my happiness and my Vincent and try and hang onto them for as long as I draw breath." Then Deborah smiled at Sabrina, almost as if she were grateful, she'd been asked the question.

"Thanks for answering my question and sharing your thoughts, that's very interesting, thank you" Sabrina replied. When they had both been single women, they often shared their time and thoughts and Sabrina thought it more than a co-incidence that on the very same day, they'd both ceased to be single women, but in different ways. Jeff hadn't moved in to live with Sabrina and she expected they'd get married. She hadn't quite worked out what was taking him so long to propose to her but she knew she needed to be more patient. She knew that Deborah didn't want to believe in God but that Vincent had some belief, but not in the way she herself, fully believed. Sometimes they had talked about God, but not recently. In some ways Deborah was still something of a puzzle to Sabrina and she wondered if she was a puzzle to Deborah or even Jeff. Well, she'd had two questions answered today and all the others could keep for other days.

The Devil's Riding School

Vincent and Deborah were walking very slowly to the letterbox at the Devil's Riding School. However, this was no slow stroll hand in hand, rather that parts of the walk took them over some unusual and very slippery rock formations and neither wanted to end up on their backside or break a leg. While a volcanic crater, it was unusual in being very wide and flat and at one time in the very distant past would have contained a lake. The best views of it were obtained from green mountain where its concentric rings could be seen. It wasn't a long walk and at the letterbox they sat down for a cool drink and a snack after they'd written in the visitor's book, and had a read through some of the previous entries.

"Do you realise that Charles Darwin may have once sat at this very spot?" Deborah asked Vincent.

"I thought he went to the Galapagos Islands" he replied and added "you told me it was Joseph Hooker that came here".

"He did, but he came here as well but didn't stay long and in fact visited here several years before Hooker's visit. They were close friends but never came here together. At that time the island looked quite different and Green Mountain wasn't green at all." She replied. Anyway, tomorrow it's time to start on something else from that era, which is replacing the water pipes. It'll be a big job, even with vehicles and small mechanical handling equipment. We could put it off for years but then again if we had a sudden unexpected problem with the desalination plant, we'd be very sorry we didn't do it earlier. I'm a great believer in planning ahead and not putting off tomorrow what can be done today." She told him.

"I thought you said something about a heritage project had ensured the island would have a water supply?" he replied.

"Yes, I did, the catchment areas and tanks and even a wind pump are all in working order, the missing part is the pipes that lead from the mountain to the tanks in Georgetown. Some of the original pipes are missing, others broken, so we have to lay replacement pipes and they are all cast iron, like the originals." She told him

"Why couldn't you have used that thick blue plastic pipe?" He asked.

"I think it would have needed to be buried and while that was doable, with a mini back-hoe I couldn't be certain how long it would last. With cast iron pipe I already knew how long the original lasted and there was less of a risk something would go wrong, so it was a safer bet, albeit a more expensive solution." She replied and added "Are you ready to wander back now?"

"Yes" he replied and he followed Deborah back the way they came across the NASA road and along the obsidian trail.

Obsidian

"Can you keep your eyes out for obsidian and perhaps kick up a bit of sand?" she asked him.

"What's Obsidian? I've only heard of the Obsidian Hotel." He replied.

"Obsidian is a form of natural glass but it's jet black in colour. It's a kind of semi-precious stone and can be made into decorative things or even set in a clasp to make jewellery. It can also be made into a knife blade. I think the Mayan's used Obsidian knives even for cutting rock. I don't do anything with the pieces I find but I might one day. I also don't often find any pieces but then again, I don't often look. But since we are at one of the most likely places on the island to find some, I wanted to have a look for some." She told him.

They walked slowly through the sandy part of the Obsidian trail and they each picked up several pieces of obsidian that varied from very glass-like to more stone-like, but all with very sharp edges. Deborah was pleased with what they had found which they carefully put in their rucksacks before walking over to where they had parked.

The pipeline

On the drive back Deborah explained a bit about the history of the water pipeline, of which the first part dated back to 1830 and other parts a year or maybe two years later. It was of four inches in diameter and at least six miles in length and in use for over a hundred years. The pipes were sold by a Mr Edward Bailey of No 272 High Holborn, London, England who was a Brazier and Ironmonger and who may also have manufactured them at the premises. "It's odd to think the apocalypse has destroyed that old building, and the rest of London, that survived so long yet some of his old pipes are still here on the island. I'm open to ideas as to what to do with them when we lay the new pipes. I'm even going to use lead and oakum on the new joints, just like the originals. Well not personally I suppose. We could use some sort of pipe glue but there's no guarantee it will last the length of time we want it to last, whereas the traditional method is already proven. I also thought about lining the iron pipe with plastic pipe but it seemed a bit 'belt and braces' and even more expensive, so I abandoned that idea. This is one of most important projects on the island and the tried and trusted methods of the past represent the least risk."

Vincent nodded as she talked and was quietly impressed that she'd been able to plan all of this. He'd seen the pipes on the 'Hansel' and had wondered why they were taking them to Ascension Island. He'd never imagined that he'd be on the island laying those pipes under the supervision of an amazing woman whom he loved, and who loved him.

Deborah had called a meeting for anyone wanting to volunteer with the pipeline, and she was encouraged when she saw a good number of attendees. "Ok, thanks everyone for turning up to this evening meeting about re-laying the water pipeline from Green Mountain to Georgetown. It will be a challenge for us but probably less of one than it was when the pipeline was originally laid because we haven't got to dig a tunnel through part of the mountain, that was done for us a very long time ago! I plan on starting at the top of the mountain and working downwards. We will need several teams handling the pipe, from loading at the warehouse, to unloading at the mountain at first, and then progressively nearer to Georgetown. We'll also need a pipe positioning team and a pipe joining team or maybe just the one pipe joiner. There will be some complex work where the pipe fits into the various tanks and of course we'll need to undertake some testing," Deborah told everyone present.

"We'll be eating at the Red Lion for the early stages of the work and then as we work down the mountain, we'll probably eat at one or two unoccupied houses in Two Boats, we'll open up for that purpose." Deborah told them. Since there were no questions, she thanked them once more and everyone left. The next day everyone arrived on time in Georgetown and began loading up some pipe. With each length of pipe being six feet long, it wasn't possible to send up many pieces in a vehicle. But even if they could send pipe faster up the mountain, it still had to be physically carried from the Red Lion to the water catchment area tank system and joined to it.

After a while the teams settled into their routines and there was a steady flow of pipes moving up the mountain. Everyone marvelled at how challenging a task this would have been originally even with a lot of the donkey work being undertaken by, well, donkeys. At the top of the mountain the first joint had been made and it was slow work getting each section of new pipe in place and even that couldn't be done before an original 1830 era piece had been replaced. They'd agreed to remove old pipe as they laid new so they could be certain it was being placed in its optimal position. At the end of the first day while a lot of new lengths of pipe were roughly laid in position, sometimes next to a complete or broken section of original pipe, very few pieces of pipe had been connected up. Deborah realised the task was going to be slower and more difficult than she had envisaged.

"Don't look down-hearted darling, you always knew it wasn't going to be a five-minute job and there's no reason for concern," Vincent told Deborah while giving her a gentle sideways hug.

"Yes, I know, I guess I'm an administrator rather than a civil engineer." She replied. Then after ensuring she personally thanked everyone, they drove slowly back to Georgetown.

Over the next few days, which turned into weeks, the pipeline project gradually proceeded. The work also picked up pace, once no pipe had to be manhandled up the mountain. Thanks to the hard work of the Ascension Island Heritage Society, before the apocalypse, they had drawings, which some of the Americans called schematics, of the pipeline. The original design, including the use of break tanks to reduce pressure, was well thought through and section by section the pipeline was completed.

"Well, Alan, since you worked so hard on this project, I thought you might like the honour of testing the system, though you might want to have a test wash, with the first water, rather than drink it" Deborah told him. Alan made some calls on his radio and further up the mountain various valves were slowly opened. The valves weren't all part of the original design but prudent additions, that would help run temporary bypass pipes, if any of the cast iron sections ever broke. It wasn't a true test because each section had been tested at every break tank, and everyone knew this, but nonetheless there was a large cheer when Alan turned on a tap in Georgetown and there was a steady stream of water.

Chapter Fifteen – A tall ship

With all the effort of training for the Dew Pond Run and then laying the cast iron pipeline from the mountain to Georgetown, both Deborah and Vincent decided they wanted to relax a bit but had spent enough time on Green Mountain to prefer the warmth of the beach for a change. As much as they enjoyed spending time at Comfortless Cove, they decided to go to English Bay beach. While it was less suitable for swimming because of the large waves, known as 'rollers' that crashed onto the main part of the beach, it was nearly always less crowded than Comfortless Cove, despite being much larger.

Deborah was snoozing on the beach and Vincent was sitting in a rock pool. Something kept biting him on his leg and he was intrigued to see what it was. After a while he saw that he wasn't actually being bitten at all but that a small Sergeant Major fish was plucking hairs out of his legs. Having satisfied his curiosity, he decided he'd have a quick swim. The main section of the beach had a rope that stretched across the water at the furthermost point of two rocky outcrops. So, if the current caught a swimmer, they could catch hold of the rope to prevent themselves being swept out to sea and being washed up on the coast of Brazil. However, Vincent decided he'd take his swim on the other side of the outcrop, where there was no safety rope.

Vincent wasn't a strong swimmer and he never liked to swim out of his depth and liked to always be able to stand up whenever he wanted to. At first everything seemed ok and then he suddenly realised he was being caught in the current, only yards from the shore. He went to stand up and found he was out of his depth and couldn't touch the bottom of the sea bed. He immediately started to swim the short distance towards the beach using breast stroke, his preferred swimming stroke, but found he wasn't getting any nearer to land. He'd heard front crawl was a more powerful, faster stroke, so he switched to it and was alarmed to realise he was now gradually getting further from the beach, going backwards while trying to swim forwards. He switched back to breast stroke and put in every effort he could muster and very gradually he was inching back towards the beach. Between the beach and his position there was a large solitary rock and he decided if he could get close enough to grasp it, he could then climb on it and once on the other side he'd be back within his depth.

Vincent was near to exhaustion when he was finally within reach of the rock and grabbing it managed to pull himself up on it, where he sat gasping for breath. He was relieved, both that he hadn't been swept out to sea but also that neither Deborah or anyone else would discover how foolish he'd been, and it was a mistake he would never repeat. He eventually felt enough of his strength return to move over to the other side of the rock and waded to shore. He was just finishing drying himself off when their radios sprung into life.

"Deborah, Vincent, Henry and everyone else, we have something on the radar about the size of a small ship, it's not moving fast but it's not moving slow either. Wait one, we're getting a call on the radio." The duty island radio and command centre operative announced in his broadcast to all radios.

They then listened to the message from the vessel.

"Ascension Island, this is the captain of The Sprite. Are you free of the pandemic virus and nuclear fallout over? I say again, Ascension Island, this is the captain of The Sprite. Are you free of the pandemic virus and nuclear fallout over?"

"This is Ascension Island to the Sprite, we are clean, but we want to quarantine you when you arrive here. We can see you on our radar and you are moving slowly, what sort of a vessel is The Sprite?"

"The Sprite is something of a sorry vessel at the moment as we've lost a mast, otherwise we would be a magnificent tall ship." The captain told them.

"Ok, we might be able to help with that later. What's the total number of crew and any passengers?

"There's twenty-five adults and six children, teenagers. We'd be grateful for a safe anchorage, drinking water and other supplies you can spare us."

"Ok Sprite, we can supply you with water, food and any other supplies you might need. However, we'll quarantine you but we can do this while you're at anchor and we can deliver water and supplies to you. We'd also like our doctor and other medics to visit you. A RHIB will meet you and be your pilot to safe anchorage. Acknowledge them when you see them, over."

"Ascension, we confirm and look forward to seeing your RHIB." The Sprite replied.

Deborah was driving the Land Rover to Georgetown with Vincent as her passenger so he could call out his defence volunteers and get the RHIB launched. Some of the volunteers were already at the quayside and Arnold already had the RHIB on the water and the engines running. The intercept was smooth and since the 'The Sprite' was expecting them, there was no gunfire. A line was thrown to the RHIB from the Sprite and it was then given a gentle tow to Clarence Bay.

"Did you see that Captain, they're armed to the teeth" Roger, the first mate, told, rather than asked, the captain.

"Yes, I did but they never concealed their guns nor aimed them at us" he replied and added "I don't think we've got anything to worry about, they seemed friendly but business-like. But if we do have something to worry about that's all we can do, worry."

"Ok everyone I want everyone on deck for a briefing" the captain announced. Once everyone had assembled, he began his briefing. "Well, we are now in safe anchorage in Clarence Bay, Ascension Island. We don't know much about the islanders except that while seeming friendly and offering us assistance, they're heavily armed, but non-threatening so far. They have instructed us that they will subject us to quarantine, which sounds a bit aggressive, but it is their island and a right and proper precaution. They have offered us any medical assistance we need and promised to deliver water and supplies to us daily. I think it's safe to assume they will be watching us and making sure we don't launch a dinghy and pay the island an unauthorised visit. They told us they saw us on their radar and given they also have a very long military runway; they might have all sorts of capability we don't want to tangle with. I can't imagine they will be able to do anything to help us with our broken mast, so don't get your hopes up."

So, for the next two weeks the islanders used the Ascension Frigate to ferry water and food to The Sprite. They learned that it was a two-masted brig but it had lost one mast in a storm. The crew and passengers on the Sprite passed the time as best they could and grew anxious about what plans the islanders would have for them, despite the daily delivery of supplies.

With the two-week quarantine period passed without any illness on 'The Sprite', it was time to pay them a visit and invite them onto the island. Mindful of what had happened with the Admiral, Vincent deployed most of his volunteer defence force when Deborah boarded 'The Sprite', on their first visit to it. The volunteers all looked more professional now and less like an armed mob, having been kitted out in US military clothing. Vincent observed that most people on the ship looked extremely nervous at their arrival and he made sure that no-one was within spitting distance, let alone shoving distance, of Deborah.

"Good morning everyone, please relax. This isn't a show of power, or my private army. It's simply that they want to protect the interests of the island and its assets of which they see me as one." Deborah then turned to Vincent and beamed a smile at him before speaking. "Vincent darling do you think you could put your pistol in its holster?" He nodded in reply and put his pistol away. He also turned to the defence force and indicated for them to shoulder their arms which they did with synchronised military precision.

The crew and passengers visibly relaxed and Deborah spoke to them again "I'm not sure how much you know about Ascension Island but it is steeped in the history of the Royal Navy and thanks to their foresight we can supply a suitable tree, a Norfolk Island Pine, for you to re-mast your ship with because even if you never plan to leave, I'm sure you'd want to see it restored to its full glory. On the other hand, if you do want to leave, I'm sure you'll want to leave with the mast replaced."

"Really? We have a ship's carpenter who would relish the challenge" the captain excitedly replied. "Well welcome aboard 'The Sprite', I'm not sure we can offer any hospitality equal to what you've already given us, but you're welcome to what we have. I think firstly though we ought to introduce ourselves" the captain told them before introducing each one of his crew and passengers.

So, Deborah and Vincent spend the next half hour or so drinking tea with the captain, while the defence volunteers were made welcome and given tours of the ship. Deborah told the captain what history of the island she could readily recall, the nautical parts anyway.

The captain explained they were at sea when the global crisis first began and they decided they would try and find a safe haven and see what happened. Initially they had taken a similar voyage to the yachties but had anchored off shore from St Helena for some weeks after already having lost a mast in the storm. They had hoped some sort of relief plane might land at St Helena but none did. They were loath to sail on to Ascension in case they found it was plague decimated or had been attacked and was 'cooking' in nuclear radiation. They still had reasonable supply levels of food and water so could sail on past Ascension, but had no general agreement where to go to next. In the end they did decide they would sail to Ascension as it was the next nearest land from St Helena and were pleased their radio message was heard.

After a fairly pleasant day for everyone, Deborah agreed to send out the RHIB the following morning to collect anyone wanting to live on dry land for a while and also any volunteers to work on felling a pine for a new mast. Then having said their goodbyes, they left and returned to the island.

"What do you think my darling?" Deborah asked Vincent. Vincent hadn't yet stopped hesitating to reply when Deborah addressed him like that, because it always took him a split second to realise, he was being spoken to.

"They aren't likely to give us much trouble, and probably no trouble. The only odd thing is why they don't seem interested in staying here. What do they suppose they are going to find anywhere else in the world? A few looked like they might want to stay and I guess they are the passengers rather than the crew. The island's population will need those teenagers, if it's going to survive long term. Oh, and yeah, giving them one of those tall trees for a mast isn't going to be simple, unless you can get a pack of donkeys to drag it." He replied smiling at her.

Dry land and a new mast

With the volunteers from 'The Sprite' having been collected and after some re-introductions and housing arranged for those wanting to live on the island for a while, the discussion about re-masting began.

"We can saw or chop one of the pines down but it will be a fair amount of trouble, not to mention getting it to Georgetown will be a challenge, or maybe just hard work" Frank advised.

Frank was of course correct because of all the diverse selection of equipment on the island the one thing they didn't have was a chainsaw. Also, most of the saws were small woodworking saws and not really practical for safely sawing down a massive Norfolk Pine. After a fair amount of discussion, it was decided a suitable tree would have to be felled by traditional axes, but even they were very much on the small side. As things turned out, felling one of the pines actually turned out to be a lot of trouble and a long job. Eventually one of the outermost pines was felled and a mixed team of islanders and ship's crew set about removing all the branches so what was left was the main trunk itself. The ship's carpenter was very pleased with it but everyone wondered how to transport it to the quayside at Georgetown. The volunteers from the 'The Sprite' promised that whatever happened they would bring enough rope.

It was Frank who suggested a solution. "We could go to the car scrapyard and get some complete axle and wheel and tyre assemblies to make a couple of bogies and tie the pine onto them?"

"I could help, I've worked on cars all my life" Paul, one of the Yacht people volunteered and with some other volunteers from the ship, they agreed to meet in the scrapyard and cannibalise what they could, to make the bogies in the morning of the following day.

After looking around the scrapyard, Paul took charge and split the volunteers into two teams, with each team working on a separate vehicle that he'd identified. Frank had brought a large selection of tools, including a cutting torch but it still took a couple of hours to get what was to become the bogies, free of the rest of their respective vehicle. They decided to fit a long extension end, comprising of two girders that met at a point to fit a towing hitch too and a means of attaching one bogie to the other. The end result all looked pretty rough and untested as to functionality. It was hitched to Vincent's Land Rover and very slowly, along with a small convoy of other vehicles, they set out for the NASA road and Breakneck Valley. Once they'd arrived it was apparent their difficulties weren't over.

"Well Vincent, you could try and drive up the valley but to be honest there's a risk you might get stuck. I suggest we use all the rope we have and the winch cable on my truck and see if it's long enough to reach the pine" Frank suggested.

"Sounds like a good call Frank and you're more of a local than I am. Let's just hope we have enough rope and cable" Vincent replied. While regretting they didn't have a quadbike, the gang of volunteers manhandled various lengths of rope and cable out from Frank's truck. The task got progressively harder because the further they were away from the truck the further they had to carry the rope. Vincent supposed that the original plan in the 1800s was for the donkeys or the Royal Marines or sailors to manhandle the pine all the way to Georgetown. They must have been tough in those days he thought. On the other hand, this was the one task they'd never had to undertake and as far as anyone knew, no pine tree had ever been cut down before, and this was the first re-masting undertaken using a tree from the island.

'The Sprite's volunteers were as good as their word and didn't run out of rope and after a lot of to and froing the pine was connected by rope and wire, and Frank winched it in as far as his winch cable on this pickup, would allow. Then the cable was wound out and attached further back on the rope length to the pine and the process repeated, until eventually the pine was at the edge of the road. Since it was about midday the volunteers decided to have a lunch break. While they were working hard, they didn't feel cold but once they'd stopped working and a bank of low cloud rolled over the mountain, some of them felt a little too cool and put on long sleeve tops while they ate.

Once everyone had finished eating and tidied up, Frank manoeuvred his pickup truck with the nose and the winch facing the bogies. With everyone grappling the pine they first dragged one end round and then managed to raise it high enough up to sit on top of what would be the rear bogie. Then Frank slowly and carefully winched the pine along the top of the rear bogie and then onto the front one. While he held the cable tension using the winch, the volunteers lashed the pine firmly onto the bogies.

"What do you think guys? I suggest we use my pickup to tow because it's bigger than Vincent's Land Rover" Frank asked the volunteers.

It was the mechanic, Paul, who replied, "There are no brakes on the bogies and it's a steep downhill drive, so I agree and suggest we have a long rope from the rear bogie to the front of Vincent's Land Rover, so if you pick up too much speed, he can use it to aid with braking." Everyone agreed this was a good idea and someone suggested that if Frank gave a continuous toot on his pickup truck's horn, it meant he needed braking assistance. Someone else suggested that if the Land Rover saw a speed greater than 30 mph, Vincent would give a continuous toot and apply braking to the Land Rover; with a view to holding back the load. So, with everyone in agreement, the convoy left with an additional vehicle in front of Frank's as a bumper car in case all else failed.

The NASA Road was one of the newer roads on the island, albeit built in the mid-1960s and also in good condition since it never saw a lot of use, and even less after the NASA tracking station had closed down and the buildings occupied by the island's scout troop. It was also the first time a pine for a tall ship mast had ever proceeded down the road! The convoy set off, never exceeding 15 mph and less through some of the sharper corners. Before long they were on a straight and level road so they stopped to check nothing had moved during the descent down the NASA road. Vincent knew on their left-hand side was the crater known as the Devil's Riding School, where himself and Deborah had been only the other week. With everything checked, they were soon on the move again and without any drama or incident, they were at the quay in Georgetown.

The ship's carpenter decided he wanted an authentic re-masting experience because he might never get the opportunity to re-mast a traditional sailing ship again. Consequently, the Norfolk pine would be transferred to 'The Sprite', that day and he'd work on it aboard ship, rather than the quayside. The dockside crane was used to place it on a pontoon and from there it was transferred to 'The Sprite' using traditional block and tackle.

Over the next few days there was something of a holiday atmosphere on the island, as some islanders took a visit to see a tall sailing ship for the first time, while the crew and passengers from the ship toured the island. One day a fishing competition took place from 'The Sprite' and that evening there was a fish barbeque in the evening.

"Sabrina, was it a good thing when we all arrived or a bad thing, a burden? I mean, is there really enough stuff to go around?" Jeff asked.

Sabrina wrapped herself around Jeff as well as she could manage and kissed him before replying. "It was and is the best thing ever for me, you're arriving here, and an answer to prayer. I'm still the deputy administrator for the island and have a good idea of what goes on and what needs to go on and how much stuff there is. I'm confident there's more than enough to go around. Of course, we are at the mercy of the weather and potential clouds of nuclear radiation drifting our way, or all the fish dying but even if all those things happened, we could live in the bunker for months and months eating packet food. We could easily cope with the thirty or thirty-one people from 'The Sprite'. There's plenty of empty properties and enough farming and fishing to keep everyone busy. So, don't worry about them and anyway I think most of them will leave and I'll bet Jo Cockburn will go with them; we've spent more time with her parents since the ship arrived than she has" she replied.

"Thanks for reassuring me" he said and added "Are we both invited to this dinner?"

"Yes, but Deborah had to suggest that I accompany you as I wasn't on the original list" Sabrina replied laughing.

After the long task of re-masting 'The Sprite' was complete, the captain invited a number of islanders to a ship's dinner/banquet. Not just islanders who might be described as 'the great and the good' but rather those people who had by sheer hard work managed to get the pine tree to Georgetown and then to 'The Sprite'.

With the dinner eaten and after-dinner brandy being served, the captain sat down to talk to Deborah. "Well Deborah, the answer to your unasked question is both yes and no. Some of the ship's company, what are really our passengers as it were, will accept your offer to stay. The rest of us, at least for the next year or so, want to sail on and see what has survived of our world. We realise the risks and the challenge of this but see it as an adventure. Also, Jo, the Admiral's daughter, wants to join us and we've accepted her on to the crew where we think she will be a great asset. Her parents aren't too happy about her decision but accept she is young and will only grow restless here, so they have given her their blessing to leave." Ian told her.

Deborah smiled before speaking "There are no surprises in what you are telling me though I wish you were all staying. We'll all miss you and the sight of your lovely ship at anchor in Clarence Bay. The keen photographers and videographers are looking forward to seeing your sails unfurled and I think you'll be given quite a send-off. I'd have been happier if you'd have taken some arms and ammunition but can understand why you've declined." Then, after a lot of handshakes and hugs all-round, the islanders left and waved goodbye as they departed on the RHIB.

As Vincent and Deborah were lying on their bed that evening, she asked him "You look a bit glum. Are you sorry to see the crew leave?"

"No, I don't mind them leaving or leaving behind some good people, including youngsters for us. It's just I feel sad for that old bastard, the Admiral. He's lost a daughter but hasn't gained a son. Well, he might gain a son but only if 'The Sprite' does return in a year or two, and he might not live long enough to see that. I bet his head still hurts now and again from the bruise my pistol muzzle gave him. I'm more used to dealing with faster moving rogues and following through" Vincent told her before falling quiet.

Deborah realised that Vincent had let his guard slip slightly, once more, and she knew that having realised it, he'd speak very little for several days. She didn't like it when he was quiet and introspective but it was a price worth paying for the glimpses not only of his past but of the kinder and caring part of his nature, he kept concealed, guarded even. "The Admiral and Petunia will be ok. They've practically adopted Jeff and Sabrina as their own. The Admiral is helping Jeff with his sailing technique and they've been around the island a few times in his yacht. Jeff and Sabrina are also treating them like the parents they never had, so everything is working out ok" she told him.

Vincent smiled "Great, I feel better now, can we just go to sleep tonight?" and, not waiting for an answer, closed his eyes.

Chapter Sixteen – A wedding and Boatswain Bird Island

Deborah sat down at her desk and found an envelope addressed to herself and Vincent. She smiled after opening the envelope and found it was an invitation to the forthcoming wedding ceremony of Miss Sabrina Triumph and Mr Jeff Learoyd. How exciting, she hadn't been to a wedding in ages! The date was in two weeks' time and she guessed Jeff had decided to make a move sooner rather than wait until later. Since it was a church wedding, she guessed Rev Simon would handle all the paperwork, not that it really mattered, or did it, she thought to herself. She realised that she wasn't married to Vincent and there was an old-fashioned phrase that used to exist for such circumstances. Yes, 'living in sin' that's what it used to be called.

An adventure

"Say Vincent, are you up for an adventure?" Frank asked.

"I think you know the answer already, which is I'm always 'up' for an adventure. What sort of adventure and how do you know I've not already done it already?" he replied.

"Camping overnight on Boatswain Bird Island – you haven't even set foot on it have you?" Frank replied laughing.

"Is it big enough for a tent and how are you even going to get on it?" Vincent asked. He was of course as keen as mustard to visit the island. He'd been interested in it ever since he'd been close to it on the Spire Beach rescue, before the apocalypse. At one time in the past, it had been the final retreat for many of the island's rare bird species but after the successful eradication of the island's cat population some years before Deborah's arrival, all the species could now be found on the main island. Boatswain Bird Island itself seemed to have sheer rock cliff faces with no cove to moor even a small boat.

"We won't be the first visitors because in nineteen twenty there was a short-lived attempt to extract the guano for export as fertiliser. Then no-one apart from the occasional 'Saint' fisherman landed on the island until nineteen fifty-eight, when a British Ornithologists Union expedition spent several nights here. They wrote about it in a book, which I have a copy of. Lastly the wildlife film maker Cindy Buxton, and her assistant Annie Price, filmed a documentary on it in 1984, so we knew a little bit of what to expect before some of us made our own first visit some weeks ago.

"There is a landing platform which we've already rebuilt and we also recleared a safe footpath. Part of the adventure will be to study the birds and report back to the new island conservation group. We can expect to see:

Boatswain birds, Storm petrels, White-tailed tropicbirds, Red-footed boobies, Brown boobies, Masked boobies, Black noddies, Common white terns and Ascension Frigate birds. The plan is for you and I, Brad, Alan and Simon to take Jeff along with us since he's yet to see any boobies, so we thought he ought to see some before he gets married" Frank said before bursting out laughing and continuing "It's also a kind of pre-marriage blokes party without alcohol. You still interested?"

Vincent had got to know Jeff a little bit because he sometimes accompanied Sabrina when she visited Deborah. They'd talked a bit but hadn't found they had much in the way of common interests. "Yeah, but I don't know him that well, maybe I could go some other time."

Frank's expression changed to a more serious one before he spoke to Vincent. "Perhaps you don't realise you would be doing him a great honour by coming with us. You are fast approaching the status of a living legend and he looks up to you, as most people do. Let me just run through why that might be so. You arrived on the island and stayed when everyone else was leaving. You led the rescue of Eddy Mannock with some boat handling skills and courage the rest of us didn't have. You recruited and trained the island defence force, which no-one else could have done. You supported Deborah in everything she did. You saved the island from the Admiral and helped him change to become a better person. Then you won Deborah's heart. You won the Dewpond run this year and your team won the team prize. So, everyone looks up to you but more than that, you are kind and friendly to everyone and humble in a way few men could manage. You're a role model for all the men on the island and no less for Jeff than any other. He'll have his challenges and his hands full, so needs people like you and friends like us to see him through those times."

Vincent felt his cheeks redden slightly and hoped that Frank didn't notice. "You're more complimentary than I'm sure I deserve Frank, and I'll come if it makes Jeff happy before his big day" he replied.

The landing on Boatswain Bird Island was going to be made using a small dinghy that would be used as a shuttle between the island and the Ascension Frigate, which Arnold would pilot. On the day the expedition set out the party's wives', and Deborah and Sabrina, were there to see them off. Deborah said goodbye in a flood of tears and then Sabrina began to cry as well. Vincent looked at Jeff to give him a look of reassurance, along with a 'get used to this kind of stuff' look of nonchalance. After that they were on their way on a calm sea.

Once they reached the island Vincent realised why one of the yacht people, Jake, had accompanied Arnold. While Arnold held position in the launch, Jake had to take the dinghy back to it once everyone was on the island. Once they were all on the island, they undertook a final radio check with Arnold and then waved him and Jake goodbye. Vincent was surprised how large the island was, though you couldn't get lost on it.

"Here we are, home for today, tonight and tomorrow morning. As you can see there are lots of birds here and this is their home. One of the things we'll be doing is seeing if we can count some of them by different types, have a look at the chicks and see also if we find any of these beetles that look like scorpion's but aren't. We've agreed to total radio silence unless there's an emergency. If the emergency is on Ascension, they'll set out to fetch us straightaway, weather permitting. If we have an emergency, we'll radio for whatever help we need. However, Simon has prayed for safety, so we'll be believing and trusting in our Father in heaven for that" Frank announced.

Vincent smiled because he was with what was sometimes called 'The God Squad' or just 'The Squad'. He also knew he wasn't in 'The Squad' but he knew his card was marked and at some point, he'd have to surrender and join, though he wasn't quite sure how that happened. He knew they would have a prayer meeting later but it was all very casual. They never prayed with special words or phrases but it was like having a chat with a person on the other end of a telephone. You couldn't see the person but they were listening. He liked being at the meetings because he didn't really have any memories of his own father and he liked the idea of having one. God would be his father, they often told him. He supposed he would have to tell them that soon he would be a father himself and the responsibility of that worried him. Not becoming a father, and Deborah losing the unborn baby, worried him even more, or losing Deborah or both of them.

Pitching the tents was something of a challenge and everything they did covered them in the white dust of bird droppings. The original hut had been rebuilt by Frank and others and despite their protests Jeff and Vincent were to sleep in it, being far more pleasant than any tent. There were lots of birds and lots of bird noise and lots of exploring by the visitors. Alan took photos of just about everything while Brad took videos.

Vincent was in charge of cooking the evening meal and he'd brought along a selection of British and American ration pack meals which everyone agreed tasted a lot better than they'd hoped and made a change from fish. After dinner they had a sing song and a prayer time which Vincent quite enjoyed and he found the whole time relaxing and peaceful. He discovered that Jeff did have something in common with him after all, in that he had no surviving parents and few positive memories of them, his having largely

167

been brought up by his sister. Everyone slept well that night and were all up early in the morning.

Deborah was embarrassed that she cried so much when she waved Vincent goodbye for his overnight adventure on Boatswain Bird Island. He was with the 'God Squad' so couldn't be in safer hands. When the boat was a speck in the distance, she wiped her eyes dry and looked at Sabrina, 'I feel so embarrassed Sabrina, I don't know why I cried so much, it isn't like me at all." She told her.

"Perhaps God is working in your life and having softened your heart, you feel more vulnerable?" Sabrina replied.

Deborah felt there might be some truth in Sabrina's explanation, and it was unusually bold of her to make any statement about God and Deborah in the same sentence. Well, either way it was time to have a wander back into town; small as it was, they couldn't stand at the quayside all day, especially not in this hot sun.

Their plan for the day was to drive to Comfortless Cove and have a lazy day with some swimming and sun-bathing, which all went to plan. They hadn't been back at Deborah's home very long when they both felt a slight earth tremor.

"Did you feel something just then or did I imagine it?" Deborah asked Sabrina.

"Yes, I felt it, it was like a small earthquake, how strange" she replied.

The small earth tremor was quickly forgotten as Deborah prepared dinner. She'd been given some Wahoo and was going to grill it and serve it with some frozen oven chips and frozen vegetables. The island still had quite a large supply of frozen food and one routine task was to keep a track of how much was left and to consolidate that food into as small a number of freezers as was possible. Deborah expected that before too long the farm would not only be producing enough fresh food but a small surplus, so they could experiment with freezing some or using preserving jars.

It was late when they had finished eating, washing up and tidying things away. "Deborah, I'm going to pray for Jeff, Vincent and the others on the island and it seems silly for me to go and hide myself away to pray. So, I wondered if you wanted to pray with me, just say the amen at the end or nothing at all if you preferred?" Sabrina asked.

"Err, no I don't mind, I want them all to be kept safe" she replied.

"Dear Lord Jesus, thank you very much for giving us each a man to spend the rest of our lives with. Thank you for our homes and this island where we can live with them. Thank you for keeping them safe, and carry on keeping them safe, and help them to be able to relax and draw close to you while they are on Boatswain Bird Island. Amen" Sabrina prayed.

"Amen" Deborah added, thinking how lovely Sabrina prayed, as simple as talking to someone.

Then they both drank a mug of cocoa, said goodnight, and went to bed.

In the morning Sabrina was awake first and not so much anxious to see Jeff again but looking forward to seeing him again. She realised it was different for her than for Deborah because she wasn't living with Jeff and they never spent the night together. In some ways they both thought it was a bit silly not to, but with their wedding looming up fast, decided a few more days waiting wouldn't matter.

Deborah woke up and reached out for Vincent and realised he wasn't there because he was on Boatswain Bird Island. She smiled and wondered how well he'd slept with all that dusty guano, flies and the smell of bird poo. He'd have been woken by the birds at first light. Well, she supposed, discomfort was all part of what made a 'blokey' adventure.

After they'd both eaten breakfast and tidied away Deborah thought she might take advantage of the relaxed atmosphere to be a friend to Sabrina, and see if she had any questions, she might be able to help her with before she got married.

"I was thinking, Sabrina, if there was anything you wanted to ask me about men, that you thought I might be able to share some experience of, or err, or advice, or answer a question for you. One perhaps you might not have felt comfortable asking the Rev Simon" Deborah said.

As quick as a flash Sabrina did have a question "There certainly is, two in fact. Why on earth do men find farting funny, it's so disgusting? Do they ever grow out of it?"

Deborah didn't think it was appropriate to smile, both at the questions and that they were the only ones Sabrina needed answering and not at all what she'd had in mind. "I'm sorry I don't know the answer to your first question and the second isn't very encouraging in that I don't believe so, at least not in my experience" she replied.

"Oh. I suppose I'll grow a tolerance to it over time" Sabrina said.

They spent the rest of the day making sure nothing had been forgotten in the wedding plans, and taking things easy. However, both were looking forward to the arrival back at Georgetown of their men.

On the island everyone was looking forward to leaving and having a wash. They'd have liked to have tried a quick swim but even with a harness and rope it wasn't safe because there were known to be lots of sharks in the area. They'd had a look at some of the photos and video footage and had made sure they'd cleared up everything they'd taken with them when Frank called out to the group. He'd found one of the pseudo scorpions which was really a spider and quite small. There was some excitement while several people tried to get a good photograph of it before it disappeared into a crevice. Then they could see the Ascension Frigate appearing on the horizon so they made their way down to the landing stage.

Once they were all safely on board the launch, Arnold spoke to Vincent and 'the squad' saw Vincent nodding before he beckoned Jeff over.

"Jeff, Arnold tells me you are rapidly gaining experience handling powered craft, in addition to being a sailor and we wondered if you'd like to captain the launch back and see how close you can stay to the coast, without sinking us?" Vincent asked him.

"Yes, thanks Vincent" he replied and then Arnold handed over the controls of the launch to him. Jeff was pleased he was given the job of captaining the launch on the way back to Georgetown. The sea state was ok and so he was able to 'hug' the coastline without risk. He'd sailed round the island regularly and had begun to get a feel for when and where the currents would change.

While everyone chatted on the way back Arnold and Vincent kept an eye on Jeff, to monitor his seamanship, and every now and again, they would look at each other and either nod or smile. They'd made radio contact as soon as they'd left the island and there was a small reception party waiting for them on the quayside. They soon had the launch moored and everyone dispersed to their homes. Bird life on Boatswain Bird Island carried on as it always had, without anyone or anything from the mainland disturbing them.

Now that she had Vincent back safely home with her, Deborah began to recollect when she had last been to a wedding but nothing came to mind. She would of course need to dress up and buy a present. Well, find a present, there was no need to pay for anything. Perhaps she could make something?

"Vincent do have any ideas of what we can get Sabrina and Jeff as a wedding present?" Deborah asked him.

"Not really" he replied and added "I have got an idea of how you could give her some flowers that will last practically for ever. If you can get some sea shells, mount them on thick wire or rod and paint them bright colours, they look a bit like rose buds. You can then use some flat shells painted green to look like leaves. I bet you could also use a drill bit for glass to drill holes in a nice piece of one of your pieces of obsidian to mount them in as a base, rather than use a vase. She'd then have lovely bunch of flowers that would last for ever that's made from the treasures found on the island." He then added laughingly "'course it has to be a bunch of flowers because she already has a lovely bunch of coconuts."

"Behave Vincent, and thanks, that might work" she replied.

Most of the people on the island were very excited by the wedding and nearly everyone was helping in one way or another, especially with the catering. The islanders had re-opened the Obsidian Hotel for Jeff and Sabrina and everyone was looking forward to the wedding day and making an effort, in small and large ways, to make it special.

Vincent walked into the church with Deborah and felt at peace in his life. He almost wished this was his wedding service, albeit with less fuss and without everyone on the island being involved in one way or another. Once they were seated, he tried to think when he'd last been to a wedding. It took him a while but then he remembered a time when he had a girlfriend who'd been invited to one, and he went as her guest. As slow as he realised he was, with some things, at that time his impression was that she thought they ought to be next. Not long after that, they went their separate ways and he knew he'd hurt her feelings badly. On Boatswain Bird Island, he'd learned a new thing and that was to bring just that sort of regret to God and so there and then he did so, for both of them, and left and trusted it to God, being outside time, to have put right what he had done wrong, well the way he'd done it. He was then interrupted in these thoughts by the sound of the bridal march and along with everyone else he stood up.

After he'd completed the wedding vow part of the service, Simon began his address. Sabrina and Jeff were 'regulars' and they'd said he could pretty much preach whatever he wanted and, unusually for him, he felt slightly nervous.

"I'm sure this isn't the part of today that you've all been waiting for so I'll try and keep it short but interesting for you all. All of us here today are what are called Gentiles, meaning we are not Jewish. God's plan was for the Jews to be his chosen people and he sent his son to reconcile them to him. However, most rejected him but ourselves as the Gentiles became God's adopted people, as it were. Today God loves us as his adopted family as he does his chosen family.

"I think there is an interesting parallel to ourselves as islanders, though none of us were born and bred here; and the yacht people. We were like a chosen people, and certainly we are a group of people that survived the apocalypse. Then the yacht people arrived. I believe we have adopted them into our island family just like God adopted us all as Gentiles into his family. Certainly, here today Sabrina and Jeff are now joined together and are a new family.

"Of course, Almighty God doesn't need a wedding service any more than a piece of paper to say people are joined together, what we call married to each other. He doesn't even need to hear the promises they make to each other. As far as he's concerned being joined together, err, well you know what I mean, is kind of the marriage act" the vicar said boldly though noticing several people were smiling.

As Simon continued with his short address, Deborah stopped listening to what he was saying because she was thinking about the joining together part of what he'd said and wasn't quite sure she did know what he meant. Did he mean having sex was getting married? She supposed he did mean that. She did understand about God not needing to see a certificate of marriage, it would have taken years for writing and records to have been invented. Well, anyway she was very pleased for Sabrina and Jeff. She guessed Sabrina might be a few years older than Jeff and that he might have his hands full. Then she smiled because with the figure that Sabrina had, he would certainly have his hands full. She was aware she was being nudged and realised that Simon had finished speaking and they were now going to stand up and sing a song.

Sabrina looked radiant as she walked back down the church aisle, hand in hand with a smiling Jeff. Outside it was a lovely sunny day and someone was organising everyone for the photos. Vincent kissed Deborah on the lips and just as he did so someone took their photo. Deborah felt relaxed, it had been rare for Vincent to show any affection in public so he must be relaxed as well.

The reception was at the Obsidian Hotel and everything went very well, with everyone well behaved. It was late when Deborah and Vincent drove back home and they quickly fell asleep.

Chapter Seventeen – Trouble

It had been several weeks since Sabrina and Jeff's wedding and life on the island was busy but settled. Deborah was in her office when suddenly she felt her desk tremble, then not only her desk but the whole building shook and for a second, she thought the island was under some kind of bizarre attack. She ran outside and could see a distant cloud of smoke. Then there was a long, low rumble followed by an explosion. She could hardly believe her eyes and ears. There it was, the one thing she hadn't planned for, a volcanic eruption! She knew Ascension was a volcanic island with forty cones, but it hadn't been active as far as history had been recorded and was supposed to be dormant now. Perhaps the nuclear war had created seismic shock waves that had changed the order of things. Well, one expert missing in the island community, as far as she knew, was a volcanologist.

Well, there was no point in sounding an alarm, everyone on the island could see what was happening. The question was what to do. She was interrupted in these thoughts by her office phone ringing and she dashed back into her office and picked up the receiver.

"I suppose you've seen it. I think it's Broken Tooth Crater" the voice told her.

"Yes. There's nothing we can do about it. I can't believe it's happening" Deborah replied. She pondered the irony in that while expecting and planning for surviving a nuclear war she never expected that a dormant volcano on her volcanic island might erupt. It could be worse and might even be yet. Still, there was nothing important on that side of the island. She supposed the volcano would throw out ash or lava away from the island, but if another dormant cone erupted, they could be in real trouble. She knew one half of the island was much older than the other and so long as Green Mountain was ok, they ought to be ok. They could also evacuate to the bunker.

It wasn't long before a number of vehicles arrived in Georgetown square and a crowd of locals had gathered, so Deborah addressed them. "Ok, as you can see Broken Tooth has erupted and is throwing up some ash and smoke. I don't know if it's also producing any poisonous gas but even if it is, it's being blown away from the island." She told everyone present.

"I think we need to evacuate Two Boats. It's quite close to Broken Tooth and if poisonous gas is produced and the wind dropped suddenly, then everyone there might die, even in their sleep if it was at night." Henry suggested.

"There are eight houses occupied by the yacht people and four other houses occupied and we can easily accommodate them into houses in Georgetown. The islanders in the four houses might not be that keen to leave them, especially one couple who've lived there for a long time." Sabrina told Deborah.

After a short discussion, it was decided to leave everyone who wanted to stay in Two Boats there, but put a twenty-four watch on the volcano from a safe distance, mostly to watch out for a drop or change in the wind direction or increased activity, such that it might throw out hot ash or even lava that would be dangerous. As things turned the wind direction didn't change and the South Easterly Trade winds were blowing the ash cloud mostly into the sea. Everyone that lived in Two Boats was nonetheless invited to leave if they wanted to but none did, and as agreed, Deborah wasn't going to force them to move and they covered the volcano watch between themselves. There were no storage sites or significant assets at Two Boats other than the historical two boats themselves, which would survive pretty much anything except a lava flow.

It was the middle of the night when a huge rumble woke Vincent and Deborah and they were both hardly out of bed before their radios burst into life. "It looks to be spewing out lava now, quite spectacularly. The good news is that it must be flowing out on the coast side because there's nothing coming this way" the voice told them.

"Thanks for the update, if you need us to do anything, or need any help, let us know." Vincent replied. Then looking at Deborah, he got back onto the bed and went back to sleep.

They both ignored the series of tremors and noise throughout the night and got up at the normal time. It was strangely quiet. "Perhaps it's finished?" Deborah suggested.

"Maybe. Shall we have a drive over and take a look?" he replied, to which Deborah nodded. He took their two titanium flasks and filled them with cold juice and smiled to himself. There wasn't much of a saving over a stainless-steel flask but all these little weight savings added up and he wished he could have had kit like this years ago.

The roads were deserted once they'd left Georgetown and after they'd parked at Broken Tooth there were a few more vehicles there than they'd expected. They could see several expensive cameras on tripods and enthusiastic owners waved at them. Neither of them was a keen photographer but the island was something of a photographer's paradise, and photography was a keen pastime. They realised that photographing an ash cloud is one thing but a full-on lava eruption at night, would have been quite something else. Deborah supposed that the photographers were taking a certain amount of risk but she hadn't declared the area off-limits. While the island needed every person it had, and couldn't afford to lose any of them, or have anyone incapacitated, they needed something to prevent them getting bored, despondent or depressed.

"Morning Deborah, Vincent. I think you've missed the excitement, the eruption's over and Broken Tooth appears to have gone back to sleep. Miranda is flying a drone over it now and has already flown over the lava flow, although there's a fair amount of steam as it's flowed into the sea. The island is a bit bigger now but not usefully so as far as we can tell," the photographer, whose name was Colin, told them.

The following days and then weeks gradually became less anxious for everyone on the island and most believed what was something of a freak eruption, may well have been due to the after effects of the nuclear apocalypse. Everyone relaxed and began to settle back into post apocalypse island life and had simpler worries such as what to drink when the tea and coffee finally ran out.

Big Trouble

"We're intercepting some radio messages that appear to be Chinese. They are coming from some distance away and are coded. There are no replies to the messages they are sending, so we suspect this is a lone Chinese military vessel that's survived the apocalypse. We have no idea what it's doing in the South Atlantic. It might be a supply vessel for a submarine or a small or medium size warship. The steady increases in radio signal strength suggests it's heading in our direction. We won't be able to see it on the radar for a while yet" Brad advised over the radio to Deborah. This wasn't the sort of news Deborah ever wanted to hear. She was just getting over severe morning sickness and hoped to be able to take things a bit steadier with her pregnancy.

No sooner had Deborah broken the news to Vincent he had gathered his Island Defence Volunteer Force together and once all were present, sat them down. "There's bad news and there's good news. The bad news is there appears to be a Chinese vessel, which could be a warship, bearing down on the island. They are likely to want to land and take just about whatever they can from us, possibly even the whole island and enslave us. The good news is that we are going to deny them landing and engage them in battle. We are a formidable fighting force with the home territory advantage. They may be battle weary and battle weakened already, or they may be deserters or no more than pirates. Either way, if their ship's main guns or missile batteries are operational, we will come under heavy bombardment. Some or our all of us might die or be injured." Vincent then hesitated before speaking again "So, I want to apologise now for offering you the chance to leave the force, without criticism or shame." He told them.

The volunteers all shook their heads and Vincent grinned at them. "Sorry about that, now we need to run through some battle plans." He told them. "Most of the island will evacuate to the bunker and they will be safe from any kind of bombardment but they aren't wholly invulnerable with air intakes being the weakest point, which could potentially be stopped up altogether, though I think that's unlikely. We have to have a flexible plan with some assumptions. We can plan to initially engage them at sea, using the M47s and heavy machine guns from the RHIB and the launch. This would have to be a hit and run operation and we'd only take them by surprise once. They'll have a radar watch but if we wait close to shore, we might surprise any landing party and overcome it. If they send up a helicopter, we will seek to bring it down with small-arms fire but only from two of our land positions and that won't be easy.

"However, if they choose to land in force with multiple boats, if they have that capability, we are unlikely to initially destroy more than two boats and we can't risk losing either of our ours. It might be better then to sink their lead boat, and then lay a massive smoke barrage and escape to launch a land attack on their landing party. We aren't all going on the boats because I want a land force as a back-up in case our boat teams are incapacitated, sunk or killed in action. Remember, if your boat sinks, you'll be hard pushed to swim to shore and will need the other boat to rescue you if they can, but if they've coming under heavy fire, outnumbered or out gunned, their priority is to live to fight another day not risk their lives or the mission trying to save you.

"We will have a single land team split over two fixed positions with myself mobile. The job of the land team will be to provide cover to our boats and draw in enemy fire. I'll be leading the land team. Arnold will captain the RHIB, with the callsign Marine One and I've asked Jeff to captain the Ascension Frigate with the callsign Marine Two. But Naomi will have operational command of both boats and she will be Marine Forces Commander and second in command to myself. If we lose one or both boats and the enemy has boats still on the water, we must prevent them landing if we can. If despite our efforts they do manage to land, we have to engage them but be prepared to lose that firefight, withdrawing to Green Mountain; as fast as we can."

"To enable do that we need to leave a vehicle with the keys in it at Comfortless Cove and another at English Bay Beach. So, if one or both boats are forced or called to fallback they can land or beach there. The occupants of the boat should drive to Two Boats and then make their way to the Red Lion on foot, being less likely to be seen, and regroup. Radio silence should be maintained. I'd expect any hostile landing party to seek to consolidate their position in Georgetown and that will buy us useful time. On the mountain the surviving force members will seek to engage the enemy in a series of hit and run raids or ambushes. Depending on the strength of their numbers, the resistance they've encountered and that they are hopefully sailors and not commandos, the hostiles may choose to retreat. If hostile numbers are large, our last and second option is to seek assistance from the bunker, which would surely result in a heavy loss of life for our friends and families but ought to result in a decisive victory, albeit one that would still leave that Chinese ship off our shores which we'd have to hope would accept defeat and look for a softer island. They might choose to fire a barrage at us all the same, if they have enough ammunition.

"Finally, retreating to the bunker isn't an option for us but if anyone is badly wounded or for any reason whatsoever decides to go to the bunker, there is no shame in doing so. Ok, other stuff. We have some extra kit we are going to use for the first-time, body armour. We didn't wear it when we intercepted the yachties or the tall ship because I hadn't found it at that time!

"Oh, and another finally, you don't have to tell me but I want to tell you, between ourselves as soldiers, you may never have killed anyone before, but I have. It's one thing to shoot and kill someone from a distance but less pleasant when you see them face to face, eye to eye, even if you are shooting them rather than stabbing, slashing or cutting with a knife or using your bare hands which I've done, because I had to. At such times, we have to realise if we don't kill them, they will kill us and we are fighting not only for our own lives but those of our friends and loved ones.

"The Chinese have signed the Geneva convention but this ship may contain deserters or plain simple pirates, so if you choose to surrender whether or not you are injured, there's a risk they will kill you in cold blood. Or they might even interrogate or torture you. I can't imagine they will surrender to us because they have a ship and they can leave in it. However, if anyone does surrender to us, we have to accept that and take them prisoner. We'll use the police cells which should be big enough. We'll make some more detailed plans now and this is all we'll be doing until we have to get in position ready for when they arrive. Are there any questions?" Vincent said.

Vincent looked at his team and for a split second they looked at each other and then they jumped up stood to attention and shouted in unison "NO VINCENT."

A lump rose in Vincent's throat and he nodded at them and beckoned to them to sit down before telling them "You are the best team I've ever worked with, and some of them were exceptional. Let's get into that detailed planning." Then he started to discuss battle manoeuvres and outlined roles and responsibilities of the commanders, himself-included.

"Vincent, this is Henry. Two things. Firstly, we are evacuating to the bunker now. Secondly we've received a radio broadcast from the Chinese ship which called upon any inhabitants on the island to surrender to the People's Republic of China and reminded English and American inhabitants that they are at war with us."

"Ok thanks Henry. That's very useful because it sounds like they aren't certain they know we are here or that we can mount a defence. I am sure we are ready for them. Look after everything and see you later" he replied.

Henry shook his head in disbelief. How could Vincent be so calm at a time like this, and confident we'd even all be around later to talk about it.

Vincent was just finishing the last of his preparations and had just finished briefing Deborah, when he came up against one thing he hadn't foreseen or planned for and that was her. "Ok darling so what position do you want me to take up?" She asked him.

"Surely you will be in the bunker?" he told her half question, half statement.

"You forget I'm the commanding officer, your commanding officer and I insist I have an operational role." She replied, almost through gritted teeth.

Vincent looked at Deborah and realised that she was correct and that she was also a soldier. The problem for him was that she hadn't trained as part of his team. Before he had chance to reply she spoke again. "We agreed we would spend the rest of our lives with each other and never leave each other and be together always."

"Yes Deborah, I agreed that. Ok, I want you to man an M2 heavy machine gun set up in the back of your Land Rover, tailboard down, with a firing arc across the quayside steps. If I radio or signal to pull back, you'll drive back in stages, stopping and waiting for anyone and everyone to join you and then one will drive, one will man the gun and everyone else will hang on, putting some rounds down according to what they are capable of doing" he replied with a sigh.

Deborah was impressed but puzzled. Had he planned a role for her all along but waited until she'd pushed for a role, or had he simply made up that brilliant idea on the spot? There wasn't time to find out now, she'd have to get someone to help her get a gun and belt ammunition in the back of her Land Rover and they'd need to give her an instant basic lesson in loading the belt. Reflecting on that, she decided he had just made up that idea on the spot and was relying on someone working the gun for her.

Henry had most of the rest of the Island in the bunker and had secured it. He'd undertaken communication checks and checks of everything else he could but wasn't relaxed. He guessed they'd be heavily outnumbered and it would be a bloody battle but hoped it wouldn't be. He regretted not being trained as part of Island Defence Volunteer Force but also knew that Deborah wouldn't have agreed to it.

Alan and Frank weren't in the bunker but they were at the Pyramid complex and were feverishly working their way through a complicated check list. Eventually they stopped working and looked at each other. Alan broke the silence. "It's charging, but slowly, there's nothing we can do now but wait" he told Frank.

Through his binoculars Vincent could now see the ship. It was an old looking medium size warship, dirty and bearing Chinese insignia it could well be a Jiangwei Class Frigate. All his team had to do now was wait. Eventually the ship came in close to the shore and slipped its anchor. It aimed its deck guns and some kind of missile battery at the island. A key part of Vincent's strategy had been to maintain radio silence and trust the team to follow the plan. From his vantage point he could see a small boat being launched and to his dismay a helicopter rose from the back of the ship as well. He knew the RHIB would intercept the boat and engage it but if it did so too far from the harbour, the helicopter would chase the RHIB and quickly be out of the range of his fixed positions. The RHIB would have a job to down the helicopter and deal with the boat. The Ascension Frigate wouldn't appear for a single enemy boat. The helicopter was also unlikely to come within the fairly short effective range of an M47. There was nothing for it, it would need accurate hits on the helicopter from small arms and before it quickly moved out of range or flanked them. This fire would need to be from land, leaving the RHIB to deal with the boat as they'd planned. It was a serious oversight not to have foreseen the Chinese would have launched a helicopter and a boat simultaneously rather than one or the other or two or more boats, and he kicked himself for it.

Naomi, one of the 'Saints', had turned out to be the best marksmen amongst the volunteers but since Vincent hadn't figured on needing what amounted to a sniper's shot at a moving helicopter, she was on the RHIB. So, it would be down to himself to take the helicopter out. He looked around and noticed the jib of the dockside crane was at almost a perfect forty-five degrees. Ditching his binoculars and slinging his spotting scope around his back he darted across to the crane and began to climb the jib, quickly reaching the top. He re-gained his breath because he needed to be able to hold and release it slowly for good shooting. The helicopter was moving in his direction. It was within range now and coming in towards him almost head on. He waited and then once he thought he could see the pilot; he fired several quick shots in succession at the silhouette in the canopy. The canopy didn't look as if it was breaking but then the helicopter suddenly veered off at a tangent to the sea and then crashed into it, throwing spray and debris into the air.

The boat launched from the destroyer was now closing fast towards the harbour and Vincent was trying to get down the crane. He got as far as the cab when he could hear gunfire and some ricochets off the steel of the crane's jib. Then he heard some rapid gunfire and guessed the RHIB had engaged the Chinese boat. He was now able to get away from the crane and ran clear of the square. He could see the RHIB had now turned to make a run from the boat and someone had used the smoke grenades. The RHIB was also dangerously close to the shore. There was then some fresh gunfire from his left and he knew that Hannah had engaged the Chinese boat with the heavy machine gun from the land position. Firing from the boat ceased and clearly out of control he watched it crash into the rocks. Then Hannah laid down a lot of rounds over the wreckage and he doubted anyone would have survived.

Deborah felt helpless as she watched Vincent climb the crane because she guessed he was going to try and shoot the helicopter down. She saw a second boat had appeared from behind the destroyer and it was concentrating its fire at Hannah's position and then her machine gun had fallen silent. She saw the Ascension Frigate appear from behind the cover of the coast and behind the second Chinese boat and laid down some decent firepower on it but a large calibre gun from the destroyer opened fire and just missed the Ascension Frigate before it produced a large amount of smoke but also ceased following the second boat. It had clearly had to pull back and it would be difficult for it to get close enough to re-engage the second boat, which had the greater supporting fire power from the destroyer.

Vincent knew they were in a tight spot and he knew he had to get to the heavy machine to engage that second Chinese boat, before it was in the harbour. He turned and looked behind him at Deborah and she could see he was looking at her. He blew her a kiss and before he had moved, he heard her scream.

"NO VINCENT. NO STAY PUT" she screamed at him.

Ignoring Deborah's scream for him to stay put, he made the sprint of his life to the forward firing position and was knocked off stride at one point and he knew he'd been hit in the thigh by something, most likely a bullet. He reached the position where the heavy machine gun was and could see Hannah was unconscious. Her helmet looked to have withstood an impact but remained intact. He knew he didn't have time to do anything for her, at that moment. He pushed her gently to the side of the gun and then quickly checking the belt, fired a series of long sweeping bursts at the leading boat, causing it to suddenly change direction.

Then there was a huge explosion and he saw the boat explode. Good, someone, probably from the RHIB, must have hit it with an M47. He changed position and sought to put some rounds down on a third boat that had been launched but it swung back towards the ship. Then just as he feared, the ship fired a salvo of shells from a forward gun. He heard them whistle over his head and into Cat Hill and guessed the Chinese were either rotten shots or more likely, they wanted the quayside intact and didn't plan on damaging it needlessly.

Vincent shook his head and shouted into his radio "We can't fight this, everyone withdraw now to our agreed fallback position." Then he saw a short red flash and the ship's superstructure exploded. What the fuck was that he thought! Then there was a second red flash and a cloud of steam rose from somewhere near the middle of the ship which then began to sink rapidly. He looked across to his right just in time to see two more red flashes in quick succession make direct hits on the remaining small boats. The red flashes were some sort of massive laser beam being fired from the Golf ball at Pyramid Point.

"Sorry to anyone left who can hear us, we've never fired this sucker before, even for a test and it took longer than we'd hoped to get it charged up. Acknowledge over?" Alan said breathlessly.

"This is Vincent, thanks, we're bloody grateful. Can you get a message to the bunker and get them to send some medical staff because we have living and possibly dead casualties?" Then everything blurred for Vincent and he lost consciousness.

"Bunker command this is Alan, the Chinese destroyer and all Chinese boats are sunk. Can medical teams proceed with speed but caution to the quayside? There are casualties." He told them with an edge of anxiety to his voice.

"Acknowledged and response despatched" Henry replied from the bunker while wringing his hands together. He knew that the medical teams were already close to the quay because they had decided to deploy half their teams outside the bunker in a field ambulance, they'd parked at the rear of the hospital despite his misgiving about their doing so. He turned to look at Sabrina who nodded and Henry knew Sabrina had relayed the message to the medical team and that the bunker team were also now leaving to assist. What he didn't understand was what had happened. Deborah had given him a running commentary but then had ceased transmitting any message. He prayed to God she was still alive. He'd heard the sounds of the battle in the background of her commentary and he had battled within himself, not to start shaking. He'd rather have been there to help rather than be in the bunker but Deborah was the boss, and a soldier, and she'd put him in command of the bunker and he knew it was the right decision. What he also couldn't understand was how the ship had been sunk, surely Vincent's team didn't have the means to sink it. He wrung his hands again.

Deborah was lying prone by the corner of the church and could just see their now somewhat battle scarred RHIB race across the bay and then slow down and circle what wreckage remained of the first boat and then proceeded at high speed to where the water was bubbling and dirty where the Chinese destroyer had been. There was lots of wreckage but no obvious survivors. She watched the RHIB turn around and saw the bow rise and she knew it was now seeking out the Ascension Frigate. "This is the Marine Force Commander. We have located Marine Two, advise your orders Vincent?" what sounded like Naomi, asked.

"This is the Commanding Officer, undertake a final sweep for survivors and then proceed to the quay unless you have casualties, in which case both boats proceed immediately to the Quay." Deborah replied.

The defence volunteers on each boat looked at each other and wondered what had happened to Vincent. Deborah had sounded calm so they guessed he must be ok. They did have casualties who were being treated by those without injury and so proceeded to the quay at maximum speed with the RHIB arriving first.

Deborah got up and ran in the direction she had seen Vincent running. She quickly realised he must have been running to the machine gun emplacement and when she got there it was a shocking scene. Hannah looked to be dead and there was a lot of blood everywhere. She found Vincent unconscious and while he only seemed to have a small wound in his thigh, she could see a lot of blood pumping out from it. He must have lost more than a pint already. She took her Swiss Champ out of a pocket and unfolding the scissors, cut his trousers open in both directions, roughly centred on the wettest part. She could see the wound now and put one hand on it and then the other. As she pressed as hard as she could, the flow of blood subsided. Now she faced the long wait for help to arrive. As she sat with Vincent she wept. She had lost the first love of her life and it would be too much for her to lose the second, it would be more than she could bear.

With every breath in her lungs, she screamed out to God, "DON'T LET HIM DIE." Then she was about to scream out again when there was a reply.

"I won't let him die Deborah." But it was not God in heaven replying but Doc Caskey, and he had a volunteer medic with him. Doc Caskey set to work on Vincent on the spot and he found the bullet had torn through his leg and caught an artery. He didn't think Vincent would die but he wasn't so sure whether he could save his leg unless the bullet had passed straight through it. He radioed for two stretchers and when he found the exit wound his volunteer medic was already attending to Hannah. His hospital, while much nearer than the bunker's medical facilities, was less suited to dealing with bullet wounds. But he was confident he could at least stop the bleeding and stabilise Vincent at the hospital and move him later if he had to. He looked up and could now hear Hannah groaning. He could also hear Deborah sobbing. He was more worried about Deborah than his other two casualties. If she went into shock nothing might save her. He took a deep breath and with his spare hand tapped her shoulder to catch her attention, before speaking to her. "Commanding Officer, your Second in Command will live but is incapacitated. I need you to direct my follow up medics and assist them with the casualties from the RHIB. I want them all in the hospital. Also, I want two blood donors from the bunker who are blood group A positive to be at the hospital, as soon as they can get there. OK?" he asked her.

He was encouraged when she snapped to and after bending down to kiss Vincent turned away and began to talk into her radio. Doc frowned and when his volunteer looked up at him, he decided he needed to explain himself. "I have two professional rules and I've just broken both of them in quick succession. My first rule is not to make a medical promise I can't be certain of keeping. The second is to not be emotionally involved with the patient or their loved ones." He shook his head and set back to work on Vincent.

Once everything returned to normality it turned out that Hannah had been knocked unconscious by a chip of stone flying up under her helmet, rather than a bullet. No-one from the island had died. It was assumed most of the Chinese sailors were eaten by blackfish or sharks or entombed within the wreck of their ship itself. However, some bodies were found washed up on the rocks and it was decided to bury them at sea over the position where the warship had been sunk. The Rev Simon did the honours and in this he was assisted by the Admiral, Arnold and Jeff. Other willing volunteers being unable to assist since there were in hospital under strict doctors' orders.

And so, in all the years of history of the Island the first and perhaps last major attack on it had been repulsed and won by combined: South African, St Helenian, British and American forces – islanders one and all.

The islanders had never seen the effects of the pandemic or the nuclear apocalypse but had heard the effects second-hand from the yacht people and the tall ship sailors. They had felt the world change but in so many ways they had escaped its ravages, until their own island battle had been fought. The care-free mood on the island was absent for a long time afterwards. Most of the Island Defence Volunteer Force had been injured and even after the bandages and splints had been removed from them, they could see that the healing process would take time and that some movements caused them pain. They had scars they didn't need to display nor hide. Everyone could see the damage to the RHIB, and they could see the new small craters on the island that hadn't been caused by a volcano. What they also knew was that they had saved their friends and families. No-one thought of the battle as a victory over the Chinese but a victory in survival. There was no celebration afterwards and no victory ceremonies or parades or medals awarded.

Chapter Eighteen – In for the long Haul

It had been four years now since the third World War which they generally called the apocalypse. Deborah reflected that it had taken a long time to adjust to a life that didn't have the routine of pre-apocalypse times, a routine she'd missed. Her world, along with everyone else's, had shrunk and it had taken some getting used to but she'd managed it, along with Vincent's help. However, he'd adapted quickly, probably because his pre-apocalypse life had never seemed to have had any routine at all to it.

Life on Ascension had changed but not dramatically. There was a number of things of which stocks of had been used up some years ago. Most of them weren't missed and the islanders had got used to not having them. The lack of sugar and fizzy drinks was probably a good thing because the only dentist on the island had died of old age the year before. Also supplies of toothbrushes and toothpaste were one of the things that had all been used up.

Deborah looked at her watch and smiled. It was an expensive Superocean II Breitling with a white face that she'd never had to completely pay for because she'd bought it pre-apocalypse on finance. Her only regret was that she hadn't bought half a dozen of them. The American Base Exchange did still have a fair stock of watches but most of what were left were battery powered and while there was a supply of batteries, they'd run out in a few years' time based on the current rate of consumption, so she was glad hers was an automatic and that so were Vincent's. She smiled when she remembered his confession about ending up with a duplicate set of watches. He'd also explained that, unusually for him and his experience of watches, he was keeping every single one of them.

It was getting late and she needed to think about getting back to Georgetown before it got dark and then she spotted them, lots of little turtles scampering down to the shore as fast as their little flippers could propel them. She picked up one that was heading in the wrong direction and like picking up a small clockwork or battery-operated toy, its flippers increased speed until she set it down again. Off it went, now in the right direction into the surf and then onto a long voyage of life and discovery. Having checked they'd all now reached the sea; it was time to return home to her husband and son. She was grateful that Vincent had turned out to be a great father as well as husband. Their son, Duncan Philip Irving would be safely in his bed by now and he would have been read a bedtime story and shown the pictures in the story.

Not quite all alone

Deborah was reminded that it was about this time of year when they had encountered 'The Sprite'. She remembered how magnificent it had looked when, in full sail, it disappeared out of sight. Everyone knew there was a strong chance it might never return and so far, it hadn't. However, like most of the islanders she harboured a secret hope that it would return and Captain Ian and his crew would have lots of tales to tell. Of course, it would be too late for the Admiral and Petunia, as they'd both died peacefully last year, within days of each other.

No more yachts meant there had also been no more yacht people but there had also been no more warships either. She gave a slight shudder when she remembered seeing Vincent unconscious in a pool of blood lying next to Hannah and the machine gun. There had also never been any more planes landing on the runway, though they tried to keep it as clean as they could and it seemed in reasonable condition still.

However, they weren't alone in the world. Occasionally they picked up radio messages, but they were always in a foreign language and they had agreed a policy to only reply to messages spoken in English of which there had been none. They'd agreed that policy because they didn't want some potentially hostile warship, submarine or plane bringing trouble.

The island wasn't quite the same as it had been all those years ago either. Broken Tooth crater, now generally just called Broken Tooth was active from time to time. The islanders weren't troubled by this, believing lots of small eruptions meant there was less likelihood of a single massive one. The infrastructure of the island was in very good condition, and the fact that two of the passengers from 'The Sprite' that had stayed on the island were civil engineers had been an enormous blessing.

The biggest change on the island though was that there were lots of new young children. Their own Duncan was the oldest but Rev Simon's son, John, was only a few weeks younger. There was a gap of many months before Paul and Polly's baby daughter Davina, then Naomi the marksman had given birth to a boy she given the biblical name 'Nimrod', though most people associated it with the old sub hunting jet plane, to her occasional annoyance. Sabrina had given birth to twins: Julia and James and there were lots of other children as well, which had kept Doc Luke Caskey and his wife busy.

Peace

Deborah reflected that she was at peace now with not only herself and her past but also the living God. She'd never really understood at the time what dear Jane Briggs was trying to tell her when she explained 'she'd found Jesus'. What's more, she learned much later that Vincent had even less of an idea what Jane had meant than she had, despite him already knowing that God would give him peace.

She had her faded and well-worn concise guide to Ascension Island written by John Packer, a Cable and Wireless employee, a long time ago, in her hand and once more turned to the Epilogue and smiled. There it had been all along, the truth of Christianity by the man who must have loved the island so much he wrote a guide to it, way back in 1968. A man who, like her own Vincent, had visited Boatswain Bird Island. Then in his Epilogue he expresses an awareness of nuclear weapons and concern about mankind. His concerns were largely unheeded by mankind yet some of the survivors of the world he knew, lived on the island he must have loved very much. Perhaps he had prayed it might be saved and populated by godly people.

"You look deep in happy thoughts again – are we off to search for obscure cryptogams again this weekend on Green Mountain, or specimen collecting on the obsidian trail or searching for another hidden cave?" Vincent asked before bending down to kiss her on her cheek.

"None of those things, I'm just grateful for everything we have, here on this island, Ascension Island, in the South Atlantic Ocean" she replied smiling.

Printed in Great Britain
by Amazon

71736882R00111